"LET'S SUM UP, SHALL WE?"

I said, "Currently, I have no money, you have no money, I'm on the brink of professional ruin, and I just drove halfway across the continental United States to the one place I never want to see again."

"That's right," Skye said. "Oh, except don't forget about Bob and the baby."

"Of course."

She clasped both hands under her chin. "Does Flynn still hate your guts?"

"In a word, yes."

"What *happened* when you guys broke up?"

I sighed. "It's a long story."

MY FAVORITE MISTAKE

A NOVEL

BETH KENDRICK

New York London Toronto Sydney

An *Original* Publication of POCKET BOOKS

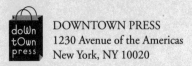
DOWNTOWN PRESS
1230 Avenue of the Americas
New York, NY 10020

This book is a work of fiction. Names, characters, places and
incidents are products of the author's imagination or are used
fictitiously. Any resemblance to actual events or locales or persons,
living or dead, is entirely coincidental.

Library of Congress Cataloging-in-Publication Data

Kendrick, Beth.
    My favorite mistake : a novel / Beth Kendrick.—1st Downtown Press trade
pbk. ed.
      p. cm.
    ISBN 0-7434-7034-6 (pbk.)
        1. Women—Minnesota—Fiction. 2. First loves—Fiction.
        3. Minnesota—Fiction. 4. Sisters—Fiction. I. Title.

    PS3611.E535M9 2004
    813'.6—dc22   2004050034

First Downtown Press trade paperback edition August 2004

10 9 8 7 6 5 4 3 2 1

DOWNTOWN PRESS and colophon are
trademarks of Simon & Schuster, Inc.

Manufactured in the United States of America

For information regarding special discounts for bulk purchases,
please contact Simon & Schuster Special Sales at 1-800-456-6798
or business@simonandschuster.com

For my mom,
who always has the best insights about life, love, and Page Six

ACKNOWLEDGMENTS

My thanks to:

Susan Mallery, a wonderful mentor, whose advice and generosity made all the difference.

My brilliant editor, Amy Pierpont, who makes me do the best work of which I am capable (damn her!).

My agent, Irene Goodman, who believed in me from the beginning and introduced me to *The Godfather*.

Megan McKeever, who never once hung up on me on the five thousand occasions that I called to ask really stupid questions about the publication process.

Barbara Ankrum, who encouraged me through a long and scary first draft and made sure I got enough protein along the way.

The "La-La Sisterhood": Chandra, Corinne, Doris, Teresa, Valerie, and Julie. I probably *could* write a book without taking time out every week to gossip, complain, and eat too much cheese . . . but why *would* I?

ACKNOWLEDGMENTS

The Majewski family, who helped me "research" bar-hopping in the North Woods.

The Minnesota natives, Catherine Johnson and Jason Hein, who taught me everything I know about hot-dish, hockey, and what to wear when it's thirty-five degrees below zero.

And, of course, the LBC, who is better than Kerry Wood and Russell Crowe put together.

The only way to prove that you're a good sport is to lose.

—ERNIE BANKS,
FORMER CHICAGO CUBS SHORTSTOP

1

I would just like to state for the record that I tried to say no. In fact, I *did* say no. But my sister, as usual, refused to hear it. And then she dragged my credit rating, ten years of pent-up guilt and my ex-boyfriend into it, so what was I to do?

This was late June in Florence and I was holed up in a narrow-halled hotel near the Piazza del Duomo. Skye and I were thirty minutes into a intercontinental AT&T marathon. Between the crackling overseas connection and her wet, honking noseblows, details were sketchy. But all signs seemed to indicate trouble on the marital front.

"Mitzi!" she shrieked. "Her name is fucking *Mitzi!*"

My brother-in-law had a long history of dallying with poodle-named women. Before he married Skye, there had been a

Brandi, a Lulu, and even, if the rumors can be believed, a Kiki.

"Mitzi, huh?" I said. "That cuts like a knife."

I did not point out that since Bob, ruddy-cheeked and shifty-eyed, had left his second wife for *her* after a few illicit trysts in a pickup truck, this situation was not quite the Stonehengian coincidence she was making it out to be.

My sigh stirred up a flurry of dust motes on the windowsill. This was not new territory for us. I turned back to the laptop perched on the hotel's spindly legged end table and put my Big Sister voice on autopilot while I started to proofread my latest attempt at a travel article. "Sweetie, I know you're upset right now—"

"I think that there should be laws against calling your children bad seventies porn star names!" she sobbed. "The rule should be: What if your daughter wants to grow up and be a senator? Who's going to vote for Senator Mitzi?"

"Okay, just calm—"

"What am I going to *do?* Bob is the love of my life! How could he dump me like this? No one *ever* dumps me." She paused. "Now I finally understand how you felt all those times."

I held my breath, counted to ten and tried to ignore the hot prickling in my chest.

"Faith? Are you even listening? I'm totally serious. I'm killing myself!"

This was my cue.

"Suck it up, Skye. Come on," I barked like a sergeant demanding six A.M. push-ups. "This isn't the spirit that won the West. You're not going to kill yourself over some chick named Mitzi and your jackass husband. First of all, you know you can do better. By your own admission, that guy Lars or whoever has been panting after you for weeks."

Ragged breathing over the line, but I thought I could hear a smile creep in.

"Second of all, have some dignity. My God. Don't give the whole town something else to talk about. Our family has already provided enough scandal for one generation, don't you think?"

A feeble cough.

"Third, this phone call is costing you about a million dollars and if you kill yourself, I'll have to pay for it." This was pretty much a done deal, regardless. My family had always had amnesia in matters of the heart and outstanding debt.

The note of hysteria in her voice melted into playground pleading. "But I *need* you."

I scrolled down to the next page of the draft for my article on Italian gelato. "Keep your shirt on, dude. I just need to double-check a few facts for this article, and then I'm flying back to California."

Since I moved to Los Angeles after high school, I had noticed some alarming changes in my diction. Along with a San Fernando slide-whistle lilt, the word "dude" had crept into my vocabulary, supplanting nouns, verbs, and exclamation points. I realized that this cut my subjective I.Q. in half, as effectively as snapping a wad of sugarless gum all day would do. But it had displaced the earnest Midwest intonations of my childhood, and I couldn't say that I was broken up about it.

"Look, Faithie, I need you to come to back home for a few weeks. I can't deal with this all by myself. I can't."

"No." I made my stand. "I live in California now. If you need me, you know you're always welcome there. But I am not going back to Minnesota."

"Come on! You haven't been home in years." I could hear Kleenex rustling against the earpiece.

"No."

"I really need you. I don't know where Bob went, and I think that—" cough, cough "—the bar might be having a little bit of trouble. Moneywise."

I stopped proofreading. If Skye was willing to *admit* financial glitches, I knew we were looking at ten pounds of trouble in a one-pound bag. "Define 'trouble'."

"Um, I'm not really sure."

"Well, you better get sure right now. What kind of trouble? Exactly how poor am I going to be?" I closed my eyes, once again cursing my own weakness. Three years ago, Skye, in the throes of her first divorce at the tender age of twenty-one, had suckered me into handing over all my worldly assets to help her buy and refurbish a ramshackle backwoods tavern, which she dubbed "The Roof Rat" and immediately turned over to Bob's management. That was back when I still co-owned a juice bar in Santa Monica (long story), before I gave it all up to travel the world and write "Street Food," a tiny little column in a tiny little food magazine for which I earned a tiny little salary. I started out writing about fresh produce and juice in California, then progressed to hot dogs and pretzels in Manhattan and beignets in New Orleans. Now we were into the European fare—gelato in Florence, crepes in Paris—you get the idea.

Why, one might well ask, would I give up regular income and stability for jet lag and isolation?

Well. Family life and stability had never been my strong point. Exhibit A: the conversation currently in progress.

"My life is falling apart!" Skye gasped. "How can you complain about money at a time like this?"

"I can complain about money because I have to pay my rent." "That bar is my only investment, and I'm not expecting to make untold millions, but I warned you about Bob—"

"Stop yelling!" she yelled. "God. It's only been two months since I sent you the last check."

"This deal was your idea, Skye—you're supposed to send me $2,000 a month. The last two months have netted me negative $4,000 and some strongly worded letters from Visa. I understand you're going through a rough time right now, but again I ask you: What has the bar done for me lately?"

She whimpered. "This isn't my fault! Bob took a lot of cash with him."

"Well . . ." I threw my hands up and looked toward the ceiling, searching for divine intervention or at least a modicum of patience. "I thought you guys were talking to a financial counselor. What happened to that?"

"Bob said we couldn't afford to pay someone else to manage our money."

I closed my eyes. "Jesus H. Christ on a Popsicle stick. Skye, I swear . . ."

"Don't be like this, Faith, I can't take it. Bob always handled the money and the vendors and everything, and now he's gone.

I don't know what to do about the bar. I'm in deep trouble."
She started crying again, big heaving chokes.

I fought the urge to remind her that I was not on the Academy Awards nomination committee and gritted my teeth. "I'll try to help you out with the bar. But you know I am not going back to Minnesota."

"Yes!"

"No."

"Please!"

I remembered the time she'd worn her new red galoshes out to recess in first grade. She'd waded into a puddle of mud and gotten stuck in the thick brown sludge. Squirming and squalling, she'd refused help from her teacher and the principal. Finally, they'd had to call me out of a spelling test so I could lift her out of her boots and carry her to the asphalt. She'd wrapped her arms and legs around me like a koala learning to scale a eucalyptus tree.

I thought about Skye as a ringletted six-year-old. I thought about my credit rating.

But then I thought about all the reasons I'd had to leave Minnesota in the first place, and I held my ground. "Listen. We'll work something out, okay? Don't go Lady of Shalott on me."

"Lady of who?"

"Never mind. I'll fix this when I get back to L.A."

The broken wailing resumed. "Everything's falling part, and I'm all alone, and the memories, Faith, the *memories* . . ."

I rolled my eyes. "Listen. I head back to California next

week. Send me all the legal documents and financial accounts for the bar, and we'll take it from there."

"And, what should I do about Lars?"

I blinked. "Nothing. Listen. Skye, are you listening to me?"

Sniff. "Yuh-huh."

"I don't care if it's raining men. Wait until we find Bob and get this whole Mitzi situation sorted out before you get the next victim lined up. I'm begging you."

"But—"

I dropped my head into my hands. *"Begging* you."

She paused. "Okay. But I really think you should try to get out here, because—"

"No!"

"For a week!"

"No!"

"A weekend!"

"Bye, now. Say hi to Mom." I hung up the phone, leaned back in my chair, and tried not to drown in my sister's anxiety and fatigue. She was a grown woman. She had to learn to clean up her own messes. I couldn't just keep dropping everything to bail her out every time she made a mistake. She knew she was asking for too much this time. I was perfectly justified in drawing the line at the Minnesota state line.

Right?

I shut down my computer, rubbed my temples, and grabbed my hotel key off the table. Maybe a walk and some gelato would clear my head. And my conscience.

*   *   *

Florence in the summer smells like a backwoods bar. If you close your eyes and plug your ears against the mosquito whine of *motorini,* you can smell the ripe melange of smoke and sweat charged with emotion. So it was not surprising that I spent much of my time there thinking about my hometown, finding familiar pieces of my past in a language and culture I didn't understand.

I was wandering through the Piazza della Republica, trying to stay out of the tourists' photo ops, when my cell phone rang. This was highly unususal—hardly anyone called my cell when I was on the road, which I almost always was. I dug the phone out of my leather tote bag and frowned at the unfamiliar number blinking on the little blue display: 612? That was Minneapolis. No one in the 612 area code ever called me. No one in that area code even had my number . . . except all the legal and medical forms on which Skye had listed me as the "person to contact in case of emergency."

Oh God. My shaking fingers fumbled with the phone, and I had to swallow hard before I said, "Hello?"

"Faith." The male voice on the other end of the line was tense and determined.

The deep timbre of that voice resonated through my memory. This was not some anonymous E.R. orderly. I closed my eyes, and through the static connecting us all the way across the Atlantic, I knew it was him. I still recognized his voice, but I couldn't say anything at all.

He cleared his throat. "This is Patrick Flynn."

I took a deep breath. "I know."

Ten years' worth of silence stretched out between us, both of us thinking things we would never give words to.

"Hello?"

"Yeah, I'm here." I pressed the phone against my ear. "Well, I'm in Florence, I mean, but . . ."

"I know. I won't keep you." He sounded neutral now. Brusque. "I just wanted to let you know what's going on with Skye."

I frowned. "She told me."

"All of it?"

I sat down on a wrought-iron bench and listened as hard as I could. "Well, yeah, I guess. She told me about Bob and the bar, and she wants me to come to Minnesota."

"But you're not coming." This was a statement, rather than a question.

"Um." I winced. "No."

"Why am I not surprised?" Cold seeped into his voice.

It was pointless to try to defend myself to him, so I just said, "There's nothing I can do there that I can't do from Los Angeles."

"Is that where you're living these days?"

"Didn't Skye tell you?"

"I didn't ask." He shoots, he scores.

"Oh." I desperately wanted to ask why he'd finally tracked me down now, after all these years, but at the same time I was afraid to know. To know where he'd gone and who he'd become without me. "Listen, Flynn—"

He cut me off before I could finish saying his name. "Did she tell you about the baby?"

I jerked the phone receiver away from my ear, stared at it, and then slapped it back against my head. "The *what*?"

"Left that little tidbit out, did she?" He gave me a second to absorb this, then forged ahead. "Here's the deal: she has no idea where Bob is, she's about to default on the bar mortgage, the creditors are threatening legal action if she doesn't pay up in thirty days, and she's pregnant."

I wrapped my fingers around the cool metal of the bench. "Are you sure?"

"I would never call you unless it were a dire emergency."

Touché. "Okay, I get it. Message received. You're mad at me—"

"I took her to get a blood test at the clinic. She's definitely pregnant. I can help her with the financial aspects, but for the Bob situation and the pregnancy, she needs you."

"I don't think I'm really the right person to—"

"She doesn't have anybody else. She's too ashamed to tell you, but she needs you."

Actually, she did tell me, but I rolled my eyes and blew her off.

I watched the afternoon sunlight filtering through the plaza and tried to discern the sound of his breathing. I heard nothing but static. Slow, muted minutes stretched out between us.

Finally, he spoke up. "Don't give up on *her* when she needs you most."

I winced at the pointed emphasis in his voice. "Listen, Flynn, there are a lot of things I wanted to tell you."

Both of us lapsed into silence again, and when I opened my mouth, nothing spilled out except a soft sigh.

"Do what you want. I have nothing else to say." He clicked off the line.

I closed my eyes, listening to the growling hum of passing

traffic, and my memory rewound to the days when we couldn't say enough to each other. To the day when I was just learning to drive and ran head-on into a gnarled ash tree. After my father had made and broken a year's worth of promises to give me lessons in his pickup truck, Flynn agreed to supervise me. That winter, my senior year of high school, we had commandeered my parents' new Ford for parallel parking practice and extended, window-fogging make-out sessions on the vinyl bench seat that still smelled of the dealership.

The weather had been mild, by Minnesota standards, so I had not been expecting ice on the slushy back roads. The bare trees were black against the heavy beige sky, but my spirits were soaring—I came, I saw, I conquered the Ford Ranger. Distracted by Flynn's hand on my thigh and giddy with my new-found prowess with the stick shift, I had loosened my death grip on the steering wheel and turned to give him a kiss on the cheek. At which point, of course, all hell broke loose, in the form of a vast patch of ice dusted lightly with snow and a cat streaking across the asphalt.

In the grand tradition of neophyte teenage drivers, I hyperventilated, stomped on the brakes, and spun off the road. We slammed into a tree to the sound of screeching metal and a dull clunk, which turned out to be the front bumper of my father's new truck wrenching off and hitting the ground.

I did the only thing I could: I succumbed to hysterics. I started to cry, and then Flynn started to laugh, and we fell into each other until we calmed down, kissing and whispering under the freezing, desolate twilight.

When we finally returned to my house, Flynn insisted that he be the one to face my parents' wrath, telling my father, "Well, Mike, the bad news is that we messed up your new truck, but the good news is that your bumper is the same color as the duct tape we used to fix it."

Now, staring down at sun-bleached cobblestones half a world away, my throat closed up. I hadn't thought about that accident in years. The snow and the wind screaming away outside the truck's cab. The damp heat inside next to Flynn. That must have been about six months before our high school graduation; the two teenagers curled up against each other in that Ford didn't know how bad things were about to get. How hidden hazards could send you spinning even when the summer sun was shining.

I knew now. I knew because I had finally stopped spinning. I could feel, really *feel,* the force of gravity pulling my body to the ground. The faces-and-places kaleidoscope of the last few years finally stopped churning.

I had to go home. I wasn't sure if I could help Skye any more than she could help herself. I wasn't sure that I wouldn't make everything ten times worse. But I had to try.

The time had come to stick a toe back into the murky, shark-laden waters of the Land of 10,000 Lakes. And, God help us, the next installment of "Street Food" would feature fried cheese curds and walleye-on-a-stick.

2

I like to fancy myself a decent travel writer, but I am a very bad traveler. Yes, yes, it's all glistening with irony. The very first time I flew cross-country, I realized that my childhood fantasies of growing up to edit a glossy European fashion magazine, hopping on the red-eye to take in the latest spring lines in Paris and then continuing on to Rome for a quick espresso could never be realized because the jet lag would kill me.

I don't mean it would "kill me" in that I would be disoriented and in need of two cucumber slices for my puffy eyes. I mean that the flight attendants would have to collect my cold dead body along with the empty soda cans.

But the trip back from Italy was not too bad, relatively speaking. As the plane began its descent into Los Angeles, I white-knuckled the armrest and peered out the window at the sprawling city. Pulsing grids of lights checkerboarded out toward the vast black ocean. Strings of headlights snaked up the freeway.

When you are airborne, it's obvious that the city is larger than the state of Rhode Island, but when I first drove into L.A., I had no sense of this sprawling panorama. I could only see the view from the ground while I blinked up at the sun from rock-bottom. I hoped that the sun would dry and harden me like the brittle terra-cotta tiles on the rooftops. I wanted to get lost in perpetual energy and motion, in the daily commutes on 65-mph highways. But it turns out that constant sunshine only buries the dark places in deeper shadows, and a morning spent crawling through miles of gridlock gives you too much time to think. And, raw and pale after that long Minnesota winter, I didn't want to think at all, because every thought brought me back to Flynn.

The unfortunate truth about Flynn and me is that we never ended things properly. There was a lot more walking than talking. Our story had no ending, until yesterday's accusatory phone call.

I would never call you unless it were a dire emergency. He'd come a long way from *Faith, will you marry me?*

In occasional moments of weakness or solitude, I couldn't help but try to mentally rearrange the fractured pieces of our past and compose an alternate future for us. Goethe said, "There is nothing in which people more betray their character than in what they laugh at." And we used to laugh at everything. Like hyenas. When I was fourteen, I fell through the black ice on Flatbush Lake and after they fished me out, somewhere between hypothermia and death, Flynn held my hand in the ambulance and made me laugh until the paramedics yelled at both of us.

And yes, I know: Pining is for suckers and trees, and can't we all please move on from high school? I didn't *regret* leaving. Realistically, he and I had more issues than *National Geographic,* and we never could have worked it out. He had pushed me away and I had pushed ahead, and now I had what I always wanted—a safe, warm little life under the California sun.

Back on Flight 867 to Los Angeles, the pilot announced that we would have to wait on the tarmac while the runway cleared of traffic. I gazed out the window at the concrete, which was cracked and speckled after years of baking in the summer heat. The dirt of my childhood, the dirt we buried my father beneath, was rich and dark and loamy. In early summer, you could smell the ploughed acres like a cool mountain spring. The overturned fields sloped against the sky like wet desert dunes.

My father. I remembered that he built a yellow plywood hutch for my pet rabbit, Mr. Popper, when I was starting grammar school. I remembered scooching over in bed so Skye could climb in and cling to me when we heard my father slamming out the front door and into the still winter night. When he still lived at home, we weren't allowed to wake him in the morning, so we tiptoed around the fetal form on the couch, the fitful sleeper who smelled of stale cigarettes and whiskey.

It was surprising, how quickly my father's life had faded from my memories. But I remembered his funeral. Skye and my father's new wife had screamed at each other over a bottle of moisturizer just before we left for the church. And afterward, when I returned to L.A., brittle and wrung-out from the memorial service, my boyfriend Thom broke up with me at the airport.

Thom was representative of my California boyfriends—a lost cause with great bone structure who worked occasionally as a model and more frequently as a bartender. His car had always been cluttered with head shots of himself and crumpled cocktail napkins smeared with lipstick and scrawled phone numbers that I tried not to ask about.

Now, sitting on the tarmac on the flight from Rome, I tried to congratulate myself on all the progress I'd made since that unfortunate airport break-up two years ago. I had pretty much given up Thom and his ilk, as I had pretty much given up dating altogether. (I got too tired of seeing sides of myself I didn't like reflected in the dating pool.)

At least I had the sense to keep moving. To stay flexible and restless. Until now. Now I was about to drive to Minnesota and throw myself directly into the path of the Little Blond Engine That Couldn't.

Fifty-five hours, two Holiday Inns, and far too many drive-thru cheeseburgers later, I met up with Skye in Minneapolis. She claimed that she wanted to go into the city to shop, that she wanted to drive with me for the last sixty-five miles to Lindbrook.

This was a lie.

What she actually wanted was to wait until I had spent three days on the highway and had invested too much time and energy to turn back. She wanted to soften me up, then drop her bombshell in the middle of the cornfields where no one could hear me scream.

When I pulled up to our rendezvous point in the gray concrete parking lot at the Mall of America, my sister scrambled into my decrepit black VW Golf, a breathless blonde whirlwind with high heels and even higher drama.

"Faithie!" She smacked my cheek with a resounding, wet kiss. "Thank God you're here. I missed you!"

I unbuckled my seat belt and hugged her back, amazed by how prominent and fragile her ribcage felt. In the midst of marital apocalypse, she retained the air of a fresh-faced sprite too busy with pixie dust and eye shadow to remember to eat dinner.

"What's going on?" I asked. "Are you trying to get down to your birth weight?"

She threw a bulging blue shopping bag into the backseat. "What?"

I held up my pinky finger. "This is what you look like."

"Yeah, I wish." She flung herself back against the passenger seat. "I guess with Bob, and, you know . . . everything . . . it's possible I lost a few pounds."

I shoved my sunglasses up on my forehead and scrutinized her midriff for any sign of a telltale bump. Flynn hadn't said how far along she was, but it had always been my impression that mothers-to-be should not be interchangeable with swizzle sticks.

But better to hold off with the sisterly nagging and just plunge ahead with The Unpleasantness.

I tried to look stern. "Listen, Skye. I know you're pregnant."

Her willow-blue eyes widened. "You do?"

I nodded. "We have to talk about this."

"No, we don't." She shook her head, her pale curls bouncing off her shoulders. "How did you know?"

I remained poker-faced. I'd decided back in Nebraska not to reveal my sources—Flynn and I had enough to deal with without adding breach of confidentiality to the mix. "Psychic Hotline. Who cares how I know?"

"Ugh." She pursed her lips and dug a single, pink-polished fingernail into the corner of her mouth, a habit she'd had since childhood. "Small-town gossips are the *worst.*" She used her other hand to point imperiously at the keys dangling from the car's ignition. "Drive."

"I'm not your chauffeur," I huffed, dropping the pregnancy gambit and playing right into her hands.

"Of course not." She patted my wrist as I started the engine. "You're my big sister, here to save the day."

I backed out of the parking space. "Why couldn't Mom save the day for a change?"

"She wanted to go canoeing in the Boundary Waters with her new boyfriend, Doug. She said you're better in a crisis than she is."

Our mother had been saying that since I was thirteen, which was why I'd spent my high school years giving Skye curfews and signing her dismal report cards. "Great. So. Does Bob know about the baby?"

"Are you going to keep bringing that up? Because if you are, this drive is going to take, like, *forever.*" She hitched up her rainbow-striped tube top.

I gave her a look and lowered the sunglasses back over my eyes. "You want some cheese with that whine?"

"No, but I'll take some crackers with my cheese." She readjusted the rearview mirror and applied peony pink lip gloss, then tilted her head to study me. "You look good, Faithie. Very L.A. fabu. Except what is going on with your hair? Did you sleep in a wind tunnel?"

"I didn't, actually. How kind of you to mention it." I had long ago resigned myself to life as a walking recessive gene. Wavy red hair, blue eyes, skin that burned at the mere mention of sunlight. Ideal for beachside living.

"Here, I'll fix it." She beamed at me and dug a comb out of her purse.

I threw up my palms to ward her off. "I can brush my own hair."

"Don't be so stubborn. You need to look your best." She grinned. "I know someone who's all anxious to see you."

My whole body tensed up as she tried to drag the comb through my tangles. "Who?"

She giggled. "Lars, of course! I've been telling him all about you!"

My lungs released the breath I hadn't realized I'd been holding. "Oh."

She blinked and studied my face. "Why? Who'd you think?"

I shook my head. "No one. Stop scalping me and let's hit the road."

Which we did. And then, on a desolate stretch of Route 57, with nothing but miles of open horizon on either side of us, she dropped the bombshell of Bikini Atoll proportions.

"You know, you have a terrible attitude," she declared from her post in the passenger seat while I muttered about the downfalls of a culture which espouses ice-fishing and refers to the popular children's game as "duck, duck, gray duck" rather than "duck, duck, goose." "What are you so snarky about, anyway? You grew up here. It's your home."

This was mortifying but true. God knew I had played a few rounds of "duck, duck, gray duck" in my day.

"I may have grown up here, but it is *not* my home."

"Sure it is," she insisted, waving to a passing eighteen-wheeler. "You've lived here longer than any other place. How come you hate it so much?"

I sighed. "I don't *hate* it, I'm just not small-town material. And after the whole thing with Dad leaving—I had a lot of good reasons to move away after high school."

She popped open the glove compartment, presumably foraging for gum. "You took off to California like a bat out of hell with a weasely bass player."

"That is neither here nor there. I'm very happy in L.A. now."

"But you're hardly ever there," said the Sun-In Sage. "You just keep bouncing around the world all by yourself. Don't you ever get lonely?"

"No. And don't start with the Phyllis Schlafly rhetoric. I like my life the way it is."

We watched at the reflection of our car in the shiny silver tanker truck crawling along in front of us. A redhead, a blonde, and a whole lot of baggage under an empty blue sky.

She started to gnaw her bottom lip. "So . . . guess what?"

My big-sister Spidey sense started tingling. "What?"

She stared down at the cluttered floor mats. "Well, um, I think I told you this before, but you know about Flynn, right?"

I sat up straighter and adjusted the seat belt across my chest, bracing myself for the fresh horrors about to unfold. "What about him?"

I tried to imagine what might have become of my childhood love. Raising eight rowdy children with a nagging wife, a rotting white picket fence, and a mangy spaniel? Living a wretched, unfulfilling existence in a van down by the river, surrounded only by ESPN and empty beer cans? Starring in a tell-all reality TV series in which past girlfriends are hunted down and made to pay for their crimes?

"Well . . ." She picked at her cuticles. "You know that he's the other co-owner of the bar, right?"

I swerved to the side of the deserted highway and slammed on the brakes. The safety belt strap dug into my chest. The road stretched out in front of us, a black ribbon receding into amber waves of grain.

I cut the ignition, unbuckled my seat belt, and turned to stare down my sister.

"*What?*"

She widened her eyes and blinked. "*What* what?"

"Flynn is a co-owner of the bar? Are you fucking kidding me?"

She avoided my gaze and shredded a gum wrapper. "He owns a third of it. I thought I told you when I faxed you the copy of the loan application that—"

"No, you did not tell me. I *definitely* would have remembered that."

"Oh." She shrugged one delicate shoulder. "Well, you should have read the contract more carefully. I asked him for help to buy it right after I asked you, and he said yes."

"Then, why the hell didn't *he* co-sign the mortgage?"

"He didn't want to."

"He didn't want to," I repeated. "Smart guy. He gets off scot-free while you and I get sucked down deeper and deeper into the financial sinkhole. How convenient."

"No, no, it's not like that! He's helping out. He's bartending and stuff at night. He's going to help all summer."

I closed my eyes and rested my forehead against the black plastic steering wheel.

"Flynn. Is working at the bar. Right now."

"Uh-huh."

"Did you tell him I'm coming?"

"Not exactly."

"That's it." I put the car into gear and executed a neat three-point turn across the double yellow line. "I'm going back to Los Angeles."

She gasped. "Faithie! Nooo!

"I'm dead serious. If you want to get back to Lindbrook, you have ten seconds to get out and start hitchhiking." I lunged across the front seat and shoved the passenger door open.

She wrapped both hands around her seat belt and howled. "Don't leave me! I really need your help. I mean, with all your restaurant experience . . ."

Six years ago, I worked as a cocktail waitress at a club in Los Feliz. The job involved ferrying Pinot Grigio and Johnnie Walker Blue to record producers and sitcom actors. Then I bought a juice bar, which I sold because I couldn't stand getting up at four A.M. every day to hit the organic produce markets. How this made me a crackerjack candidate for a managerial position in a backwoods tavern called "The Roof Rat," in which they served a regional beer called "Pig's Eye," was unclear.

"You do not need me. You have Flynn." I pointed at the car door. "I'm going back to Cali, baby."

"But he can't do everything!" She layered her voice with a Styrofoam squeak and played her trump card. "What about the baby?"

I closed my eyes and balled up my fists, the better to really concentrate on seething. "I am going. To kill you."

"You'll hardly ever see him. I swear to God, Faithie! He lives up in Minneapolis now, and he's been driving down to help me out every night since Bob left. But he has this big important job in the city . . ."

I couldn't resist taking the bait. "What's his job?"

"He works for the new NHL hockey team in the cities."

"The Polecats? Flynn works for the St. Paul Polecats?"

"Yeah, I guess. He's kind of a workaholic."

"He is?" I paused. "Is he married?"

"No."

"Girlfriend?"

"Maybe." She turned her attention back to her cuticles, bored with this line of questioning. "I don't exactly keep track."

My foot remained firmly on the brake. "Let's sum up, shall we? Currently, I have no money, you have no money, I'm on the brink of professional ruin, and I just drove halfway across the United States to the one place I never want to see again, all to face personal and financial humiliation with a man who hates my guts and doesn't know I'm coming. Is that about right?"

"That's right." She nodded. "Oh, except don't forget about Bob and the baby."

"Bob and the baby. Of course."

She clasped both hands under her chin. "Does Flynn really still hate your guts?"

"In a word, yes."

"What *happened* when you guys broke up?"

"It's a long story."

She waved a hand as if dismissing her butler. "Don't worry. It'll all be fine."

I thought about his chilled, clipped voice on the phone line in Italy. "It will not be fine. In fact, it will be the exact opposite of fine."

"Why? Just because you guys used to date?" She looked

amazed. "I'm sure he doesn't care about all that anymore. It's been, like, ten years. He probably doesn't even remember your passionate, star-crossed whatever. He's a *guy.*"

"That makes me feel *so* much better, Skye."

"You're welcome." She beamed. "Besides, we need you. You're so good at math and bossing people around. You know about making drinks and running a business. The family business. And besides, what were you talking about before? Oh yeah, your credit rating. Think about that."

We listened to the rustle of the wind in the open fields. Finally, I turned the engine back on, jerked the car through another three-point turn and started off toward the Land of Lutefisk.

"Damn it, damn it, son of a bitch."

Skye let out a delighted whoop. "This is going to be great, Faithie! You won't regret it!"

I already regretted it, but I was too far gone to turn back now.

3

Twenty miles of cornfields later, I remembered why I'd been in such a hurry to flee America's heartland ten years ago.

Skye, having depleted the chewing gum reserves, slouched into her seat, as close to a supine position as she could achieve in the overstuffed Volkswagen. I was trying to watch the road while simultaneously whipping myself into a frenzy about the upcoming reunion with Flynn. I had given up on subtlety and resorted to interrogating my sister in a loud, high-pitched voice.

"Do you guys ever talk about me?"

"Not really." She blew a big pink Trident bubble and crossed her eyes, watching it balloon past her nose.

"Well, does he ever ask about me?"

"Not really." The bubble popped.

I gritted my teeth. "What does 'not really' mean?"

"I don't know! It means stop asking me. What's the big deal, anyway?"

"Look. I just want to know where I stand. It's been a long time since I've seen him, and I need to know what to expect. You dragged me into this mess—the least you can do is prep me."

She slowly scraped the gum off her cheeks and popped it back into her mouth. "Why so nervous? Seriously. What on earth happened when you broke up that you're still so antsy about the whole thing?"

"I'm asking the questions here."

"Whatever." She sighed, all put-upon and penitent. "He never mentions you. Mostly we just talk about how much money the bar is losing and what we should do." She squirmed in her seat. "Why *did* you take up with that bass player, anyway?"

"I don't want to talk about it."

Eventually, I stopped badgering the witness and stared out the windshield at acre after acre of undulating golden grass. Trying not to think about the river at the edge of the town where Flynn and I had grown up together. We had made endless discoveries in the clear, cool water and the silty gray muck underneath. When we were young, it was all about tadpoles and turtles and other wholesome Mark Twain critters. But our late adolescence was spent in large part lying on the riverbanks, tangled up in a gasping urgency, exploring each other. We delved into the savage, lovely wilderness that can exist between two people who are too desperate and too young to realize that you can get lost if you forge ahead too quickly. And we got lost, all right. We found that river together, and we left each other on that wet, grainy shore, but I wasn't sure what remained of the deep, dark undercurrents between us.

"Here we are. I guess." My sister's voice was flat as we whizzed past a giant bronze statue of Paul Bunyan (don't ask), which was flanked on either side by a white clapboard sign welcoming us to Lindbrook.

"Yep." I studied the Jackson Pollock bug splatters on the window. "The bar's where The Penalty Box used to be on Main Street, right?"

"Yeah, but we can't go straight there. We have to go see Lars first."

"Forget it. I'm your underpaid business consultant, not your bad boyfriend enabler."

She clapped a hand to her heart. "How can you say that? You haven't even met Lars! He's totally different from Bob. And Jason. And Dave. And Seth."

"Allow me to refresh your memory. You are pregnant with your AWOL husband's child, are you not? Isn't it a tad early to return to the dating circuit? Let's not be a ground ball for the Jerry Springer recruiters."

She giggled. "I'm not dating him—yet. Besides, we have to go see him because he's got my house keys. I gave them to him before I left so he could fix the kitchen sink while I was gone."

"What happened to your sink?"

"Oh, it got clogged or something because I put Bob's fishing

tackle down the disposal when I got mad. Here, pull over. There it is, Minne-Motors. That's his auto shop!"

"Minne-Motors?" I parked the car. "What does that even mean?"

I had expected my return to Lindbrook to be marked with a rush of bittersweet déjà vu. I had expected to be overwhelmed with total recall of my childhood days. But when I finally stepped out of the car and onto the sidewalk, I was struck not by how much things had remained the same, but by the slight changes in the landscape. Like the McDonald's down the block. That was new. Garish golden arches now soared over the familiar brick storefronts and the grassy public park.

"Come on!" Skye pranced in place on the sidewalk, scattering an orderly parade of black ants. "I can't wait for you to meet Lars! And I really have to pee."

The proprietor of Minne-Motors had obviously not invested a lot of time or money in interior decor. Piles of grease-streaked chrome crested between open-hooded, disemboweled cars. The walls were dotted with rusty out-of-state license plates, and the metallic pounding of mechanics at work almost drowned out the Guns 'N' Roses blasting out of a tattered black boombox.

"Isn't this great?" My sister yelled over the racket.

She dragged me over to a gutted green Honda, where her latest ticking time bomb of a suitor was replacing a tire. Lars was everything I'd expected, a big sister's nightmare. Clad in jeans and a smudged white T-shirt, smelling vaguely of WD-40, he wore his blond hair in that style so perennially popular with Minnesota maintenance men—the mullet.

Skye turned on the full-voltage charm.

"Hi." She raised her chin and smiled at him, the afternoon sun streaming through her curls like a halo.

Lars stumbled to his feet and scuffed the ground with one well-worn boot toe. He was roughly the size of the Tower of London. "Hey."

It was hard to tell, but it almost looked like he was blushing under those grease stains and that swarthy farmer's tan.

"This is my sister, Faith." She grabbed my fingers and forced them into a handshake with the Human Harley-Davidson.

He sort of grunted by way of introduction, but his eyes continued their all-access tour of Skye, who was still doing her rendition of sugar and spice and everything nice.

She flitted off to the Minne-Motors version of a ladies' room, leaving Lars and me to stare blankly at one another for five minutes in an effort to get to know each other better. It was all the time I needed to ascertain that the man had the wit and personality of an anvil. When my sister returned from the bathroom, she demanded her apartment key.

"Sure, babe." Lars dug through his jeans pockets, frowning at the array of loose change, Swiss Army knives and begrimed store receipts he unearthed before handing over a glittery pink keyring. "I had to replace the disposal rotor in the sink. It's not a good idea to put wire and lead weights in there."

"Of course. How silly of me." Skye wrapped her slender white arm around his bulging bicep, then turned to me. "Now let's get out of here and go home. I need to change." She frowned down at her tube top. "This shirt is totally sweaty. You should really get your car's air conditioner checked out. In fact, I'm sure that Lars here would be happy to—"

"No time for primping." I gave her a look. "We need to start dealing with the bar—and other, more pressing matters—posthaste."

"I have to change," she pouted. "And I live right upstairs from the bar. It'll take two seconds."

Lars regarded her with the same pitying expression as he might an abandoned kitten shivering in the gutter. I rolled my eyes and gave in.

"Oh, fine. But you get two seconds only," I warned.

"Okay! Lars will drop me off. It's his lunch break." She tugged him toward a gleaming silver motorcycle in the parking lot.

I trailed behind them, closing the door as "Welcome to the Jungle" started pounding out of the boombox. I started for my car as they roared off down the street, but froze in place as a familiar figure rounded the corner a block ahead of me. He was tall and dark-haired with broad shoulders. I scrutinized the back of his head and his gray T-shirt, my heart pounding like a kettle drum.

And then a dog barked and bounded across the street. The man turned to greet the black and white spaniel, and as soon as I saw his profile, I exhaled, the tension eddying out of my chest. It was no one I knew. Just a tall, dark stranger.

I started the car with shaking hands. I knew exactly where to find Skye's bar—I had vivid memories of darting in there twenty years ago, red-faced and stealthy as I tried to convince my father to come home for the evening.

Returning to Lindbrook had been a huge mistake, the equivalent of rowing out to the center of a lake in an aluminum canoe during a lightning storm, brandishing a titanium golf club, and yelling "Bring it on, God!"

When I parked on Main Street three minutes later, I kept my seat belt fastened and stared at the dusty brick facade of the Roof Rat. The bar was constructed like a Midwestern version of a classic Italian palazzo—a small, squat building with a business on the first floor and living quarters on the second floor. A large picture window showcased the bar's name in fanciful turquoise letters (Skye's nod to redecorating). I could see neon signs inside, glinting against the glass.

The House of Bad Karma cleverly disguised as a backwoods watering hole.

What finally forced me out into the open was the humidity. Without the air conditioner cranked up to eleven, the Golf soon assumed the properties of a terrarium under a blazing sunlamp.

I grabbed my battered suitcase out of the backseat and lugged it around to the sagging wooden steps.

"What took you so long?" Skye demanded, throwing open the door. "Gosh, it's hot."

"You got that wrong. It's fucking sweltering." I tossed my bag on the floor and assessed Chez Skye.

She had painted the living room walls lemon yellow, offsetting a threadbare purple loveseat and a huge red sofa in the shape of a pair of lips. The floor was carpeted with old newspapers and discarded wardrobe choices, and she stepped over a fuzzy pink sweater on her way to turn on the air conditioner.

Atop the scratched wooden coffee table lay several issues of *Cosmopolitan,* a copy of *Field & Stream,* and an overflowing ashtray. Guessing that the ashtray and *Field & Stream* were artifacts from happier days with Bob, I scooped them up and carried them to the trashcan in the kitchen.

Automatically, my hands started to clean up the mess my sister had left on the counter—boxes of Pop-Tarts, half-empty coffee mugs, bananas far past their prime.

Skye appeared at the kitchen door, twisting her hair up into a topknot. "What are you doing?"

"Listen up, buttercup. I came here to save both our asses, and as God is my witness, that's what I'm going to do. But you need to cooperate." I opened the dishwasher and tried to locate the silverware drawer. "If you're going to spend all your time drooling over Sven and the art of motorcycle maintenance, this isn't going to work."

"Hello? I *am* cooperating," she protested. "I'm getting changed right now to go to work." She emphasized her point by retrieving a powder-blue halter top from the top of the refrigerator and disrobing in front of the sink.

"Okay. Putting on darling little outfits is not what I need from you right now."

She stuck her bottom lip out. "Then what do you need?"

"Long-term, I need you to come to the bar every day ready to work. I need you to help me sort through the financial stuff you have down there. I need you to pay attention so this kind of thing doesn't happen to you again." I ticked these items off on my fingers and tried to look stern.

"I'm listening," she said with her head in the freezer. She emerged with two frostbitten grape Popsicles, handed one to me, and smiled. "What about the short-term?"

I thought this over while I stacked plates in her cupboard.

"Have you decided what you're going to do about the baby?" I finally asked, raising an eyebrow at her flat stomach.

"Um . . . no?"

"Then you have to do three things. One, make an OB-GYN appointment as soon as possible. See if they can get you in tomorrow. Two, watch out for Lars . . ."

"You are so paranoid." She twirled the Popsicle in her mouth and did not, I noticed, agree to my terms. "What's three?"

"Three is . . ." I deposited the clean spoons in the silverware drawer and let my hair fall down over my face. "Flynn's coming to bartend tonight, right?"

"Yup."

"Then here's what we're going to do. We're going to go down to the bar now, and you're going to show me all the accounts and receipts. But you need to let me know when Flynn shows up. Do *not* tell him that I'm here until I get a chance to tell him myself. I will handle him. Okay?"

"Okay. I promise." She nodded solemnly. "I will let you know the second Flynn gets here."

"Good. Now let's get ready to go."

As we headed for the bedroom, the damp, mosquito-riddled

heat brought back memories of my childhood summers, spent languishing in front of whirring portable fans, playing lethargic games of Uno and sweating.

"Jeez, look at your arm. You're going to be a crispy critter tomorrow," Skye said. "Didn't you use any sunblock?"

"Half the bottle."

"Well, you're all freckled and pink and gross. What should I wear with this top? I need to look good." She peeled off her shorts and surveyed the floor for clothing options. "How about this?" She fished up a miniscule white skirt.

"I don't know." I frowned down at my gross, pink, and freckled arm. "What's typical Roof Rat attire?"

"Oh, you know. A bar is a bar. Just wear what you'd wear to go clubbing in L.A."

"In L.A. I'd be wearing second-hand Prada and a canister of pepper spray. Ugh. I feel like roadkill. I need to take a shower." I could not face *anyone,* let alone the ex love of my life, with sunburned limbs, insomniac bags under my eyes, and wind-tunnel hair.

"No time to shower. Here, borrow my lip gloss. And let me do something with your hair." She pounced on me again with the comb.

"Ow! Knock it off, that really hurts!"

"Faithie, no offense, but you're a buzz-kill and a half today," she said, continuing to yank my hair out by the roots. "What is the matter with you?"

I pulled away and struggled into a white tank top and a black cotton skirt. I felt tight and hot all over. The sunburn had gotten under my skin and into my blood. "Nothing's the matter with me."

"Then stop acting like something crawled up your ass and died. Let's go!"

So we trooped out the door and down the back steps, Skye still swiping at me with the comb. Every step we took toward the gray metal door to the Roof Rat brought me closer to outright panic. Because I was really back. I was back, my old boyfriend was back, and, just like the song, there was gonna be trouble.

4

"All right. Let's have a look at this place." I tried to steel myself for the task ahead.

Skye was having trouble with the dead bolt. Maybe this was a sign. A sign that I should *not* go into the bar.

But then the door swung open, a portal from the orange Minnesota sunset into shadowy layers of spilled Pig's Eye and cigarette smoke.

"Come on! This is going to be great." She bounced past me, flicking on lights inside the bar.

I ignored the coppery taste tingling in my mouth, set my jaw like a new recruit and marched inside.

* * *

My sister had told me the bar was in trouble, but even I couldn't imagine how much trouble until I saw it with my own eyes.

It was bad. The main barroom seemed to be styled in North Woods Nouveau. Mottled maroon floor tiles were scuffed beneath the thick maple chairs and tables, and the chipped wooden bartop had clearly seen better days. A cracked cloudy mirror, an enormous stuffed moose head and a stuffed gray muskie wearing an expression of eternal disdain hung alongside the collection of neon beer signs.

"This place has got a lot of character," I said truthfully.

"Don't you love it?" Skye grinned. "I bought the moose head after I divorced Jason. Found it at a garage sale. And wait 'til you see what I did to the women's bathroom! Come on, I'll give you the grand tour."

But the grand tour began and ended with the back office, because I went Leona Helmsley as soon as I saw it.

I stood at the office door and tried to pick my jaw up off the floor. "Skye Geary, what the hell were you thinking?"

She peered over my shoulder. "Um, what do you mean?"

The back office looked like the aftermath of pledge week. I could barely discern a desk under a rainforest's worth of fashion magazines and, inexplicably, *The AKC Guide to Choosing a Dog*. Pastel hair clips littered the thin beige carpet, and the white walls were plastered with pictures of Hollywood heartthrobs.

I gaped at a brooding Colin Farrell and tried to absorb the magnitude of this disaster. "Hell. We should file for Chapter Eleven right now and save ourselves the angst."

She clutched at my shoulders. "How can you *say* that?"

"Look at this place. It's like Britney Spears's tour bus. Clearly, I just wasted three days driving out here."

She took a step back and turned both of her palms toward me. "It's not that bad. I know where everything is, I promise. I have a system—"

"And what's with the *Tiger Beat* collage?"

She crossed her arms over her chest and stuck her bottom lip out. "Bob let me decorate however I wanted."

I crossed *my* arms over *my* chest and leaned back against the doorframe. "Well, there's a new sheriff in town, honey."

She bowed her head, then blinked out at me, lost and forlorn.

I wasn't buying it. "I mean it. We have to get our act together. Now. Go get me a trash bag, please."

Her head snapped back up. "What for?"

"I'm assuming that there are invoices and profit and loss statements under all this crap?"

"Well, yeah, but . . ."

I jostled past her and stormed into the barroom, where I rummaged around until I found a lone green Hefty bag next to the garbage can. "Aha!"

My sister stayed hot on my heels as I charged back into the office.

"Faithie, please, no! I'm begging you! Give me half an hour to clean this up myself. Give me ten minutes!"

I kept going. "Skye. We have thirty days as of last week. Time is of the essence. Your ten minutes are up."

I ripped into Russell Crowe. She howled.

"Trust me," I said, balling up Orlando Bloom and Hugh Jackman along with sticky bits of tape. "This hurts me more than it hurts you."

My sister stayed in the doorway and wailed pitifully as I tossed her "system" into the trash bag.

"That's my favorite—"

"We're throwing it out!"

"I haven't even read that issue—"

"Out!"

"Not the nail polish!"

"Out!"

And so it went until the desktop was visible. I was sweaty and exasperated by the time I had unearthed the creditor bills and the payroll information, but Skye seemed near tears, so I gave her a consolatory pat on the back.

"Trust me, sweetie. The new system will be much better. Now, where's your computer?"

Her big blue eyes watered. "We don't have one. We just use an account ledger."

"Naturally. It's only the twenty-first century. All right, then, where's the ledger?"

"One of the desk drawers?" she guessed.

I sighed. "What about the receipts?"

"The floor safe. I think."

After a moment of silent hysteria, I smiled gently at my sister and said, "Okay. Go open the bar. I'll be back here figuring out how this place runs."

"Are you sure I can't help?"

"The best way to help is to make sure we're doing lots of business," I said. "Go open the bar. And, hey—remember what I said before? About talking to Flynn?"

"Yeah, yeah." She tossed her hair. "I'm not a total idiot, you know. I'll bust in here as soon as he walks through the door. I promise."

"Thank you. Oh, and what's the combination to the floor safe?"

She slapped the comb—now full of the hair she had ruthlessly yanked out of my scalp—down on the desktop. "Nine-oh, two, one-oh."

But of course.

Whatever the combination to the floor safe was, it wasn't 90210. It took me a good five minutes to determine this, five minutes trapped under the desk on all fours, sweating and cursing while my head thudded against the overhanging wood and my knees chafed raw against the cheap, scratchy carpet.

I thought about the girlish fantasies on parade throughout Skye's home—charm bracelets, pastels, clean-cut Hollywood heartthrobs. What would life be like for her baby? With a mother who was still waiting for life to turn into a fairy tale and a father who would forever be chasing the newest pretty face? After about a second's worth of deliberation, I decided that the kid would be better off having no father than a father like my own—restless, smothered by his children's very existence.

I was giving the alleged lock combination one last shot when I heard the slow, deep male voice in the bar.

I jerked my head up against the desk and smacked the shit out of the top of my skull.

My thigh muscles were burning, my head was smarting, but I froze where I was and strained with every pore in my body to detect activity from the barroom. Was that him?

Poking my head out from under the desk, I closed my eyes and turned my right ear toward the door. Which facial muscle should I tense in order to improve hearing acuity?

And then I heard solid, steady footsteps heading down the hall, heading toward me.

"Relax, Skye. I got it. I'm all over it. I'll be in the back room if you need me."

Oh my God. It *was* him. I knew Flynn's voice when I heard it.

This was it. The big reunion.

I remained in my catcher's squat under the desk, mouth open and mind reeling, searching for the best way to handle this. It felt like the tide was coming in, fast and freezing, and a single coherent thought crystallized in my head:

I was so not ready for this.

Any nanosecond now, that door was going to burst open, Patrick Flynn was going to stride through, and he was going to look at me and see that I was just as big a mess as I was when I left him. If not bigger. And I was going to look at him and see—well, I didn't know what I would see. I was about to stare down the consequences of my past choices.

So I stopped peeking out from beneath the desk and did what any rational woman would do: I ducked back under and burrowed deep into the corner between the floor safe and the wall.

The door swung open.

The view was very limited from my shadowy enclave, but I saw two scuffed brown hiking boots and several inches of clean blue denim appear through the open doorway.

And then I heard humming. He was humming . . . he was humming the *Mission: Impossible* theme?

The boots started toward the desk and I shrank back against the cool plaster of the wall, squeezing my eyes shut, hoping that this would somehow help to make me invisible.

The humming stopped.

And then I heard the hollow click of plastic against wood, directly over my head.

Oh, shit. The comb. Skye had left the comb full of my red hair sitting there on the desk. He sucked his breath in. I was afraid to let mine out.

The silence stretched out into ice ages.

"Faith?" He said this word in the same low, quiet tone he'd been humming with, but I heard it. I turned my face up toward the raw, unfinished planks of wood under the desktop.

"Yes?" I whispered back.

The boots took two giant steps back toward the door.

"Faith?" His voice sounded louder and startled and not very pleased.

"Yeah?" I called back, trying to sound nonchalant.

There ensued another very long pause. I attempted to wriggle out from under the desk while holding down the hem of my skirt and finally managed, with no dignity whatsoever, to crawl out. My cheeks flushed as I stood up, brushed off my bare knees and prepared to reckon with the man I'd run away from ten years ago.

Flynn filled the doorway with his wide shoulders and tall, lanky frame. The watery fluorescent light cast the contours of his face into sharp, shadowed angles, but I could see the boy I'd left behind in this dark, handsome man. I could see him in those hooded sepia eyes and the thick brown hair. I could see him in the curl of that mouth and the long, straight planes of those cheeks.

He looked unbelievably pissed off.

He crossed his arms and leaned back against the wall. His posture was relaxed, but his voice was edgy when he spoke. "What's going on here, Geary?"

I wiped my palms on my skirt and tried to disguise the fact that my hands were trembling.

"I can explain," I said. "Skye gave me the wrong combination to the safe, you see, and—"

"Get the hell out of here."

"*What?*"

He cleared his throat. "I said—"

"I heard you. They heard you in Duluth." I looked into his eyes and tried to find a trace of the safe, sweet boy I'd known. I got nothing but flinty Clint Eastwood hostility.

"Then get going."

"You call me, *in Italy,* and beg me to come out here and now you're telling me to get lost?"

"I would hardly call that begging." He stared at the wall behind me. "And you show up, in my bar, unannounced and uninvited. What do you want me to say?"

"Skye invited me," I sputtered. "And it's not *your* bar. And what ever happened to good manners?"

"I'd say we gave up on good manners a long time ago." He smiled tightly and shook his head. "I told you to help with Skye's personal life, not her business problems. This bar is my responsibility, and I can't have you in here. Especially if you're trying to crack my safe."

"It's not just your responsibility." I took an involuntary step back and my skirt brushed against the desktop. The smooth, cool wood pressed into the backs of my thighs. When had he become so surly and brutish?

"Really." He took another step toward me. His shoulders blocked my view of the door. The only escape route.

"That's right." I crossed my arms over my chest, mirroring his defensive posture. "It is *our* bar and *our* safe. Skye obviously neglected to mention this, but I'm a co-owner of this bar, too. So one third of this safe I'm cracking is legally mine."

Another step toward me. His face didn't betray any shock or surprise, but I could see a small muscle flexing in his jaw. And as he approached, I recognized the familiar scent—part sun-dried laundry, part lawn clippings, unmistakably Flynn.

"Well, do me a favor then and stay out of *our* office," he said. "I have a lot of work to do and I don't need this"—he gestured to the air crackling with tension between us—"getting in the way."

There was a charged, angry silence as we sized each other up.

The faint clink of glasses drifted in from the barroom. Finally, I couldn't stand to think about all the things we weren't saying.

"Skye's safe combination isn't working," I blurted out.

He shoved his hands into his pockets. "That's because I changed it."

I softened my tone. "Look. Flynn." He flinched slightly when I spoke his name aloud. "Let's start over. I'm here to help."

"I don't want to start over. And I don't need any help."

"Oookay." I took a deep breath and exhaled slowly. "Well, then, I need *your* help. How's that?"

"Faith Geary admits she needs help?" He raised his eyebrows. "Should I be getting ready for the apocalypse?"

I put my hand on my hip. "Cease and desist, Flynn. I know you're mad, but we have to make peace."

"I'm not mad, and I have a lot of work to do."

"You're not mad?" I raised my eyebrows.

He shook his head and folded his arms. "Nope."

"Really? Because you *seem* a little angry."

"And yet I'm not." He lowered his voice each time I upped the volume.

I opened my mouth, then closed it again. "What's the combination to the damn safe?"

"Ninety-nine, thirty, nine."

"How am I supposed to remember that?"

"Jersey numbers. Wayne Gretzky, Bobby Orr, Gordie Howe."

"Of course. The holy trinity of the Church of Hockey." I

rolled my eyes. "Getting out of Minnesota was the best decision I ever made."

"Oh, come on, don't say that." Flynn looked at me with a hint of the sly, wicked humor I remembered. "Not marrying me was the best decision you ever made."

And with that, he turned and left me with the leaden weight of his words in the pit of my stomach.

So I did what I always do. I ran.

My feet took off for the orange exit sign down the hall. As I crashed through to the damp falling dusk, I could hear Skye shouting, "Faith? Flynn?! Oh, damn it!"

I caught up with myself in the car and clenched the keys so tightly I cut my palm. The first evening stars winked down as I started the engine and peeled out onto Main Street.

I headed for the highway. For the road that would take me back to California. But when my headlights illuminated the road sign reading PILLERTON, 3 MILES, I realized that not only was I going the wrong way, but I had been driving for fifteen minutes with absolutely no recollection of the journey.

The only thing I could think about was the sharp chill in Flynn's eyes. If the man who'd once loved me more than anyone else in my life could look at me like that, what did that say about me?

I pulled into the first parking lot I saw. Once I turned the headlights off, it was just me and the vast open spaces spreading into the gray horizon.

I yanked the keys out of the ignition and flung them to the floor. And then I folded my arms on the steering wheel and cried.

I cried until my mouth was briny with salt and my anguish succumbed to exhaustion. I cried for all my failed attempts at love and for the people I'd let down. I cried for the capsized childhood that still haunted my hometown and for Skye's unborn baby, who would surface from the womb into a life sentence of capital *K* chaos. I cried because I'd barely slept in three days.

And that was how I ended up taking a nap in the Kmart parking lot in Pillerton, Minnesota.

A tinny ringing sliced through my sleep, and I jerked back to consciousness with a gasp. My right hand groped for the snooze button, but there did not seem to be one handy.

In fact, I seemed to be sitting up, staring over the hood of my car, in a parking lot flooded with insanely bright halogen lights under the night sky.

The tapping persisted, and I turned my head to the left to discover a ferocious neck cramp and a round, smooth-faced woman striking the window of my car with her keys.

"Oh, good." Her voice filtered through the glass. "I was hoping you weren't dead."

I stared at her as the events of the last few hours came rushing back. "Dead" would actually be an improvement on my current state.

I rubbed my eyes and rolled down the window a crack. "No, I'm not dead."

She nodded and shifted her hold on the baby on her hip. The infant, roly-poly in pink overalls, regarded me with drool-laced censure. "Good to know. We don't get too many corpses turning up at Kmart around here, but"—she shrugged—"there's a first time for everything."

Upon further inspection, I could discern part of a second child's head behind her dress. An unruly black cowlick popped out from behind her long denim skirt.

"Are you all right?" The woman still appeared concerned.

That voice. I closed my eyes and did a quick flip through the mental Rolodex. She seemed so familiar. I turned back to her and took in the curly chestnut hair, the huge amber eyes, and the authoritative, no-nonsense posture.

"Leah?"

Her face lit up and she smiled, cocking her head as she searched my face for clues.

"Leah Metter?" This was unbelievable.

She nodded. "Yeah. I'm sorry, but I can't seem to place—wait . . . Faith?"

I mustered a shaky smile. "Yeah."

"I'd recognize that red hair of yours anywhere!" she shrieked. The baby remained unimpressed.

I scrambled out of the car and we hugged, lurching around the parking lot in a crazy, awkward dance.

"Oh my God, Leah Metter! I can't believe it's you!" I tried to reconcile the Leah standing in front of me with the Leah I remembered from childhood.

"I know. It's actually Leah Goldberg now." She flashed the simple gold band encircling her left ring finger. "I've changed a lot since high school."

This was the understatement of the century. Leah Metter had been our regular babysitter through elementary school and junior high, and I'd always regarded her with a shy sort of awe. The only Jewish girl in a county high school of four hundred students, she was the type of self-assured free spirit who wore Birkenstocks before they were faddish and listened to the Ramones instead of Garth Brooks. After graduation, she'd gone off to UC Berkeley, and I had always assumed she'd progressed to international espionage or radical third-world revolutions.

Never once had I imagined that she would come back to Minnesota, acquire a husband and two children, start wearing silver hair pins with conservative Talbots outfits, and find me napping in total disgrace in a Volkswagen outside the Kmart.

"What are you doing here, anyway?" She pried the baby's fingers from their death grip on my hair.

"Here in Minnesota or here in my car?" I stalled.

"Both."

"Well, it's kind of a long story. Basically, I'm here to help out my sister."

"Skye?" She said this in the disapproving tone of voice you might use to mention "mink coats" or "tabloids."

I nodded.

"Yeah, I heard that Bob ran off with some hussy from Faribault. What a jackass." The baby stated to fuss, and Leah bounced the infant in her arms. "Look, it's almost seven, and I have to feed these two ASAP. Have you eaten yet?"

"Well, no, but—"

"Then it's settled. You're coming home with us." She smiled

at the baby on her hip. "This is Rachel. She's eleven months."

Rachel opened her mouth, gave me a gummy pink smile, and squealed. I was never sure how to act around babies, but I smiled and squeezed her tiny hand, which she reciprocated by waving a plump fist and announcing "Bye-bye!"

"And the little terror back there is Eli. He's five."

"No, Mama! Rex!" piped up a voice from her skirtfolds.

"Oh, excuse me. I forgot, honey. Faith, please allow me to introduce my son, Rex."

Rex, *né* Eli, was a pale little boy with thick dark hair and luminous black eyes. He clutched a small Kmart bag in one hand.

"Hi, Rex. I'm Faith." I knelt down to shake his hand, and he greeted me with the solemnity of a CEO meeting a new administrative assistant.

"Hello." His handshake was firm and perfunctory, very professional for a five-year-old wearing grass-stained jeans.

"Why is your hair so red?" he wanted to know.

Leah shushed him with a single raised eyebrow. "Come on, now. Everyone back to the car. Forward, march."

Rex hup-two-threed to a teal Camry parked a few spaces away, and Leah turned to me.

"Are you all right? You look like you've been crying."

"I'm fine, really," I told her.

She looked at me for another long moment. "We'll talk about it later. Here, help me get the kids strapped in, and then you can follow us in your car." She smiled ruefully. "By the way, we're hoping the 'Rex' thing is just a phase. I don't know what goes on in that kid's head. One day he just showed up at preschool and announced that he would no longer answer to Eli, only to Rex. So the teacher figured what the heck, except now half the boys in his class want to be called Rex, too."

Leah opened the passenger side door with her free hand, laughing at my stunned expression. "You're back in Minnesota. No one locks their car doors here."

She leaned in to strap Rachel into a car seat while I wrestled with Rex's seat belt, then walked around to the driver's seat and started the car. A soothing, syrupy version of "Little April Showers" drifted out of the stereo speakers. This was the consummate family sedan, complete with little baggies of goldfish crackers in the ashtray and Wee Sing audiotapes in the glove compartment.

"I'm starving, Mama!" Rex cried from the backseat.

"We'll eat as soon as we get home. I hope you like fish sticks and macaroni and cheese, Faith."

"What's not to like?"

Leah and Rex sang along with the tape deck, and Rachel clapped her hands and gurgled with laughter. No one was paying any attention to me, but I was full of the nervous, eager hope of a stray dog suddenly adopted.

5

I'm going to be a deejay when I grow up," Rex announced through a mouthful of bright orange macaroni. "I will spin the wheels of steel. My name will be DJ Question Mark."

I swallowed the broccoli I was chewing. "A fascinating career. What made you choose that name?"

"It sounds mysterious." He scraped up the last bite of his macaroni and donated it to the Goldbergs' mixed-breed retriever. The dog licked up the pasta in a frenzy of snuffling and tail-wagging.

"Hans Gruber! No!" Leah's command came too late, and the caramel-colored dog sat back down and panted up at Rex with the plaintive eyes of a famine victim. "Eli, I already fed him dinner. Don't give him anything else."

"Rex, Mama!"

Leah rolled her eyes and wiped the baby's mouth with a damp napkin. "I beg your pardon, Rex. All right, I believe it's almost bedtime for the lights of my life. Stan, would you do the honors?"

"Of course." Stan Goldberg was wiry and good-looking in a tax-attorney sort of way, with a seemingly endless supply of patience and good humor. He rounded up the children with promises of lightning-fast baths and a dramatic reading of *Where the Wild Things Are*. Rex bestowed orange-tinted kisses on Leah's cheek, and then three-quarters of the Goldberg family retreated up the stairs in a fading hubbub of laughter and high-pitched chatter about the importance of question marks.

Leah and I were left with the remnants of dinner. The kitchen was small and warm, with clean white walls decorated by Rex's drawings, tan tiles on the floor, and a large glass patio door. I caught my reflection between the Yu-Gi-Oh decals plastered all over the window. I looked like a photographed negative of myself, dark and shifty against all these crisp white lines.

"Thank you so much for dinner. The least I can do is the dishes." I rose from my chair and started gathering up glasses and plates.

"Thanks." Leah leaned forward and rubbed the back of her neck with both hands. "I'm exhausted. Rachel got me up at five-thirty this morning, and we didn't get a nap."

The kitchen counter bore testament to this. It was cluttered with pacifiers, shattered graham crackers, and half-empty plastic juice cups. As I carried a handful of forks to the dishwasher I noticed a cactus parked between a huge, motherly fern and a sturdy aloe plant. Leah obviously had a green thumb, even with prickly, arid things imported from the desert.

I felt more at home here than I'd felt in any apartment or hotel room in my adult life. As I ran my hands under a stream of hot water, a dam overflowed somewhere inside me, but I honestly wasn't sure if I was jealous or just longing for this kind of kitchen, for the kind of a family life I'd never had.

"Stan's great," I told her. "Your whole family's great. You're really lucky."

"I know." She smiled. "When I left for Berkeley, I never thought I'd come back, but then I met Stan, and it turned out his family is from St. Paul. Once I got pregnant with Eli, it was all over. Our parents were dying to get their hands on my first-born, and since everyone was here in Minnesota . . ." She shrugged. "It seemed like a sign. So we moved back, and Stan opened the bakery down on Second Street, and now we don't have to drive to Minneapolis to get good challah."

"Wait. You guys own a bakery?"

She laughed, her brown curls bouncing against the faded blue denim of her shirtdress. "Yeah. My mother was shocked, too. I'm a part-time baker with two kids and a semi-checkered past. Who knew?"

"I'm ready to adopt Eli right now." I redoubled my efforts to scrub the stubborn fish stick residue off the plates.

"Well, you're welcome to take him off our hands any time, and I *do* mean *any* time. He can be a handful, and—" She broke off as I leaned over to grab a bottle of dish soap. "Faith Geary, is that a *tattoo?*"

I immediately tugged down the hem of my tank top, which had gapped up from the waistband of my skirt.

"Um . . . sort of." I wrenched at the back of the shirt again.

"Well, shuck my corn. What is it?"

"It's a little red heart." This was, at least, part of the truth, and I did not want to provide further details.

Leah's eyebrows practically reached her hairline as she grinned at me. "No offense, but you turned out nothing like what I would have expected. You were always kind of the Tori Amos sister, and Skye was the Tori Spelling. Do you know what I mean?"

Sadly, I did.

"You were always so quiet and shy . . ."

I bit back a laugh.

" . . . and you were always just so *together.*"

This time I did laugh. I couldn't help it.

"You were! You were like this cute little English professor, with those colored dividers in your notebooks and your shirts buttoned all the way up to the collar, telling Skye to do her homework. You were nine going on forty-five. And don't give me that look, you know it's true. I figured that you would have graduated first in your class, married that guy Flynn, and become a Sunday school teacher with five kids by now."

The bubble of mirth in my throat soured and sank into my stomach, where it settled like a lead bullet.

But Leah was on a roll. "And now look at your life. It turned out to be so exciting! Skye says you live in L.A. and travel all over the world. You got a tattoo, you still have all that gorgeous hair, and you obviously eat nothing but tofu and salad. You're a walking, talking, local-girl-makes-good story."

I swallowed hard and tried to smile.

"To think I had you pegged as a nice little introvert married to some stoic Minnesota boy." She shook her head. "And Skye, who I was sure would take off for Hollywood after high school, is still living here, wearing her sorority girl outfits and running a bar into the ground. So I guess it just goes to show you . . ."

To my utter mortification, I burst into tears for the second time in two hours.

Leah was out of her chair and across the kitchen faster than I had imagined possible. She enveloped me in her soft, secure arms, the same maternal strength I remembered from childhood.

The feel of her collarbone under my cheek reminded me that first of all, I hadn't seen this woman in ten years, and second of all, I was getting snot all over the Talbots ensemble. I tried to squirm away.

"Faith. I am so, so sorry. I apologize."

I covered my eyes. "No, it wasn't you. I just . . . remember how I was sleeping in the parking lot?"

She nodded and waited.

"Well." I took a ragged breath and sat down. "Remember that guy Flynn?"

She nodded again.

"I saw him tonight for the first time in years. And it did not go well." I rubbed my forehead with my palm.

"Oh boy. I heard you left town after graduation, but I never did get the whole story on what happened with Flynn. I assumed that it was just a high school sweetheart thing—that you guys just grew up and grew apart."

I twisted my hands together in my lap—a lover's knot with chipped pink polish and sunburned knuckles. "Not exactly." I exhaled slowly. "He wanted to get married, so I took off to L.A."

"I'll make some tea." She picked up a blue kettle and filled it at the sink. "So is that still a problem?"

"Flynn and I had a very intense relationship," I said, drained, defeated and yet somehow unable to abort this archeological dig through my interpersonal failings with the one potential friend I had in Lindbrook. "It went way beyond the high school sweetheart thing."

She smiled. "I guess you were elementary school sweethearts, too. Middle school sweethearts."

"Hell, we were in the same kindergarten class. And he was always hanging out with my family because he didn't have one."

She tilted her head to one side. "He didn't have a family? But I think I remember meeting his mother at Wendy Drake's wedding."

"Well, I mean, yes, he *has* a family, obviously, but his mom was a single parent. She worked constantly—and I do mean constantly—so mostly he stayed with his grandparents. It was all very Charlotte Brontë."

She nodded.

"His grandparents lived right up the road from us, and they were nice, but sort of staid and stodgy. That's why he started coming over to our house. Even though my family was a mess, at least there was always something interesting going on. My mom and my sister sort of adopted him. We were best friends until we hit high school, and then we were crazy in love, too." I paused. "Emphasis on the 'crazy.' It was like every emotion we had was magnified to the tenth power." I propped my chin in my hand. "Who knew it would all eventually lead to a nervous breakdown at Kmart?"

Leah looked puzzled. "I'm not quite getting the Kmart connection. So you broke up with him. That was ten years ago. You guys were teenagers. Of course you broke up. Probably much healthier in the long run than getting married when you were clueless, penniless, and eighteen years old."

She rummaged in a cupboard for mugs.

"You don't understand. This was all right after my father left the family. And my heart was broken and I wanted to leave, too. I was dying to get out of here and go live somewhere exciting and exotic. And Flynn knew this, but he asked me to marry him anyway. He gave me an ultimatum—get married or break up. Just to hold on to me, you know, to keep me here. We didn't even know where my father was at this point, if he was dead or alive or what." I sighed. "So I said no, and Flynn said he didn't ever want to see me again, and that's when I took up with the bass player at The Penalty Box."

"Oh yes, the infamous bass player." She laughed. "I heard all about that and I wasn't even in the state at the time. Well, so he proposed and you left him. So what?"

"We had sex for the first time the night before."

She turned to face me. "Hmmm."

I stared at the floor. "Exactly. I was just so upset. When I needed him the most, he wasn't there for me. We did it, and then all of sudden, he's in my face, demanding a lifetime commitment while we're watching my parents' marriage implode. He was trying to force me into the whole white-picket-fence cliché, which was—and still is, mind you—beyond terrifying."

"So you wisely said no."

"And when I did, he wouldn't even look at me. We turned everything inside out. All that intensity. Raging, hormone-addled, *adolescent* intensity. I flipped out and left for California."

Leah fished two tea bags out of a blue ceramic canister. "Cut the guy some slack. He was only seventeen. Seventeen-year-old males are not known for their emotional maturity."

"Neither are seventeen-year-old females. The bass player was the last straw for me and Flynn. I never called. I never wrote. He never called. He never wrote."

"I have to ask. What happened with the bass player?"

"Hank?" I tried to smile. "Oh, I got exactly what I deserved on that front. Once we got to L.A., he took up with another redheaded groupie, nabbed all the furniture and my crappy gold-plated jewelry, and I never heard from him again."

"Let the wild rumpus start!" Rex streaked across the kitchen floor, soaking wet and stark naked. He left a trail of bath water behind him on the tan tile floor.

"Stop running, you'll slip!" Leah yelled.

Gleeful and giggling, Rex scampered into the family room, where Hans Gruber started to bark.

"Excuse me for one moment, please." She stood up, marched into the family room, and returned a few moments later with the drenched desperado slung over her shoulder. After relegating Rex to the bathtub, she returned to the kitchen and handed me a mug of tea.

"Well, welcome back to the least exotic place on earth. How long are you staying?"

I wrapped my fingers around the cup and waited for the warmth to seep into my hands. "Hard to say." I'd given her the CliffsNotes version of Skye's money troubles, leaving out a few minor details, such as the pregnancy. "Until Skye sorts her life out or Flynn has me killed, whichever comes first."

She looked incredulous. "Why is he still holding a grudge?"

I shrugged. "Why do men do anything?"

"Point taken." She sipped her tea. "You know, I used to be mystified by males. Then I got married."

"And now?"

"Now I just try not to ask too many questions." She winked. "The answers are too frightening. But one thing I have figured out is that men are just as sensitive as women. But they refuse to acknowledge it, even to themselves. Look at this from Flynn's point of view. He slept with you. He proposed. Men really hate to put it out there. And when they do put it out there and then get trampled, they don't usually deal with it very well."

"Yeah, but a *decade* later? It's time to forgive and forget." Riiight. Just like I had.

Leah put her hand up. "Hey, don't tell me. The two of you need to sit down and talk it out."

"Easier said than done." I practically gnashed my teeth. "I tried to start the 'dialogue of healing,' as Oprah would have it, today. But somehow, we ended up having a fight about hockey instead."

"Yeah, that'll happen." She nodded as if this were a totally normal occurrence.

I fought the urge to bang my head against the wall. "He picked a fight and then refused to talk. I was sweet as pie and he just stonewalled like there was no tomorrow."

She looked at me. "You were sweet as pie?"

"I was!" I insisted. "What happened to the man? He never used to be like that. I'm going bankrupt over this stupid bar, and Skye's hooking up with the biggest no-hoper I've ever seen, and then Flynn looks at me like I'm something a stray cat threw up . . ." I trailed off and watched the wisps of steam rising from my tea. "Okay, I'm done with the pity party."

She smiled. "Well, if you two are going to work together, then you'll have to straighten this out sooner or later, right?"

I swallowed. "I guess."

"Postponing it is not going to make it any easier. If I were you, I'd go talk to him immediately. Start fresh."

I rolled my eyes. "Right."

She shrugged. "Why not?"

"Because the last time we started fresh, he told me to get the hell out and I ended up fleeing in disgrace and taking a nap in a parking lot."

"Well, things can only go uphill from there." Leah stood up, looking very resolute. "Come on. I'll walk you to your car."

"Did you not hear my story about the hockey argument? I can't go back there!"

She gazed levelly at me and folded her arms. "Not with that attitude, you can't."

"Oh, God. Don't tell me you've turned into one of those horrible power-of-positive-thinking people?"

She grinned, the same grin that Rex had. "It's my cross to bear. Now move it, my little chickadee. You're about to learn how to deal with a spurned Minnesota Man."

6

When I pulled up in front of the Roof Rat for the second time in twelve hours, the steamy July night was swarming with mosquitoes. Stale cigarette smoke and jukebox twangs escaped into the darkness every time someone opened the front door. The digital clock on the wall of the First National Bank announced that it was 10:13. The locals were just warming up.

After a few deep, carcinogen-filled breaths from the front step of the bar, I went in to face the country western music.

The first thing I saw from the shadows in the neon-tinged alcove was Flynn, pouring drinks behind the bar. He hadn't noticed my entrance, so I took the opportunity to really soak him in, without words or defenses or uncalled-for sarcasm getting in the way.

Flynn had been quite the dish even in our teenage days, but he'd improved during the past decade. He was broader now, more solid. The thick brown hair was shorter, the jawline and cheekbones now more chiseled than gaunt. His eyes were the same deep, autumn brown, but now they crinkled around the corners when he smiled.

I watched him pick up a tray piled with empty glasses. His hands looked exactly the same. He could have played the piano with those hands, or reshingled a roof. "Renaissance hands" I used to call them, when I was young and poetic and wanted to harass him.

He was currently clad in jeans and a plain white T-shirt. Par for the course. Throughout high school, he had insisted on wearing some combination of the following: white T-shirts, gray T-shirts, khakis and jeans. Any deviation from this ensemble was met with great suspicion: "Real men don't wear shorts," he'd tell me. "Bright colors are for hunting season only."

At the moment, he was talking to someone I recognized with a sinking heart as Sally Hutchins, who had graduated high school with us, the Class of 1994's answer to Lady Macbeth. Her father was the mayor and owned Lindbrook's sole real estate agency. My mother had cleaned his office every Thursday morning, and Sally never let me forget it.

Currently, she was poking at the ice cubes in her drink with a perfectly manicured index finger. She had dyed her once-brunette hair a jarring shade of crimson probably described by Clairol as "Titian Temptress."

There was something obviously amiss with a woman who voluntarily spent time and money to acquire hair like mine.

Flynn was nodding and smiling, listening to Sally. There was no sign of the embittered, mulish Wayne Gretzky disciple I'd faced down earlier that evening. I added to my growing list of problems the fact that my bar's co-owner appeared to be suffering from a split personality.

I watched the dark eclipse of his profile as he turned toward the bar. The white cotton T-shirt stretched across his shoulderblades, and I remembered how they had felt under my hands. The sound of his heartbeat and his laughter, as deep and thick as warm molasses, had been as familiar to me as my own.

A droplet of sweat curled down my neck.

I stepped out of the alcove. He didn't turn, but I saw him jerk his head up to glance into the cloudy mirror behind the rows of Jack Daniel's and Smirnoff. He wrapped his hand around the scarred wood of the bar. My shoulders slumped as his tensed into a Type-A template.

"Um. Hi." Why oh why hadn't I come up with something suave and disarming to say?

He turned back to the sink, away from the customers. All I could see was the back of his head. "How may I help you?" His voice remained steady and flat. He might have showed more affect reporting a Timberwolves score.

I lowered my voice to avoid being overheard by the many eavesdroppers straining to catch every syllable. "I don't know. I guess I just wanted to talk."

"About . . . ?"

"About . . . you know. This afternoon and everything."

"What about this afternoon?"

I sighed. Evidently, we were going to be doing this the hard way. "If you don't want to talk about today, then can we at least talk about what happened before today?" I counted to ten, then plunged ahead. "About the break-up?"

Dead silence. And then he said, in that same Timberwolves-scorecard voice, "I have nothing to say."

"Well, I have a few things to say. To start with, I should probably explain why I said no when you asked me to—"

"I mean it. I'm not going to talk about it."

I couldn't see his face, but I recognized that tone. He wasn't going to talk about it. Case closed. I tried to decide how best to proceed. "Flynn. I am working my ass off trying to be nice here. Are you going to talk about *anything? Ever?*"

He considered this for a moment. "I should probably talk about my plans for the bar."

I reminded myself that now was not the time to get territorial and petty, and kept my mouth shut.

"And I guess you can help out tonight if you want. I haven't seen Skye since eight-thirty."

I thought about Lars and feared the worst. "Okay. I'd be happy to help."

"Fine." His voice was still the vocal equivalent of a brick wall, but he had released his death grip on the countertop, which had to be a good sign.

Sally Hutchins swiveled around on her bar stool and curled her upper lip at me in the way only a small-town mayor's daughter wearing an old high school varsity letter jacket can sneer at the housecleaner's daughter.

But my years of battling celebutantes for the last parking space at the Fred Segal sale on Melrose had given me armor against Lindbrook's version of class warfare. I lifted my chin, sauntered past her, and realized that *my* hair actually might not be that bad.

Flynn finally turned around and looked me in the eye.

I smiled. I couldn't stop myself—an insane, totally inappropriate grin took over my face as I stared at the guy who'd shared such a huge part of my childhood, and whose absence had played such a huge role in my burgeoning adulthood.

He raised his eyebrows, but he started smiling, too. I didn't think he could help it either, although he rolled his eyes and tried to look impassive. "Let's get down to work."

"Whatever you say, dude."

"Did you just call me 'dude'?" he demanded, folding both arms over his chest and leaning back against the counter.

"Yeah, I guess I did," I said. "Why?"

"Oh, no reason." But he was giving me the same look of scorn he used to give to Skye when she was in the ninth grade and insisted on reading aloud from *Seventeen* magazine. He raised the hinged piece of the countertop to usher me behind the bar, and when he turned back to attend to Sally, my eye was drawn to a thin white scar on his cheek.

I had inadvertently given him that scar almost twenty years ago, when we were fighting over who got the window seat in the my parents' truck. He had always been physically stronger than me, but I was quick and scrappy, so the scuffle had resulted in simultaneous damage to the rearview mirror and Flynn's cheek. We left a lot of marks on each other's bodies throughout our first eighteen years.

I shook my head to clear my mind, horrified at my own nostalgia. Saccharine, wistful sap would not help me now. I needed money for the bar, an instant two-parent home for my sister's unborn child, and a one-way ticket back to California.

Luckily, Flynn had not witnessed my Hallmark reverie. He was too busy listening to the princess of Lindbrook's Lutheran country-club set, who was telling a joke.

"Okay. How many Catholics does it take to screw in a lightbulb?"

He shrugged.

"None, because they live in eternal darkness!" She giggled.

Flynn, to his credit, looked nonplussed.

I cleared my throat. "Flynn. Hi. Still here."

He shot a distracted glance my way, then resumed his conversation with Sally.

Apparently, he had me confused with the woodwork. I waited as he took an order for a gin and tonic and then prompted, "You wanted to discuss something?"

He gave me a curt nod. "Yeah. We're selling the bar, and I need you to sign some papers."

I blinked. "I'm sorry. We're what?"

"We're selling the bar. You're signing some papers."

"Ah. But aren't you forgetting something?"

He shook his head. "No."

"Actually, you are." I made and held eye contact. "You're forgetting two things. One, I'm an equal partner in this business and you need my consent to make decisions like that. Two, we can't sell the bar. I need the income and so does Skye."

He rested a hand on the bar and leaned casually to one side. "If you're an equal partner in this business, then how come I haven't heard about it until today? Where've you been all this time while I worked my ass off helping Skye?"

I straightened the straps of my tank top. "I've been seeking my fortune. Making my own way in the world. Sucking the marrow out of life." I decided to skip the parts about the jet lag, the sketchy model/bartender paramours and the insomniac nights. "I invested in this place and Skye runs it and shares the profits. That's how business works. You can look it up."

"Well, it's a shame you had to stop sucking and come back to the provinces." He straightened up to his full six foot two. "But don't worry, you won't have to stay long. Because we're selling the bar."

I planted my feet in the puddles of Pig's Eye. "We cannot sell this bar."

He stared down at me. "Why not?"

"Because Skye showed me the paperwork. I know all about the creditors and the debt and the mortgage. We are so far in the hole, we're practically in China. So correct me if I'm wrong, but if we sell now, we all lose a lot of money. I know *you* were too cagey to put your name on any of the loan documents, but *I* co-signed a ten-year mortgage and I'm about to get my ass sued off."

"Exactly. That's why we cut our losses, sell the building and the assets, and get out now."

"No, because then I lose my entire life's savings." I tried to ignore the panic swirling in my stomach. "Even if we sold everything in this place, we wouldn't be anywhere close to recouping the original investment."

"True." He grabbed a clean glass off the counter. "But you've got to know when to hold 'em, know when to fold 'em, and know when to walk away. That's how business works." He raised an eyebrow. "You can look it up."

I took the glass out of his hands. "Well, it's time to hold them."

"Geary. Holding on to this bar is like shoveling money into a furnace. And you of all people should know how to walk away." He took the glass back. His fingers brushed against mine, and both of us pulled back immediately. The glass dropped with a thunk to the black rubber mat on the floor.

Neither one of us moved to pick it up.

"Listen," I said. "You may not understand this, because word is you have some sort of high-power hockey management career, but I am on the verge of bankruptcy thanks to this damn place. And what about Skye? Do you want to be the one to tell her that we're going to leave her twisting in the wind?" I dropped my voice to a whisper. "Her and the baby?"

He looked away first. "We're not doing her any favors by letting her get further in debt."

I paused and looked down at the glass. "Well, if you're so hell-bent on selling the bar, why have you been driving down to help out every single night?"

"Things were different before."

"Before when?"

"Before tonight."

"Why? Just because I showed up?" I shook my head. "Flynn. You called me. Come on. You want to sell this place just to punish me?"

"I'm not punishing you." He seemed surprised. "Calling you on Skye's behalf is one thing. But I don't think it's a good idea for us to work together."

"Why not?" I asked, not sure I wanted to hear the reply.

"Because I don't want to."

Stung, I crossed my arms. "So you'd rather take a huge financial loss than work with me for a few weeks?"

He shrugged. "It's a lost cause, anyway."

"That is the most short-sighted, defeatist thing I've ever heard."

He reached into a drawer and unwrapped a package of paper napkins. "I'm telling you it's hopeless, and I'm the one with a business degree."

I called a time-out. "You are? Where did you end up going to school?"

"University of Minnesota."

"You took the hockey scholarship? Well then, why are you shuffling papers in the front office instead of brawling on the ice?"

He stiffened. "I don't want to talk about it."

"Of course you don't." I threw up my hands. "God, you're frustrating. And guess what? You might have the almighty business degree, but I've taken a few classes too, and I'm the one who actually has experience running a small business."

"Skye said you were a travel writer."

"More of a food writer," I corrected. "But I used to own a juice bar."

"You ran a juice bar. In Los Angeles. And now you're a food writer who goes to Italy."

"That's right."

"That's an abrupt career change."

I did my best imitation of his expression. "I don't want to talk about it."

"But you don't even like juice," he pointed out.

"True, but I liked the many paying customers who helped me make a small fortune out of lawn clippings, some organic papayas and a blender."

"I thought you were broke."

"I am! Because I poured all of my juice bar profits into this squalid hellhole. Skye begged me. And now she's begging me to bail it out, so that's what I'm going to do."

"It's too late."

"Why are you being like this?" I took a step toward him.

He took a step back, sending the glass we'd dropped rolling into the corner.

"I mean it. I'm trying to work things out here, and you're just being . . ." I tried to keep my voice level. "Don't you even want to try?"

"That's what I've been doing, Faith. The whole time you've been gone, I've been trying." He bent over, picked up the glass and placed it gently back on the bartop. His eyes were watching the crowd behind me. "But something's got to give."

I stared at him. "Could you be a little more cryptic, please?"

"I'm washing my hands of you and this entire liquor-licensed fiasco. I refuse to lose even more than I have already." He paused. "But if you're determined to straighten everything out, you can start with the tray of glasses back there." He turned back to the patrons and resumed taking drink orders.

"That's it?"

He handed an overfilled beer stein to a man with a Vandyke beard and red suspenders. "What else do you want from me?"

"I don't know." I mulled it over for a moment. "Nothing, I guess. I'm just curious about what you've been up to for the past ten years. Don't you want to know what else I've been doing since, you know . . ." I coughed. "Since high school?"

He picked up the dishrag and looked me up and down without a hint of the affection I used to see in his eyes. "It's pretty obvious."

My eyebrows shot up, and I could feel a red heat swelling in my cheeks. "I see."

He reached out with a gesture I recognized from years of washing and drying dishes in my mother's kitchen. I instinctively handed him a glass from the stack behind me.

"Thanks," he said. This time, our fingers did not touch.

And I realized, with a jolt of shame and surprise, that I wanted him to touch me again. I took two faltering steps backward. When the corner of the countertop dug into my back, I ducked under the bar's partition and put the thick planks of wood between us.

I bowed my head to hide my face behind my hair. "I'm going to go deal with those glasses," I informed my sandals.

"If you have time, you should probably check the condition of the ladies' room. Wendy Drake was in there about ten minutes ago, and she looked a little green around the gills."

Things just went downhill from there.

7

Leah called me early the next morning for an update on the Flynn situation, and ended up coming over to the bar for breakfast. She brought her entourage with her. Hans Gruber divided his efforts between licking the beer stains on the floor and begging for handouts, while Rachel fussed in the car seat we'd perched on the bartop. Given her status as a minor, we'd thought it best to cut her off after a bottle of apple juice.

My usual bouts of insomnia had reached new levels last night, so I'd gotten up early to pore over Skye and Bob's account ledgers. Leah's visit was a welcome respite from the vast seas of red ink I'd discovered.

"So how'd it go last night?" she asked.

"Two words: not good," I said, helping myself to one of the cinnamon rolls she'd so thoughtfully provided.

"Hmm. Well, what does Skye say?"

"About what? Flynn?"

"Yes."

"That would be nothing, because I don't talk to her about it."

"Why not?"

"She's got a lot on her plate right now, and I'm her older sister. I'm supposed to be helping her out, not scrapping with her sole reliable bartender. She's in kind of a chaotic place right now . . ."

The Inquisitor in Blue Chambray just raised her eyebrows.

"Oh, I don't know." I sighed. "My relationship with Skye just doesn't work like that. I'm not used to talking to her about my personal life. The deal is, I take care of her and in return, she loves me in spite of my many shortcomings. Besides, she never has trouble with men. She doesn't know what it's like."

Leah laughed. "Excuse me? The woman is twenty-four, and her second marriage just disintegrated."

"Yeah, but I mean, she never has trouble attracting them."

She pounced. "I see. So you were trying to attract Flynn last night?"

I realized that I had just strolled, whistling and carefree, into a steel-jawed trap.

"I . . . what?" I thought about his strong, tanned hands wrapped loosely around that white cloth dishtowel. "No. God, no."

"So you don't need any help from anyone?" Leah smiled knowingly at Rachel.

"I'm only staying in Minnesota for like, five more minutes," I ranted, "and the only reason I'm staying that long is to keep this stupid bar afloat. We dated ten—count 'em *ten*—years ago. It was *high school,* for heaven's sake."

She took another look at my face and gave up the debate. "Keep telling yourself that."

"I will."

Both of us paused at the sound of a key twisting in the lock of the front door. Hans Gruber trotted over to investigate, and I followed. Skye was never up before noon, and besides, she used the back entrance. That left only one keyholder . . . but wasn't he supposed to be working in Minneapolis? I gathered my wits for another showdown with the Man Who Didn't Want To Talk About It.

"Oh," said Sally Hutchins, yanking the door open just as I reached for the knob. "I didn't know anyone was in here."

She swept past me with a weighty blue binder in one hand and a knock-off Louis Vuitton bag in the other. Behind her trailed a portly, puffing, middle-aged man. He mopped at his brow with the sort of white linen handkerchief you read about in Victorian novels.

He surveyed the barroom, taking in the moose head, the solid wooden stools, and the cheap paneled walls. "What's the square footage?"

I marched over to Sally and cleared my throat. "We're closed. We open at five P.M. Is there something I can do for you?"

Sally plunked the binder down on the bar and started flipping through it. She didn't even glance at me. "What's your name again? Faith?"

Four years of giggling at my thrift store sweaters in homeroom and she didn't even remember my name. I set my jaw. "That's right."

"Didn't you move out to Miami or something?" She raised her head and looked back at the sweaty-handkerchief guy, looked right through me.

"Los Angeles. But I'm a co-owner of this bar, which is why I'm confiscating your key to the front door." I held out my palm.

"Oh, it's okay. I work for my dad's real estate agency. I'm just showing it to Mr. Warton. He wants to buy it." Her glance flitted past my face and landed on Rachel, who was a vision in soft chestnut curls and a duck-patterned sunsuit. She wrinkled her nose. "Is that a baby?"

"Mr. Warton can't buy this bar, because it's not for sale," I snapped.

She finally deigned to look at me. "Of course it's for sale. I've got the listing right here."

I peered at the Xeroxed flyer she held out, and sure enough, it detailed a sales listing for the Roof Rat. "No one consulted me about this."

"Bye! Got to pick up Rex from his play date! I'll call you later!" Leah headed out the door with Rachel, Hans, and a voluminous diaper bag in tow.

"What's going on?" demanded Mr. Warton, chugging up behind Sally. His eyes were small and shrewd.

"Nothing." Sally patted his arm reassuringly. "Why don't you take a look behind the counter? It's very sturdy construction." She turned to me and whispered, "Flynn gave me the go-ahead on this. I told him about this appointment last night, and he said it was fine."

"He did?"

"Yes. So you better take it up with him."

"I might just," I said, stalking into the back room.

It took me two seconds to find Flynn's cell phone number tacked to the newly de-cluttered bulletin board.

He answered his phone with a brusque "I can't talk now, Skye."

"It's not Skye, and you're gonna talk now," I informed him.

There was a long pause. I could hear a phone ringing in the background.

"Would you like to know who is rifling through the bar right now?" I asked politely.

"Oh, God. Don't tell me the fire inspector is citing us again."

"Not quite." I made a mental note to come back to that later. "Sally Hutchins is showing a potential buyer around the bar."

"Uh-huh." I could hear the faint taps of keyboard typing.

"She said she ran this by you last night and you said it was fine?"

"Uh-huh." I recognized this tone of voice.

"Patrick Flynn, stop multi-tasking and tell me what the hell is going on."

The typing stopped. "How did you know I was multi-tasking?"

"Please. It's obvious. Now. What gives? You know I don't want to sell it, but you just went ahead and okayed this appointment with Sally. They're checking out the plumbing as we speak."

I waited for him to deny this.

"Geary. Come on. You know the place is going down in flames. I'm just trying to get us all out while we can still escape with our dignity. It won't be the kind of money you want, but it'll be something. I already talked this over with Skye and she backs me one hundred percent."

My jaw dropped. "Skye said you should go ahead and sell?"

"Yep. Yesterday afternoon."

"She did not." She had *better not.*

"She did. And together, she and I are two thirds of the ownership. So calm down. And don't screw up this deal. I've got to go."

"Flynn, I am not—"

"I mean it. You better not screw this up." And then he hung up.

I stared at the receiver in my hand for a long moment, then hurried back to the barroom. I had a real estate deal to screw up.

"So that's the grand tour." I smiled at Henry Warton and did my best Melanie Wilkes impression. "What do you think?"

"Well . . ." He frowned and rubbed his chin. "The corporate records are a mess, but I might be able to do something with the building. It's a good location, and that young fellow I talked to—what was his name?" He turned to Sally.

"Patrick Flynn." She smoothed her skirt.

"He seemed very knowledgeable. He explained the taxes and the distribution of assets, and it sounds like a good prospect." He paused to give me a smirk that was part peacock, part jackal. "In the right hands, of course. You and your sister are lucky you have such a smart young man to help you out of all the trouble you've got yourselves into. He's quite a smooth talker, isn't he?"

"That he is," I agreed, wondering if we were talking about the same Patrick Flynn. "That he is."

"You should hold on to a man like that." Henry fished a cigar out of his suit pocket and lit up. He puffed away in my face and looked over the barroom as if it were his newly conquered kingdom, then turned to Sally and nodded. "Well, I'll have to talk to your father and make sure everything is inspected, but you can tell Mr. Flynn that I'll definitely be making an offer."

I smiled still wider and fell back on the most basic rule of business: when in doubt, bullshit like there's no tomorrow.

"Great!" I grabbed his hand and shook vigorously. "That's such a relief to hear. I'm so glad they finally got all of Bob's lawsuits taken care of."

Sally Hutchins shot me a look of pure cyanide.

Henry Warton frowned. "Bob?"

"My sister's husband." I shook my head sadly. "They're not divorced yet, but he did some terrible things. He ruined the whole deal with the last person who wanted to buy the bar."

"What ruined the deal?" Henry harrumphed.

"Oh, you know, just business stuff." I fluttered my eyelashes innocently, *à la* Skye. "Like, this one time, Bob claimed that when we borrowed money from him, his collateral was the assets. Does that make any sense to *you?*"

"*Yes.*" Henry loosened his tie as his face reddened.

"I'm sure everything's fine," soothed Sally.

I went for broke. "This divorce has just gotten so vicious. My poor sister. Her husband just ruins every offer we get. But he won't scare you off, will he, Mr. Warton?"

"I'm sure they've got everything cleared up," Sally said, hooking her hand through Henry's elbow and tugging him toward the door.

"They must have," I agreed. "If they're showing it to you, it must be all taken care of. I hope."

His mouth twitched under those beady eyes. "So where's this Bob character now?"

"We're not exactly sure. Vegas, maybe? But don't worry, we definitely know where his lawyers are because we hear from *them* all the time."

He was out the door in seconds, leaving only a cloud of sweat, cigar smoke, and muttered obscenities. Sally flounced after him, stopping to glare at me. "My father's going to kill me for this."

I watched the back of her green skirt and crimson ponytail swish out the door. Then I headed upstairs to find the girl who had dragged me all the way back from Europe, only to back Flynn up "one hundred percent" in his decision to sell me—and the Roof Rat—up the river.

*   *   *

As usual, confronting Skye was easier said than done.

She'd left a note on her apartment door saying she'd gone to get a manicure, and I finally tracked her down at the Upsy-Daisy Beauty Salon, curled up in a battered wicker chair in the salon's waiting area. She barely glanced up from the latest issue of *Us* when I arrived.

"If it isn't the elusive Skye Geary. At last we meet." I had fallen asleep last night on the couch at four A.M., waiting in vain for any signs of Skye, Lars, or karmic reversal. "Did you ever come home last night?"

She fluffed her hair. "Of course I did."

"Well, did you go to the doctor yet?"

She suddenly became engrossed in an article on celebrity beachwear trends. "Tomorrow."

"Way to procrastinate."

"They didn't have any open appointments." She couldn't even look me in the face while telling this blatant lie. "And anyway, where were you all morning?"

"I was working," I said. "Speaking of which, missy—"

"I know, I know, I'm going to work harder." She smiled sheepishly. "You'll see. I'm going to be slaving away at the bar from now on." She glanced down at the magazine in her lap. "Ooh, is that angora? Anyway, I'm running late today because the answering machine broke and I had to fish it out of the toilet."

I blinked. "Uh-huh. And how did the answering machine get into the toilet?"

"Well, I threw it in there, obviously. The message light was flashing after I got out of the shower, and I thought Lars might have called. So I hit the 'play' button."

"And?"

She crossed her arms over her miniscule baby-blue T-shirt. "I forgot that the first message on there was from three weeks ago, from . . . from Bob. It was from right before he left, and you could totally hear Mitzi in the background." She narrowed her eyes into dark-fringed slits of sparkling contempt. "She was in *my* bar, prancing around with *my* husband, and she was laughing."

"So you threw the machine in the toilet."

"What else was I supposed to do?"

The receptionist cleared her throat. "We're ready for you."

Skye traipsed ahead of me and pushed through some slatted yellow doors. These swung back and hit me in the shoulder as I asked, "So who was the new message from, anyway?"

"I don't know. I never got that far on the tape. But Lars, probably." She glanced around the small room filled with aproned beauticians and acrid hair product fumes, then headed for a little table in the corner.

I made a mental note to ask Leah about possible replacements for my sister's latest suitor, but Skye's next words chilled me to the bone.

"And by the way, now the toilet's clogged. I think a wire got stuck in there. I'll have Flynn take a look at it later."

I tried to keep my tone even. "You cannot call Flynn to deal with our toilet."

"Why not? Lars is in St. Paul 'til tomorrow, and Flynn's really good with mechanical stuff."

"No." I pictured Flynn filling up Skye's tiny purple and white bathroom with those shoulders of his. He'd fish a thin gray phone line out of the toilet bowl—the horror, the horror—dangle it, dripping, over the white wicker trash basket, and give me the same scornful look he'd given me last night.

I took a deep breath and forged ahead. "Speaking of Flynn. Guess what I did this morning."

She gasped. "You kissed him!"

I frowned at her. "No. Why the hell would I kiss him?"

"I don't know. You used to kiss him all the time." She took a look at my expression and briskly moved on. "So what *did* you do?"

"I fended the Roof Rat off from a potential buyer. And can you guess who arranged for this buyer to come in?"

Her guilty eyes were wide as saucers. "Um . . . Flynn?"

"That's right." I didn't even have to ask her if she'd known about this. "Skye, why did you agree to let him sell the bar? I thought I came back here to bail you out."

"Well . . ." She twisted the thin silver chain around her neck and chewed her bottom lip.

I sighed. "What do you want to do?"

"I don't know," she admitted, covering both eyes with her hands. "Flynn was here first, and he's pretty smart, and he thinks I should do what he says. But then you came out . . ."

I dug my nails into my palms. "Forget about me and Flynn for a second. What do *you* want?"

"I don't know! Maybe I should ask Lars and see what he thinks."

I managed—barely—not to strangle her on the spot.

"Hi." The manicurist sat down on the other side of the table. "Choose a color and I'll be right with you."

"We're not done with this discussion," I hissed.

"No, let's be done," Skye pleaded. "I'll do whatever you think." But I knew she couldn't be trusted to stay loyal to a voting bloc. I also knew Skye wasn't the real problem here. I needed to somehow convince Flynn to do things the right way—a.k.a. my way.

After sitting through thirty minutes of moisturizing, cuticle-trimming, and top-coating, I had devised a brilliant new strategy for dealing with Flynn. Now I just had to work up the nerve to broach the subject with my sister.

The thick, wet summer heat smacked us in the face as we left the salon and headed for Skye's apartment.

"Oh, the humanity!" I struggled to draw breath in the super-saturated air. "And the humidity!"

She raised her hand to her mouth and blew on her nail polish. "It's not that bad."

"It's like living in a big bowl of chowder."

"Hang on a second." She frowned, stopped to examine her reflection in a storefront window and gasped, "I'm bleeding!"

"You are?" I scanned her ashen face and her thin trembling limbs for any sign of injury. "What happened?"

"No, I'm *bleeding*, Faith!" Her eyes were huge and terrified. "Look at the back of my skirt! Oh my God. The baby!"

8

My mother wasn't answering her cell phone. She was off with the new boyfriend, gallivanting through the wilderness, where they probably didn't even have cell phone service. And my father was dead, and my sister was in some antiseptic enclave of the Raylor Memorial Clinic, bleeding and sobbing as the doctors tried to calm her. I was out in the waiting room. Waiting. Alone.

The only other member of our family—the unofficial member—was an hour away, in Minneapolis. But I couldn't call him. The sharpness of his tone and the anger in his face were too fresh in my mind. I'd disappointed him too many times to ask him for anything more than forgiveness.

So I was out of people to call. This was where running away

from my problems had gotten me. I had to face this agonizing uncertainty all by myself.

Part of the problem was I'd seen too many episodes of *ER*. I had no idea what was wrong with Skye, but every time I thought about the blood seeping through her white cotton skirt, my mind flashed to an image of Noah Wyle screaming, "We're losing her!" She hadn't gotten any pre-natal treatment that I knew of, and instead of marching her over to the nearest physician the minute I hit town, I'd been whining about money and trying to placate my ex-boyfriend. *Bravo*.

When at last the attending physician emerged, I was heartened by the fact that her pale blue scrubs weren't drenched in crimson. I opened my mouth to ask, but I couldn't force the words out.

The doctor seemed accustomed to this response. She cleared her throat. "You're Skye Geary's sister?"

I nodded, searching her expression for clues.

"Okay. What I'm going to tell you may come as a bit of a shock."

The look on my face must have alarmed her, because she hastened to add, "No, no, it's fine. Skye's fine." She tilted her head. "It's just that she's not pregnant."

I felt no shock or relief at this news, just sorrow that my sister had been suddenly wrenched away from yet another person she loved. I studied the anti-smoking poster on the far wall. "So she lost the baby?"

"There never was a baby. She didn't miscarry; she just started her period. I know she assumed she was pregnant, but . . ."

"But she got a blood test," I protested. "At the doctor's office. I'm sure of it. She missed her period, they did a blood test, and it came back positive."

The doctor rolled her eyes. "Probably some lab tech screwed up. You'd be amazed at the stories we hear. I have to tell you, the clinics out here aren't exactly Mount Sinai. Lab guys get the sample labels mixed up, they confuse your first name with someone else's last name . . . *they* should have to pay malpractice insurance." She gave me a tired smile. "Not, of course, that I'm bitter."

"But she missed her period," I croaked again.

The doctor sat down next to me. "It's my understanding that she's been under a tremendous amount of stress lately. And she's lost some weight?"

I nodded.

"Well, those factors can affect your menstrual cycle."

"But she was never pregnant? At all? Are you sure?" I tried to realign my sense of reality to fit these facts.

"Very sure. Sometimes these things just happen. We tested the betaCG levels in her blood serum—the hormone that the placenta would be making if she had a placenta—and the levels were so low that we know she was never pregnant. It's unfortunate, but mistakes were made." The doctor stood up as a nurse entered the waiting room, pushing my sister in a wheelchair. Skye looked drawn and gray, as if the last two hours had sucked out half her soul.

"If nothing's wrong, why is she in a wheelchair?" I asked.

"Hospital procedure." The nurse scribbled on a clipboard with her pen. "It's just a precaution. Sign here."

*　　*　　*

"Well," I said halfway through the long, silent ride home. "Do you want to talk about it?"

"About what?" Skye curled up in her seat, planting her bare feet on the dashboard. "The fact that they charged me five hundred dollars for a tampon?"

"No, about, you know. The baby. Not having it anymore."

She looked out the window at the lush green fields. "It never existed so, it's like, how can I care? I can't miss something that never existed, right?" Her laugh, though light, was brittle.

I didn't say anything.

"It's just sad, you know? Because I thought that we'd really love each other, me and the baby. We'd always have someone to talk to. And Bob would come back and be a father." She sighed. "But he's not coming back. And anyway, I couldn't be somebody's mother. I can't even remember to water my plants."

This was what had happened to her in the wake of everybody running off, first my father, then my mother and me. She'd lost all hope of ever being part of a happy family.

I could relate.

"You have me," I said. "To love."

"I know." She reached over to my hand on the steering wheel. She didn't squeeze it, just covered it with her palm. "Let's not talk about this anymore."

I groped for a topic that would make her feel better. Something light and fluffy. Something that would help her regain a sense of control. I swallowed my pride and broached the topic

I'd wanted to discuss at the beauty salon. "I need some advice from you."

After the initial shock passed, she seemed delighted. "Okay! What?"

"All right, here's the deal." I tried not to blush. "Remember when I left for L.A.?"

She nodded.

I pulled into the Roof Rat parking lot and turned off the ignition. "Well, as you know, Flynn and I had sort of a big fight. And I think he's still kind of miffed. Men. You know."

"What's he mad about? Oh, because of that bass player guy? What was his name?"

"Hank," I muttered. "No, he's mad for many reasons, most of which we don't have to get into right now."

She gave me a stern look. "I can't help you if I don't know the facts."

My dignity was long gone anyway. "Fine. If you must know, he's mad because I sort of skipped bail on our relationship. He got all bent out of shape because he wanted to get married and I said no, which is why he broke up with me. Which is why I ran off with the bass player. So really, he has only himself to—"

"He asked you to marry him?" Her mouth opened so wide I could see the fillings glinting in her molars. "You said *no?*"

"I was barely eighteen!"

"But you guys were so in love! Didn't he used to call you his little sparkplug?"

My cheeks were flaming under the sunburn I had already accrued. "Forget I said anything."

"No, no! I can help, I really can! You know business, but I know men. What do you need?"

"Well. I need to work with him at the bar," I said slowly. "And he won't cooperate with anything I want to do."

"So you need to win him over."

"Yes. I need . . ." I started to laugh. "I need to exploit my feminine wiles. But first I need to *get* some feminine wiles."

"Okay! This'll be so great." She clapped her hands. "All you've gotta do is charm the pants off him."

She painted an appealing picture. Wait, no, no—that road would only lead to disaster.

"He can keep his pants on," I said quickly. "I just want to establish a comfortable working relationship so we can help get the bar back on track."

"No problem. Feminine wiles are so easy. I am going to give you the foolproof way to win over any man alive." The mischievous spark returned to her eyes. "I don't care what you've done, he'll be yours to command."

"This doesn't involve bargaining with Satan, does it?"

Skye just smiled wickedly and rubbed her palms together. "Who needs the devil when you've got a subscription to *Cosmopolitan?*"

"Here." She handed me a twisted piece of blackened metal studded with rhinestones.

"What the hell is this?" I stood directly in front of the living room air conditioner and examined the tarnished loop of scrap metal. Short of melting this down and refashioning it into shackles, which I would then use to handcuff Flynn to the wall until he'd listen to reason, I couldn't see how it would transform my life.

She rolled her eyes. "Duh. It's my crown from junior year."

"Your prom queen crown?" I dangled the tiara between my thumb and index finger as if it were the tail of a wriggling sewer rat.

"No, my homecoming crown."

I glanced at my watch. "Look, time is money, babe, and there's a big pile of your account books with my name on them. What does this have to do with my future feminine wiles?"

"You're going to clean it off and wear it."

"Excuse me?"

"You'll see." She steered me toward the hall. "Go get a toothbrush and some soap or something."

"You'll forgive me my skepticism." But I padded off to the bathroom, where I rustled up a moldy blue toothbrush I surmised had been Bob's and a bar of Ivory soap. "Here you go."

"Great." She seemed unfazed by the origins of the toothbrush. "Okay, the first thing we have to do is scrub all the black stuff off so it's nice and sparkly."

She looked so earnest and avid and *not* preoccupied with her "miscarriage" that I decided to humor her. "Fine. But if you think for one second I'm wearing this thing, you are sadly mistaken."

"Faithie! You have to wear it. Otherwise it won't work." She lowered her voice and glanced around conspiratorially. "The thing is, if you want people to treat you like the homecoming queen, you have to think like the homecoming queen. The crown will help you. Trust me, boys love the homecoming queen. And they never grow out of it. Remember Mr. Jersen?"

I nodded. Pre-algebra teacher, mustached and polyestered.

"He asked me out at the bar last week." She shuddered. "It was really gross. But it just goes to show."

"It just goes to show what? Am I supposed to be encouraged by that?"

"Yes. If you want to start bossing Flynn around, you have to start being more charming. You know. Nice." She paused and nibbled her bottom lip, as if we might be hitting a snag here. "You say hi to everybody. You smile a lot. You pretend like everybody's interesting. If you want Flynn to listen to you, then I promise this'll help."

I rolled my eyes. "Will I be needing a glass slipper next?"

But we cleaned that crown until the fake jewels danced in the afternoon sunlight.

She beamed. "Get ready for the new you. Try it on."

In the name of sisterly harmony, I allowed her to place the aluminum circlet on my head.

I widened my eyes and waited.

"I hate to break it to you, but this is not working."

She winked at me. "Go look in the mirror."

I did, and in the bathroom, I witnessed a miracle. Adorned in this glorified piece of Reynolds Wrap, surrounded by a floral shower curtain and rumpled towels, I suddenly looked like the kind of girl who has been chosen for the final round of a beauty pageant. The kind of girl who refuses to accept a Saturday-night date after Wednesday. Who has a phone installed next to her deep marble bathtub. Who is, in short, the love child of Paris Hilton and Beau Brummell.

"See?" My sister popped into the doorway, carrying an armload of clothes and grinning. "Doesn't it feel good?"

"Kind of," I hedged. But this was a lie. It felt like a shot of tequila to the spirit. I was drunk with social power.

"Okay. I want you to remember this feeling and take it with you wherever you go. I'm going to put the crown in your car, and I want you to wear it when you're driving around." I opened my mouth but she held up her palm. "Just do it, okay? Okay. We covered the social stuff—smile a lot and always talk about the guy, not yourself, because guys think they're very interesting."

She wrinkled her pert little nose. "But now we need to do something about your wardrobe."

I raised my eyebrows. "What about my wardrobe?"

"You look too citified." she declared. "You're intimidating. You don't fit in here."

I took this as a compliment.

"You're in Minnesota now. You need to wear more colors and soften it up. Think cute and nonthreatening. Here." She handed me a plum tank top and lavender capri pants. "And also, we need to talk about your underwear."

"We do?"

"Yes. When you're dealing with men like Flynn, you have to be confident. And what makes you confident?"

I mulled this over. "A Harvard degree and a modeling contract?"

"No, your panties, you silly goose!"

And thus the eternal difference between the Geary sisters.

"If you want to be fun and sexy, you just have to start with your underwear and work your way out. I went on a total shopping binge at the Mall of America the day you picked me up, and I bought a bunch of cute new stuff that I haven't worn yet." She disappeared into the bedroom.

I yelled after her, "How do you know I don't already have something scandalous on?"

"Oh, Faithie, be serious." She returned clutching a pink bag filled with white tissue and black lace. She fished out a scrap of lavender silk. "Put this on, and put the purple outfit on over it, and then I'll do your makeup and you can go. Flynn will be much easier to handle today, I promise."

"I don't want to 'handle' him, I just want to have a civil, working relationship."

She shook her head. "That's what you say now, but I know how you two are. You're like yin and yang. Smith and Wesson. Nick and Jessica."

"That is *so* not—"

"Stop thinking with your head so much. Make sure you pay attention to your body next time he's around. What do you feel like? What is your body telling you?"

"My body never tells me anything," I objected. "Except, 'more M&M's, please.'"

"I'm just saying. You think too much and it gets you into trouble. You're always in your head. Pay attention to what your body says for a change. Now put on the purple."

"But I just wore jeans in high school and he liked me fine then."

"He'll like this better. Trust me."

My sister could be terrifyingly convincing when she wanted to be. And she did know a few things when it came to men . . .

"Listen," I said slowly. "I'll cut you a deal. I'll stop thinking with my head and listen to my body if *you* promise to stop thinking with your body and listen to your head."

She cocked her head. "What do you mean?"

"I mean, you said you'd stop conspiring with Flynn and commit to helping me save this bar. Which means we can't sell it. Which means we need to start making a lot more money, *tout de suite.* So we need—you need—to dream up ways to get customers in the door and keep them in all night. Think of yourself as the social coordinator."

"I'll be good at that!" Her face lit up. "Ooh, I have a great idea! For tonight! Leave everything to me."

"For tonight? But we open in four hours. What's the plan?"

"Trust me, you'll love it." She yelled this over her shoulder as she headed for the front door. "I've always wanted to do this, but Bob would never let me. I have to start getting everything ready. Show up at six-thirty and prepare to be amazed."

"Good evening, and welcome to 'Free Beer Till Somebody Pees'," Skye bellowed as she stood atop the bar, clad in painted-on jeans and a pink bustier, *à la Coyote Ugly.*

The bar was absolutely packed with customers—beer-bellied factory workers, twenty-two-year-old deer-hunting enthusiasts, wide-eyed young single gals and chain-smoking, rusty-voiced middle aged women. When my sister wanted to get the word out about something, she was better than Reuters. Now if only she could use her powers for good . . .

"Here are the rules: everyone who wants to compete has to get their hand stamped. Faith will do the stamping," she announced, tossing a star stamp and ink pad my way. "Once your hand is stamped, the bathrooms are off-limits to you. We've posted guards at both bathrooms and the front door." She beamed and waved to Lars and his henchmen, who gruffly nodded back. "Everyone who gets their hand stamped will drink for free."

The crowd erupted with a deafening roar of approval.

"But once somebody pees, we start charging for beer again. Okay, also, everybody here has to pony up five bucks. No, ten bucks! And the last person to pee will win a prize of"—she looked at me and shrugged—"a hundred dollars!"

"What about betting?" came a yell from the back.

She tossed her hair back and smiled. "Betting is totally permitted and encouraged. And if I were you, I'd bet on my big sister Faith, 'cause she's the stubbornest person I know!"

"Hey!" I cried. "I'm just the stamper! I'm not having any part of this."

She jumped down from the bar. "Of course you are. Somebody has to get the ball rolling."

"Well, why can't Flynn get the ball rolling?" The perfect opening to ask the question that had been preying on my mind all evening. "Where is he, anyway?"

"I told him not to bother coming in till ten-thirty." She giggled. "He'd go ballistic if he knew about this. Fire codes and blah, blah, blah. He'll be happier not knowing. Which reminds me, he called and asked how the buyer appointment went. I told him to talk to you. That man is *your* problem."

And according to Skye, I should now be able to handle him with no problem. I had spent the afternoon enduring a head-to-toe makeover, and was now decked out in the purple capris and delicate strappy sandals that strangled my toes but looked fabulous. My sister had pronounced me feminine-wile ready, but the proof would be in the Pig's Eye.

She turned back to the crowd. "All right, you guys. It is now six forty-five. You have fifteen minutes to settle up with Faith and get your last-minute peeing in!"

As the electrified mob rushed toward me, I resigned myself to the fact that Skye's taste in social events was always going to be more Animal House than Buckingham Palace. But I had asked her to help, and she was helping.

"All right, people, form a line," I commanded. "Single file. No pushing, no biting, no spilling beer on the bartenders."

I tossed ten-dollar bills into a plastic pitcher and stamped away without really looking up at faces. The hands I anointed with pink stars were workers' hands. Callused from manual labor, with fingernails tinged with traces of dirt that no amount of scrubbing could erase. These were hands like my father's, the kind of hands you just don't see in the clubs and boutiques of L.A.

But then, at the end of the line, I encountered five lily-white fingers, French-manicured and moisturized to the point of supersaturation. Bejeweled with a large and gaudy pink class ring.

The hand of Sally Hutchins.

I glanced up in surprise and stamped her flesh perhaps a bit harder than I'd intended.

"Ow!" She snatched back her hand and flung a ten-dollar bill in the general direction of the pitcher.

"Gosh, Sally, I'm ever so sorry." I gave her my best fake Hollywood simper.

"No, you're not." She clutched her hand to her chest and scowled. "Isn't it enough that you ruined my whole day? My father had a conniption after I lost that sale with Mr. Warton."

I felt an inexplicable twinge of pity for her, standing there all dour and ill-tressed.

"I'm surprised to see you here tonight," I said. "'Free beer till somebody pees' doesn't seem like your scene."

"There's nowhere else to go in this dinky little village," she sniffed. "Besides, I could use the hundred dollars. Dayton Hudson is having a sale on Monday, and my dad won't give me any money after what happened this morning." She curled her lip at me. "I really need some new espadrilles. And I can win this. I can hold it *forever.*"

"Really." I raised one eyebrow.

"Why? You think you can hold out longer?" she demanded.

I'd be damned if I folded to the woman who had made an art form of aiming the volleyball at my head in gym class. "We'll see."

She narrowed her eyes and flicked her long crimson bangs off her forehead. "Fine, then."

I put my hand on my hip. "Fine."

Let the games begin.

Flynn showed up at eight, by which time the festivities were in full swing. I was draped over the bar, tapping my pen and advising my mother's friend Mrs. Dupree to bet against Sally Hutchins, when I heard Flynn's voice behind me, quiet but unmistakably furious.

"Geary. Back room. Now."

"Hang on one second," I said to Mrs. Dupree and turned to greet my business partner.

You could set your watch by this guy's wardrobe—today was jeans and a gray T-shirt, one sleeve of which was halfway turned up around the hem. I fought the sudden urge to straighten out the folded fabric, but my little laundry reverie came screeching to a halt when I checked out the hockey player behind the Hanes.

Although his face was a mask of control, the muscles in his jaw twitched madly.

I decided to look on the bright side. What better opportunity to practice my new prom queen maneuvers? I gave him a smile straight out of the Rose Parade. "As I live and breathe, it's Patrick Flynn. How *are* you?"

This took him off guard. He straightened his shoulders and regarded me with deep suspicion.

"Get back there, now," he ordered.

"I'm right in the middle of a consultation with a client

here," I cooed. "But I'll be done in two shakes of a lamb's tail, and then I'll be happy to talk with you." I turned back to Mrs. Dupree, who had lit her second cigarette on the smoldering remains of her first.

"Sorry about that." I pointed to the list of names in my notebook. "Now, as I was saying, you might want to put a few bucks on . . ."

Flynn's strong, callused fingers closed around my wrist. My arm and breast smashed up against him as he yanked me away from the bar. When I tried to wriggle free, he clamped his other hand around my elbow.

"March." He dragged me toward the back office.

The crowd's chatter and jukebox guitar riffs faded into a long, loaded silence as we headed down the hall. He slammed the office door behind us and loosened his grip. I wrenched my arm away, chafing my skin bright red in the process, and escaped to the other side of the tiny white room.

"What the hell was *that?*" I demanded.

"That was me calling a business conference." He leaned back against the closed door.

"Do you start all your business conferences with bodily assault? This isn't the hockey rink."

"You and Skye are violating every fire code known to man," he fumed. "And I don't even know where to start with the illegal gambling."

"Oh, give me a break." I rolled my eyes. "A few bucks in a beer pitcher hardly qualifies as federal racketeering. And don't blame me for the overcrowding—that was all Skye."

"Yeah, and we're her business partners, so when the lawsuits start pouring in, we're all screwed."

He had a point. "Okay. I understand your concern," I said in the tone of voice you'd use to soothe a snarling rottweiler. "I'll go make sure every possible fire exit is clear." I took a few steps toward the door. Flynn didn't budge.

"Not so fast." He crossed his arms over his chest. The Clint Eastwood glare was back. "I'm not finished."

I waited.

"I am trying to help you and Skye out, but if I ever drive down here to find another unannounced, unauthorized peeing promo, there's going to be hell to pay."

"There's already hell to pay—have you *seen* the account ledgers?" I took another step toward him. "And as long as we're on the subject of unauthorized, unannounced business deals, why don't we discuss the prospective buyer I had to deal with this morning?"

"Good idea." I could practically see the black storm clouds gathering over his head. "Henry Warton called me this afternoon, and he had a lot to say about the way we run this bar."

I couldn't stifle my laugh. "All complimentary, I hope?"

"His exact words were 'an underfunded asylum'."

"Well, you win some, you lose some."

"I can't believe you deliberately screwed up that deal." The jaw muscles resumed twitching. "I can't believe you two went ahead with this without asking me."

"Well, *I* can't believe you tried to sell this place without asking me. Listen." I tried to rekindle the homecoming queen within.

Be nice. "Try to appreciate what we're doing here. This promo is genius—we're making money hand over fist. And it was Skye's idea. She's finally involved. Isn't that what we wanted?"

He frowned at this gratuitous mention of "we" and reverted to his tone of cold control. "You pull another stunt like this and you'll regret it."

My hands reflexively closed in a need for something to shatter. Because nothing had changed. Ten years had passed, oceans and continents had been crossed, and yet I'd been cast in exactly the same role. The stunt-puller. The black hole of dysfunction. The woman who stood between Flynn and what he wanted.

When I finally opened my mouth, my words came out clipped and crisp. "It seems to me I've said this before, but it bears repeating: you need to stop issuing ultimatums."

The anger in his eyes flared up. "*You* need to stop making bad decisions without consulting your *partner* first."

We circled each other, bristling. The squabble over the bar bets had escalated into something much darker.

Run off with one lousy bass player and pay for it for the rest of your life.

I took a step back. "I've said all I have to say."

"So have I." He nodded toward my hand. "How's your wrist?"

In all the tumult, I had forgotten about my pending personal injury lawsuit. I hid my reddened wrist behind my back. "It's fine."

He sighed and held out his hand. "Come here."

Suddenly, and for reasons I couldn't begin to untangle, I was afraid I might cry. "No."

"Come on, Faith. Let me see." His posture relaxed and his tone gentled. He gave me a hint of a smile and my stomach did a slow half-gainer.

"It's fine," I insisted.

"God, you're impossible." He crossed the room in a flash, backing me into the corner. He reached around my waist and eased my hand out from behind my back.

He cradled my wrist in both hands, stroking the delicate skin. The pink fingerprints he'd left on my forearm were fading fast, but I could see the regret in his eyes as he lowered his head to examine the marks.

"I'm sorry." His breath was warm against the hollow of my throat.

"Oh, that's okay," I stammered. "I guess we both got a little, you know, carried away . . ."

"I like what you're wearing," he said, but he didn't seem all that focused on my outfit. Rather, he was looking at me as though I were naked.

"Thanks." I continued babbling uncontrollably. "But it's not mine. I borrowed it. From Skye."

His hand skimmed up my arm and shoulder, leaving a ripple of goosebumps in its wake. I shut up. When he brushed his thumb across my chin and lower lip, I shivered against the cold plaster behind me.

I parted my lips, and he leaned in closer.

"You guys!" Skye pounded on the door. "Faith! Flynn! Somebody peed! Come on!"

"I'm sorry." We said this in unison as we leapt apart.

His expression shocked me. He looked pained. He looked reproachful. He looked the opposite of everything I was feeling.

I tried to regroup. "Did you . . . did we just . . ."

"I'll see you out there." He flung open the door. Smoke and music and a cool burst of air conditioning poured in.

Skye scooted out of the way to let him pass, then popped her head into the office.

"Faithie! What is going on in here? You look like Kim Basinger in that Tom Petty video where she's dead. I thought we covered this. You're supposed to look friendly. Now put on a happy face and get out here."

9

At ten forty-five P.M., I found the answer to Skye's prayers.

It had become painfully clear that, despite my warnings, threats, and attempts at bribery, my sister could not possibly give up dating. It would be like asking a rabbit to give up hopping. And without the specter of impending motherhood looming, she was right back to her customary routine of batting her eyes and flipping her hair at Lars, plus every other male over the age of fourteen.

But if I couldn't stop the madness, at least I could redirect it to a more appropriate outlet.

He was sitting in the shadows at the far end of the bar, using a dog-eared copy of *Anna Karenina* as a coaster for his teacup.

Tweedy and gray at the temples, he appeared to be the antithesis of Bob and Lars—a little piece of Oxford out here in the cornfields. The man was wearing an actual bow tie. I squinted, but could see no wedding ring. He clearly needed a little excitement in his life, and I knew a very exciting girl who needed a little calming down.

A reconnaissance mission was in order, but I still had a few obstacles to surmount before I could commence search-and-rescue efforts for Skye's love life.

One, Flynn. I had wanted him to kiss me in the office tonight. I had wanted him to kiss me and *then* some. My body had turned traitor and was declaring war with my mind. I wanted him, but I knew that having him would mean plunging into another push-me-pull-you struggle with explosive chemistry and hell to pay at the end. This was not part of my master plan.

Two, and only slightly less alarming, I still hadn't peed, and things were getting dicey down there. My bid for victory was going to be foiled by my own Californian obsession with hydration. I had about four glasses of water sloshing around in there. But Sally Hutchins was still in the game, so I had no choice but to think dry and cross my legs. Even if my kidneys ruptured and I died of blood poisoning, I would prevail.

Besides, refusing to hit the ladies' room was good for business. The cash register had been ringing nonstop. Even though we were charging for beer again, everyone was hanging out to see who would ultimately emerge the winner.

I squirmed and pressed my knees together, emptied the ashtray Mrs. Dupree had left brimming with cigarette butts, and visualized my tiara. Then I decided to confront Flynn, who was stationed clear on the other side of the bar, pretending the near-smooching incident had never happened.

I sashayed up behind him at the cash register. He finished his transaction, slammed the drawer shut, and refused to acknowledge me.

I cleared my throat. He reopened the drawer and started examining the receipts.

"Ahem," I said.

"Yes?" He didn't turn around from the register.

"Listen. About what happened back there—"

"I don't want to talk about it."

"Of course you don't." Grr. What would the homecoming queen do? She'd change the subject, that's what. "Who's that guy over there with the Tolstoy?"

He glanced over his shoulder at the customers. "That would be Dr. Ian Hammond."

I smiled. "Oh, really? As in physician?" Maybe *he* could take over as Skye's benefactor.

"No. As in Ph.D. He teaches English Lit. at the community college in Cannon Falls."

"But wait. If he's a Ph.D., why's he teaching at a community college out here in the boonies?"

Flynn turned around. I had to tilt my head back to make eye contact. "I don't know," he said. "I didn't realize there was going to be an interrogation. Why the full-court press? You have plans for him?"

"I have plans for Skye." My smile faded. "Turns out, she might be returning to the dating scene a lot sooner than expected."

He nodded. "I know. She told me about the 'baby'."

"She did? When?"

"This afternoon." He looked tired. "She called me after you guys got back from the hospital. She sounded awful. Just devastated. That's why I decided to come in ahead of schedule tonight. I thought she might need me." He shook his head. "Little did I know that she'd already moved on to 'Free Beer Till Somebody Pees'."

"Hey, cut her some slack. I wanted to get her mind off everything, so I asked her to help get some warm bodies into the bar. And you have to admit, she did a pretty good job."

Since Skye's pregnancy wasn't an issue anymore, both of us knew that I could return to Los Angeles at will. But neither of us mentioned this.

He jerked his head in Ian's direction. "Should I even ask what you're planning to do with that poor guy?"

"I'm trying to discourage her from dating any more shiftless louts. But she doesn't know all the details yet, so I'd appreciate it if you would keep this quiet."

He raised an eyebrow. "Isn't she seeing that guy in the leather jacket? The big, vacant-looking one?"

I dismissed this with an airy wave. "Oh please, that won't last. Now. That teacup Dr. Hammond has—what's in there?"

Flynn gave me the look Midwesterners give to Californians who spend a little too much time out in the sun. "Tea."

"Where'd you get the tea from?"

"China."

"Hardy har."

"I keep the teacup and a bunch of Earl Grey on hand for him. He's British, he's a regular customer and he doesn't like Pig's Eye."

British. And swilling tea instead of tequila. This just kept getting better. "Excellent. That's perfect."

He frowned down at me, then clamped one hand down over my bare shoulder. "Geary. What's with the jumping bean routine?"

I shifted my weight again and tapped my foot. "Well, if you must know . . ." I motioned for him to lean in. I could smell his clean T-shirt through the air filled with alcohol and cigarette smoke. "I sort of have to go to the bathroom."

He waited for more. Finally, he said very slowly and using small words, "Then go. I'll cover for you."

"I can't." I showed him the pink star adorning my hand.

"You're actually participating in this debacle?"

"Someone had to get the ball rolling. I had no choice."

"But isn't that a conflict of interest? You can't win your own contest."

"It's really more about pride than money," I explained. "Besides, I'm not trying to win. I'm only staying in until Sally Hutchins gives up."

"Why?"

I set my jaw and glared over at Sally, who was slouched back by the jukebox, her crimson hair glinting in the soft neon glow.

I was pleased to note that she, too, had her legs tightly crossed and seemed extremely fidgety.

"You guys *still* have that grudge match going from high school?" he asked.

"Hey, you didn't have to face the fashion gestapo at your locker every morning. I'll explode before I give her the satisfaction of surrender." I hopped from foot to foot, wrenching my ankles in the high-heeled sandals.

"Whatever you say. Just try not to think too much about babbling brooks. Niagara Falls. The Great Salt Lake." He brushed past me and, with a casual brotherly tousle of my hair, went back to pouring beer.

What happened to the guy who'd been looming over me a scant two hours ago, threatening retribution and ravishment? I had my vanity, after all. Vanity and the occasional impure thought sparked by a particular combination of light-colored T-shirts and dark brown eyes.

One thing at a time.

I tried to think about Arizona and the Gobi Desert as I sidled up to the Ivory Tower's answer to Prince Charming. He was letting his tea get cold as he stared at the Cubs game on TV. Absentminded on top of everything else. How very academic of him.

I watched the fifth inning over his shoulder for a minute, noticing the faint smell of chamomile and library mustiness. Not even a hint of motor oil.

"So, you're a Cubs fan?" I asked. He turned to me, his expression blank and startled over the maroon bow tie.

I pointed to the television screen.

"Oh. No, no. Not anymore. I was, when I first entered the country. You see, I was lecturing at the University of Chicago, and my colleagues introduced me to the sport at Wrigley Field. But I'm afraid I switched allegiance after the first summer or two. The Cubs have a terrible record, if I'm not mistaken."

Blasphemer. I started to re-evaluate the wisdom of introducing this heretic to my only sister.

Skye and I had been indoctrinated as devout Chicago fans by my grandfather, who had often remarked that Ernie Banks should be canonized. So the team choked every August, and had since 1908. That was hardly the point. The point was that hope springs eternal. Had this man no loyalty?

But then I remembered that he hailed from the U.K., where baseball is viewed with roughly the same degree of respect and reverence as is miniature golf.

I tried to set the record straight.

"Well, sure, they've been having a rough couple of weeks," I conceded, "but I'm sure that after Kerry Wood recovers and they play a few home games . . ." I glanced at the score and realized that the Twins were ahead 4-1. Part of being a Cubs fan was never having to say 'I'm so ashamed.'"

He lifted the teacup to his lips, leaving a damp ring on the cover of his paperback. "I admire your devotion. As the Bard said, 'Love is not love which alters when it alteration finds.'"

"He was obviously a Cubs fan."

"Dr. Ian Hammond." He offered a handshake. "We've not been introduced. I'd certainly remember that hair."

"You and every teacher I've ever had. Do you know how hard it was to skip class with this hair? The instructor always notices when the redhead's not there." I searched the room for Skye, who was mingling with her adoring subjects. "I'm Faith Geary. I'm just here for a few weeks visiting my sister."

I pointed out the family jewel, who was giggling down at a table full of slavering Malt-O-Meal workers.

"Of course I've seen her here. Every evening. She's an exquisite young lady." His eyes glazed over in a dreamy haze, no doubt picturing courtly scenes of Sir Lancelot and Gueneviere.

This was almost too easy. Why couldn't I run my own love life with the same finesse I brought to others?

He glanced at the dishcloth tucked into my waistband. "How kind of you to help your sister during your holiday. And clearly you know Patrick." He lifted his chin toward Flynn, who was back to ignoring me.

"Yes, I do. Or I did. I guess." I glanced at Flynn and tugged at the lavender camisole, making sure my tattoo was safely covered. "How did you know?"

He chuckled. "I pop by for a cup of tea almost every evening, so I have the opportunity to observe how the world wags. The attraction between the two of you is obvious."

My dismay must have shown on my face, because he furrowed his brow. "I hope I haven't put my foot in it. I just assumed that you and he were something of an item." He leaned toward me and smiled. "But perhaps it's just a sneaker."

"What's a sneaker?" I whispered back.

"In modern parlance, I suppose you'd call it a crush. A secret crush."

"Oh." I fiddled with my watchband. "I don't think so."

"No? The poor fellow looks as if he's going to keel over every time you enter or exit the room."

Now this was an interesting tidbit. "Really?" I stole another surreptitious glance at Flynn, who caught my eye, pointed to the Cubs' score, and pantomimed committing hari-kari with a pen. He did not look like a man harboring a secret crush.

Nevertheless. Compared with Lars, the professor was a catch and a half. Large vocabulary, good manners, the ability to string a sentence together. Advanced age and questionable baseball loyalties notwithstanding, this guy definitely had potential.

Everything was falling into place, so I waved Skye over.

She bounced past the crowded tables. "What's up?"

I made the introductions. She fiddled with the chain around her neck. This, naturally, called attention to the vast expanse of flesh exposed by her bubblegum-pink bustier.

"Oh, of course I've seen *Ian* here before," she said, upgrading the charm from fourteen to twenty-four karats. "You're the one who's always got some really long book. Last week it was *The Portrait of a Lady,* right?"

"Indeed it was." His eyes lit up.

She slid onto the stool next to him. "Wow. You're a fast reader. You must be smart, huh?"

And they were off.

Sometimes I forgot how good Skye really was. She was such

a master that she made it look easy. The Michael Jordan of the flirting world.

I left them to chat and went back to emptying the ashtrays scattered across the countertop.

"Mission accomplished, I see." Flynn came up behind me, reaching over my shoulder for an empty glass. I could feel his body heat on my bare legs.

"What mission?" I was light. I was casual.

"The Geary-Hammond merger." He glanced at my sister, who nodded, wide-eyed, as Ian jabbed at a Tolstoy passage with his index finger. I had to hand it to her, she actually did look interested.

"Oh, that. Well, you know Skye. A regular Tolstoy monger."

"You two get weirder and weirder," he muttered, crouching down to grab a clean tumbler. His face was inches from my thigh. If he leaned forward he would be kissing the back of my knee.

I exhaled sharply and tipped my head back. I was flooded with memories of clinging to this boy so tightly that you couldn't have fit a spare molecule between our bodies. All those nights on the riverbank, in the pickup truck, out in the fragrant fields. There was a time when I had thought he would be enough to keep me safe and secure forever.

As it turned out, I hadn't *wanted* to be safe and secure forever. But even now, after I had come full circle around the world, I still felt that he was somehow anchoring part of me. Which was just really unfortunate because, obviously, whatever we'd once had was gone.

The man was not even looking at me. He was clinking through a row of glasses, searching for a clean one. *Sneaker, my ass.*

"Geary?" I felt the warm puff of air against my calf.

"Yeah?" I breathed.

"What the hell are you doing up there?"

I'm thinking of coming right here where I stand. "I'm thinking," I said.

He straightened up and gave me a look I couldn't quite decipher. "God help us all. What about?"

"Mostly about Niagara Falls and the Hoover Dam, thanks to you."

"There is an easy solution to this problem. Trust me, they pay me to solve problems all day. Go to the bathroom."

I put my hands on my hips. "I can't. My honor is at stake."

He checked his watch. "Well, if you can tough it out for another two hours, we'll close up and you'll be home free. Good luck."

Sally Hutchins outlasted almost everyone else in the bar before she finally answered the call of the stall at 12:36 A.M. and fifteen seconds. Not that I was counting. A dull ache had settled into my abdomen and my extremities were going numb. So when she bolted up from her chair and sprinted for the lavatory, I couldn't spare a moment to savor my triumph. My sole concern was that she'd be one of those women who take forty-eight minutes in the ladies' room doing God-knows-what with lipstick and a tin of Altoids. I needed that ladies' room, pronto.

But my path to sweet relief was suddenly blocked by a mob of boisterous well-wishers, all of whom had been waiting for hours to crown a champion.

"We have a winner!" Skye clambered back up on the bar to incite the masses. "Give it up for my sister Faithie! She's going to donate her winnings to buy a round for the house!"

And Flynn, damn him, threaded his way through the cheering throngs to the jukebox. He pressed a few buttons, and the heavy bass of "Eye of the Tiger" started pulsing through the room.

The populace demanded I make a victory lap, and so, in the name of giving the paying customers what they wanted, I sacrificed my own very pressing needs for those of my public. I jogged the room's wood-paneled perimeter as best I could in three-inch heels and ended my run at the door to the ladies' room. Where Sally Hutchins remained ensconced. I knocked a bit more vigorously than usual.

"Occupied." Sally's voice oozed venom through the thin layer of wood.

I was debating whether I should break the door down or try to shove through the crowd to the bathroom by the back office, almost certainly wetting my pants in the process, when Lars's towering form emerged from the unruly crowd.

He nodded at me.

I nodded back and looked around desperately. "Yes, hi, listen, I can't talk right now, I have sort of an emergency—"

He nodded again, blond, mute, and massive. With one hand he pushed open the door to the men's room, and with the other he tugged my forearm.

"That's the men's room!" I protested. "Do you have any idea what it's like in there?"

"Empty." He nodded again and ushered me in. "I'll stand guard outside."

His voice brooked no refusal, so I stopped protesting, slammed the door, and peed.

After two hours listening to the hum of the air conditioner and Skye's soft, even breathing, I accepted the fact that I was staring down the barrel of yet another sleepless night. My body was aching for rest, my eyes felt like they were doing that spirally cartoon thing, but my mind was swirling with conflicting desires.

I groped my way through the darkness to the bedroom door, which swelled and stuck in the summer heat, and headed down the hall to the kitchen, where I settled down with a pen and pad and tried to get some work done.

It turned out that the answering machine message lost to Skye's wrath and the bathroom plumbing had been from my editor, who had called again that morning to encourage me to do a whimsical little piece on America's Heartland.

"You might as well make the most of it while you're there," he'd said. "Your family's out there, right? So talk to the locals, dig up some really down-home, off-beat places to eat."

I'd been relieved to talk to him, to reconnect with my world outside the Roof Rat. It reminded me that no matter what I had felt with Flynn in the office tonight, I had a real life waiting back in California: my apartment, my career, my usual table at

Carmine's Cafe. I couldn't get attached to life in Minnesota even if I wanted to.

Five A.M. I dropped my head into my hands, almost weepy with exhaustion, and listened to the frantic pulse of the crickets chirping outside. Why did I have such trouble completing the natural cycles? Wakefulness into sleep, motion into rest, analysis into acceptance—I simply could not finish what I started.

And that, I admitted to myself, was the problem with Flynn.

I was not finished with him. I had *thought* I was finished, but I wasn't.

When I'd left for Los Angeles ten years ago, I felt like someone had pumped me full of novocaine in preparation for an emotional root canal. I'd been numb and placid as I crossed the state line in a car filled with hung-over musicians and second-hand guitars. But even through that numbness, I could feel the raw ache between my legs, a brand new sensation lingering from my last night with Flynn. He had been so careful, so gentle with me, but my body had changed in some searing, permanent way.

I had needed to be finished with Flynn. And I'd successfully escaped my eighteen-year-old life.

So what was up with all the resurgent sexual tension between us? Seriously. You could practically hear it snap, crackle and pop.

Five thirty-four A.M. Brain wide awake, body leaden with fatigue. And I had promised Leah I'd babysit—she was coming over to drop Rex off at nine. So I padded back down the shadowy hallway and inched onto the mattress next to Skye. I wriggled my toes against the chilled cotton sheet, curled up, and finally drifted off to sleep.

I dreamed of Flynn and the ocean. The Pacific sparkling under the golden sunshine. We were lying on the gritty yellow sand together, soaking up the afternoon, lazy like cats. Lying together and not talking. Just being. Like he used to say to me, brushing a finger over my lips so we could hear the wind rustling through the grass in the dark—"Sshhh, Faith, stop thinking so much. Stop talking. Just *wait* a second with me here."

When I dreamed about the ocean that night, Flynn's body was warm and the sun was bright, and the silence between the waves was such a relief.

And then I woke up and sure enough, everything was still heading straight to hell in a handbasket.

10

Sunday morning wasn't working out so well for me. To begin with, my stomach and lower back were wracked with pain and I had to pee approximately every three seconds. Apparently, along with bragging rights and a hundred bucks, the winner of Skye's contest also got a bladder infection, no extra charge.

Leah showed up at nine sharp, and when I answered the door, still decked out in my pajamas, I surmised that I wasn't the only one having issues today. One look at the gray clouds rumbling outside, Leah's harried expression and the howling baby, and I could see that this woman had had it.

"Ah, the luxury of sleeping till nine." She nodded at my rumpled blue boxers and white tank top and jostled Rachel on her hip. "Rach, sweetie, relax."

Rachel responded by upping the decibel level.

I watched with dismay as the baby's face turned crimson. "You look like you could use a cup of coffee."

"I could use a shot of adrenaline straight to the heart. But I have to take this little diva to a doctor's appointment in Minneapolis. I really appreciate your helping me with Eli."

I rubbed my eyes, trying to reconcile the sun-soaked remnants of my dream with the sticky, suffocating summer storm pounding the stair landing.

"Um, Mama?" piped up a small voice from the steps. "I'm Rex, Mama, not Eli."

Leah rolled her eyes. "You have no idea how much I appreciate this, Faith. Honestly. Okay, Rex, you're going to stay with Faith this morning."

Rex, wearing a little yellow raincoat, peeked around the doorjamb. He grinned at me. I grinned back.

"Okay, then." She leaned down to kiss his cheek and the baby stopped crying for a minute to observe. "Be good. Faith, you are a lifesaver. If you have any problems at all, Stan's at the bakery. Meet you back here at three?"

"Take your time." I waved her away, relishing my new identity as lifesaver.

Rex and I decided to go down to Main Street and hit the shops. After we checked out the goldfish tank at the pet store, he reached up and wrapped one of his chubby white hands around mine.

"Faith?"

"What's up?"

He regarded me with wounded eyes. "Why doesn't anybody call me Rex? Why do they keep saying Eli? I changed it. I changed my name."

I managed not to smile. "I know you did, honey. But sometimes people don't understand that the name your mom and dad gave you isn't the name you'd give yourself."

He scowled. "When I tell grown-ups that my name is Rex, they laugh."

"I guess they think it's cute, and that's why they laugh."

He yanked at the hood of his yellow slicker. "I don't wanna be cute. I wanna be Rex."

"Well, when you turn eighteen, you can go to court and get your name changed to whatever you want." Leah was going to love me for this one.

"Really?" He perked up. "Is that what you did?"

I squeezed his hand. "Oh, no. Faith is what my parents named me."

Rex tugged me over to the curb and peered into the drainage grate as rainwater swirled down dark beneath the street. "Well, what name would you pick? If you picked your own?"

"Hmm. Maybe Natalia." A *femme fatale* name, very new-money and black lace.

"Natalia?" He wrinkled his nose. "Okay. You be Natalia today, and I will be Rex."

Natalia came back to bite me in the ass less than twenty minutes later.

I lost Rex at noon, in Thompson's Dry Goods store. The kid

disappeared in the blink of an eye. He was dancing down the aisle, pointing and winking at himself in the mirrored wall like a kindergarten production of *Saturday Night Fever*. He brushed against a display of folded towels, two fell down, I knelt to pick them up, and that was it. He was gone. I scanned the milling crowd for a bright yellow jacket or a ruffle of thick black hair but found nothing.

My mouth dried out as my palms started to sweat. The horrors of L.A. newscasts flashed through my mind.

"Eli?" I called. No response.

Then I remembered who I was dealing with. "Rex?"

"Natalia!" Air rushed back into my lungs as I heard the chipper cry behind me. I whipped around.

"Oh, thank God. I didn't know where you—" I broke off as Rex rounded the corner, hand in hand with Patrick Flynn.

"I found him boogying down in the housewares section. This kid's the next Ricky Martin." Flynn looked amused and surprisingly comfortable shepherding Rex along next to him. "Natalia."

My cheeks caught fire. "Yes. Well, see, we were just—"

"Picking alternate names. I heard. Rex and I go way back, don't we, buddy?"

Rex beamed up at him. "Yep. Flynn coached my T-Ball team once."

I picked my jaw up off the floor. "You *did?*"

Flynn shrugged. "Yeah." He turned to Rex. "So do I get to pick a name, too?"

The child was aghast. "No. You gotta stay Flynn." He

reached out and recaptured my hand so all three of us were linked, like a happy little family. Except none of us were related and two of us were barely on speaking terms.

"But you can still be Natalia," Rex informed me.

"Thanks." I tried to think of a way to get us out of here quickly and diplomatically. This little hand-holding chain was supremely awkward, and I just wasn't up for Flynn's editorial on my negligent childcare.

Rex tugged on my hand. "I'm hungry. Let's go to Cherry's!" He pointed at the small white clapboard cafe across the street. "And eat coffee cake for lunch."

I shrugged. "Okay."

"Coffee cake! Oh boy!" He hopped up and down, gripping our hands tighter as he lifted his feet and swung between us. "And Flynn can come, too!"

"I don't think Flynn has time for lunch right now. He's, uh . . ." I turned to Flynn, who seemed to be conducting a close inspection of a pile of scarves in front of us. "What *are* you doing here today?"

"Working." He shoved his hands into his jeans pockets. "Talking to some people. I'm trying to organize an event. You'll see."

"And the dry goods store is critical to your plan?"

"New dishtowels." He refused to look at me.

"I see." I tried to turn this conversation around. Somewhere under this stony façade was the man who'd undressed me with his eyes in the office last night. "Well, it's nice of you to spend your Sunday helping us out."

"Not really." He rocked back on his heels. "I'm just trying to bail out my investment."

I gave up. "Okay, then. Nice talking to you. Rex and I are off to lunch now." Swamped with a sudden wave of abdominal agony, I closed my eyes.

Rex stuck out his bottom lip. "Flynn's not coming?"

"Look, maybe we should just head home," I said.

The little boy's world was crumbling before his eyes.

"*After* we get a piece of coffee cake to go." I winced again, pressing both hands to my stomach. "I'm not feeling all that well."

Flynn abandoned the scarves and got all up in my face. "What's wrong?" he demanded.

"Nothing."

"What's wrong?" He met my gaze.

"You don't want to know," I assured him. "Let's just say it's a long story and it ends with me going to the gynecologist."

He nodded and dropped it. Minnesota men, as a rule, do not relish the gory details of Female Trouble.

"Flynn's leaving? This is awful," Rex wailed, wiping his nose with the sleeve of his raincoat.

Flynn knelt down. "Sorry kid, I have to do some work. But I'll walk you to the car. And you'll have to eat something besides coffee cake for lunch okay? Like lima beans and gruel."

Rex laughed. "I *like* gruel. So there."

We dashed through the rain toward my car, which was parked a block away across the street.

Things were looking up, I decided. Yes, there had been a few glitches today, yesterday, and well, ever since I got the phone call in Florence . . . but look where we were now. He was walk-ing me to my car, and he didn't even have a gun to his head. Next thing you know, he'd be kissing my feet and speaking to me in complete sentences.

Flynn grabbed Rex's wrist with one hand as we crossed the street. He placed his other hand on the small of my back to guide me through traffic.

I glanced at his face as we stepped off the curb, but he seemed completely oblivious, his eyes focused on the passing cars. I wasn't even sure if he was aware that he was touching me.

If only my abdomen weren't a writhing mass of white-hot pain, I might have been turned on.

We reached my car safely, and none too soon. The heavy gray sky rumbled with thunder and within seconds, all three of us were drenched in warm rain. I buckled Rex into the car seat Leah had supplied and turned to thank Flynn.

And that's when I noticed the look in his eyes. Somewhere on the way across the street, his attitude had changed. He wasn't looking through me anymore. He wasn't looking past me. He was looking *at* me. With an intensity that startled me.

I wrapped my fingers around the sleeves of my windbreaker. "Well, thanks for walking us to the car."

He held my gaze for a long moment. We were motionless and bright against the gray pavement and the dull windy sky. Then he leaned over and kissed my cheek. His mouth barely brushed my face, but for the space of a breath, rooted to the pavement and connected to this man, I knew where I was. I was scared, I was confused, but I was home.

Then I opened my eyes and rushed back to reality. And the reality was, Flynn didn't seem at all fazed by what had just happened. He simply turned away and headed back across the parking lot with quick, measured strides.

"So long," he called over his shoulder.

A glance into the car confirmed that Rex, k.o.'ed by the one-two punch of no nap-time and too much excitement, was already asleep in the car seat. I started after Flynn. "Hey!"

He stopped, then slowly turned around. Torrents of rain pounded down between us, but I could see that the distant detachment had returned to his eyes.

"Wait . . ." I turned my palms up toward the sky and all the wind and rain rampaging between us. "What was *that?*"

"What was what?" he asked.

"You just kissed me," I pointed out.

He shrugged. "That wasn't a kiss."

I shook my head. "We call that a kiss where I come from."

He smiled tightly. "We come from the same place."

"Okay, that is not my point." I tipped my head back, letting the rain splash onto my cheeks. "What are we doing here?"

"Why are we having this conversation in the pouring rain?"

"I don't know." I searched at the sky, hoping that a divine message would appear. Something along the lines of *Thou shalt not bear wrath against thy high school sweetheart.* "I don't know why we're having it at all, because nothing I say will make any difference. Apparently, you're going to be angry and refuse to talk about anything until I beg to play by your rules. But I don't know what those rules are. I don't. I hate to think that that look in your eyes is because of me, but I can't keep doing this. I'm through with this bait-and-switch bullshit. I'll see you tomorrow." I headed back to my car.

His voice sliced through the rain. "Don't walk away from me, Faith."

I kept walking.

"You're just going to take off?" he called. "Exit stage left, once again?"

I stopped, one foot in a puddle. "Excuse me?"

"You heard me. The minute things get tough, you turn tail and head for the hills. That's your solution to everything. You just run away."

I kept my voice even. "I suppose cowardice runs in the family."

"I didn't say you were a coward." His voice was softer now. "I didn't spend half my life in love with a coward, Faith."

And there it was again. Snap, crackle, pop.

He caught my hand in his. "And by the way, when have you ever played by my rules?"

I shivered as the rain trickled down my neck. He slipped our intertwined hands into my jacket pocket.

I took a deep breath. "I know you're still angry with me for leaving you when you asked me to get married."

He exhaled slowly, then nodded. "Yeah."

"And in a lot of ways, I'm still angry with you for pushing me away when I needed you the most. But we can't change any of that. And I'm not going to keep apologizing every time I see you. I'm not a masochist. So what now?"

"I don't know," he said. I considered this a great leap forward from the fever-pitch litany of "I don't want to talk about it." He stared at the ground. "I don't want to keep having this same fight over and over again."

"Neither do I. But what *do* you want?"

"I don't know," he repeated.

A royal blue Miata barreled around the corner, skidding to a stop just inches from my knees. Flynn yanked me back toward my car, and I stumbled into his chest. There was an awkward, mutual disentangling of fingers as Sally slammed out of the Mazda.

"What is that look for?" she snapped at me. "I'm not the one standing around in the middle of the street."

"I could have been a five-year-old," I pointed out, glancing at Rex's sleeping form through the window. "A *run-over* five-year-old."

"Yeah, and I'd tell your mother not to let you play in traffic." She clearly wanted to add "bitch" to the end of this sentence, but restrained herself for Flynn's sake. She recalibrated her mood to "sweetness and light" and purred, "Hi, Patrick."

Sally had shattered the moment I'd just shared with Flynn, and now that it was over, I was terrified by how close I'd wanted to be to him, how willing to ignore the consequences.

My eyes darted back to the VW and the sleeping child inside.

I brushed past Flynn and opened the driver's side door, then slid in behind the wheel, trying to fasten my seat belt with trembling hands. "I have to go. To the doctor."

I fumbled with the keys and glanced at the side mirror. Sally was wagging her finger and yammering away at Flynn, who was staring at the car. As I backed out of the parking space, I met his eyes.

Then I drove all the way to Skye's apartment, and I didn't check the rearview mirror once.

11

"Wait, wait, stop right there. So he kissed you or he didn't kiss you?" Skye sat crosslegged atop the kitchen counter, eating a Pop-Tart while she quizzed me.

"Yeah, you can't gloss over these parts." Leah cuddled the baby sleeping in her lap and glanced at Rex, who was studying Skye's back issues of *People*. In lieu of coffee cake, I had placated him with toaster pastries and a Popsicle.

"I told you already." I fished three ibuprofen out of the bottle. "Technically, yes, he kissed me. And then Sally practically ran me down like a dog in the street."

"And then?" my sister demanded.

"I don't know. I left."

"Playing hard to get." She saluted me with her Pop-Tart. "Good idea!"

"I'm not playing hard to get. Let's be crystal clear on this: I cannot get involved with him again. I have to go back to California soon, and breaking up with him again will kill me. Or he'll kill me himself. One way or another, I'll be dead."

"So what are you going to do?" Leah asked.

I sighed. "The very first thing I'm going to do is head over to the clinic. I have to see someone today." I winced. "Something is definitely wrong."

"Don't leave us in suspense—tell us the rest of your mini-drama," Leah said.

"There's nothing to tell," I insisted.

Leah and Skye exchanged a pointed look.

I scowled. "I told you, he hasn't forgiven me . . . and even if he has, I can't get involved. And anyway, since our little tête-à-tête was so rudely interrupted by Sally Hutchins, that's the end of that story."

Leah shook her head. "That girl always was insufferable. God's gift to the Rice County Country Club. Is she still throwing herself at him?"

"She has a thing for hockey players. And have you *seen* the hair color?" Skye huffed. "I could do better with some Easter egg dye and both hands tied behind my back."

"I don't know how to break it to him that I have to go back to L.A. soon." I put the last mug into the dishwasher and slammed the door.

"Why do you have to go back to L.A.?" Skye asked. She

didn't make eye contact, as if she expected me to start yelling.

"Yeah, that seems kind of abrupt," Leah said.

"Well . . ." I frowned. Why wouldn't I go back? Now that we'd sorted out Skye's "pregnancy," there was nothing keeping me from returning to my real life. Sure, I'd intended to help with the bar, but Flynn wasn't exactly oozing enthusiasm about that. In fact, I reasoned, I had a better chance of recouping my investment if I left him alone to run things his way. He wouldn't have to sell it to escape me.

I could leave tonight, actually. If I wanted to.

"Well . . . my editor wants me to do an article out here. So I'll be around until that's done," I finally said. "But then I have to go back."

"But can't you be a writer anywhere?" Leah asked.

I changed the subject entirely. "Men are so vexing. Why does everything have to be so damn hard?"

"Because you are unfortunate enough to have those little things called feelings," Leah said, cradling Rachel in one arm as she struggled to her feet. "Eli—excuse me, Rex—are you ready to go, bunny?"

He was deeply engrossed in a layout of paparazzi shots from the Venice Film Festival. "Can I bring this home with me?"

After we said good-bye to the Goldberg family, I prepared to make my exit. "I can't waste the afternoon wringing my hands over some stupid man. I'm going to the doctor. And then I have to get to work."

"Oh, yeah, work." Skye's face lit up. "That reminds me—get ready to be so proud of me!"

"Why?" I demanded warily.

"I landed us another promotional event thing. A real one! It's a wine and cheese party for Ian and the arts and humanities faculty at his college. They do it every summer. He's the department chair this year, and he said the Roof Rat could host it. On Saturday. Wine! Cheese! Isn't this exciting?"

"Very exciting. Except, um, we don't have any wine."

"So we'll get some! I'm going to wear my new gold lamé minidress. It is *so* classy." She closed her eyes and sighed in rapture. "I'm thinking like, a harpist, and a violinist, and waiters in tuxes passing cute little silver trays . . ."

"Will you settle for some Rachmaninoff on the jukebox and clean T-shirts?"

"Okay!" She grabbed an issue of *Us* on the coffee table and started writing all over a photo of Brad Pitt and Jennifer Aniston. "Let's start planning! I'll make a list!"

I smiled. "You do that. I'll see you tonight."

"Okay. Hurry up and recover, because I have oodles of ideas!"

There were two sure signs of impending doom at the clinic. One, "Muskrat Love" drifting out of the examination room speakers while the doctor diagnosed my bladder infection. Two, Sally Hutchins sitting directly across from me while I waited for the nurse to bring out my antibiotic prescription.

Sally's mood had not improved since our little roadside contretemps that morning. She perched primly in a mauve armchair, crossing and uncrossing her legs. At regular thirty-second intervals, she heaved a mighty sigh and rolled her eyes. I tried to ignore her and focus on the waiting room's year-old copy of *Marie Claire.*

Just as I was starting to lose myself in an article on moisturizing lotion lifespans, she flipped her hair and demanded, "What are *you* doing here?"

I put down the magazine and turned both palms toward her. "I'm just here for the drugs. What are you in for?"

"None of your business." She leaned over and snatched the *Marie Claire,* leaving me with a dog-eared issue of *Log Cabin Living.* Muttering under my breath, I resigned myself to juicy exposès on Canadian pine tree construction and chandeliers made entirely of antlers.

The nurse finally bustled in with a cheerful smile and roughly fifteen clipboards, none of which seemed to be in order.

"Okey-dokey now . . ." She frowned at the sheaves of paper in her hand. "You two are . . . ?"

"Geary."

"Hutchins."

She shuffled through the paperwork, pushed her glasses higher up on her nose, and turned to me. "Faith, we're giving you a three-day course of Bactrim for the urinary tract infection . . ."

So much for patient confidentiality.

"And Sally, hon, your doctor is giving you Septra for *your* urinary infection. That won't interfere with the antidepressants you're taking. Any questions, girls?"

Both of us just gaped at her, open-mouthed.

"Okey-dokey, then! And don't forget to drink your cranberry juice. Bye-bye!"

I watched her head back to the reception area. "Oh my God."

Sally was practically frothing at the mouth. "I'm suing. Do you hear me? I am going to go straight to my father's office, and I am suing!"

I gave up on *Log Cabin Living* and got to my feet. "Oh, simmer down. It's just a bladder infection. So what? I've got one, too."

She glared at me through slitted green eyes.

"And spare me the ice queen routine, okay? I'm not going to tell anyone about your precious urinary tract."

She slapped *Marie Claire* back onto the table. "That's not what I'm worried about."

I stared at her for a long moment before bringing up the unbring-uppable. "You're worried about the antidepressants?"

She flinched. "Keep your voice down!"

"Fine, but I don't see what you're freaking out about. I live in Southern California now. Half the population's on Prozac."

"Well, this isn't Los Angeles. This is Lindbrook, and it's not okay to be"—she glanced furtively around the empty room—"popping pills."

"Paranoid much? I'm not going to say anything, and even if I did, no one would care."

She still looked petulant and litigious.

"No one would believe me, anyway," I soothed. "I'm sure no one thinks you've got anything to be depressed about."

She snorted. "You must be joking."

"No, really." I sat back down, getting more annoyed by the minute. "You have everything you could possibly want. You have the perfect small-town life, and instead of appreciating it, you act like Cruella De Vil in J. Crew."

She stared at the stains on the flecked gray carpet. "I do not."

But I was on a roll. This little throwdown was ten years overdue.

"For God's sake, woman, you just stole my waiting-room copy of *Marie Claire*. I rest my case. Some people get the elevator, and some people just get the shaft. You were lucky enough to get the whole penthouse, and you lord it over everybody else, so I don't see why you need antidepressants."

"That's because you've never met my mother," she snapped.

"This is true." I nodded.

"You wouldn't understand." She shook out her stoplight-red hair. "I am not some witchy little princess. I happen to be very misunderstood around here."

"Don't cry for me, Argentina," I scoffed. But I was starting to think that I'd actually hurt her feelings.

"And I don't see why you're bitching about *Marie Claire* when your entire life is like a fashion magazine."

I blinked. "What, now?"

"You get to live in Beverly Hills and travel all over the world and date movie stars . . ."

I threw back my head and laughed. "I don't know who you've been talking to, but you've been grossly misinformed."

" . . . And I'm still stuck in Lindbrook, Minnesota. Living with my parents and working as my father's secretary and spending all day listening to my mother criticize my hair and tell me I should be married by now. Like it wasn't enough that I had to pledge her snobby sorority house at the University of Minnesota."

Time out. "You went to the U?"

"Yeah. Why?"

"Well, did you ever see Flynn while you were there?" Read: *Did you ever date Flynn while you were there?* This is what I had been reduced to. Pumping my arch-enemy for information about my ex-boyfriend.

"Sure." Sally played with her pearl pendant. "I saw him at every hockey game."

"You did?" *Tell me, tell me, tell me.*

"Of course. He was the star player for three years."

"And? What happened?"

"A knee injury, I think. At the beginning of senior year. I don't know all the details, but the girl he was dating said that he had like, five surgeries on his knee, and none of them worked. He couldn't play any more after that."

I began the cross-examination. "Well, who was this chick who was dating him?"

"One of my sorority sisters. Sondra Cutler. Her father was a vice president of Honeywell, and she married—"

"Hold it. Flynn dated sorority girls?" I tried to reorient my world, which had just turned upside down.

"Not just sorority girls. *Sigma Psi* girls. The cream of the crop." She crossed her ankles and tilted her chin up.

"You're kidding. Did he date a lot of them?"

She shrugged. "I don't know. He wasn't really into the groupies the way the rest of the hockey team was." She looked a little disappointed about this. "But he had some really bad break-ups."

"He, uh, he did?"

"Yes, he did, hel-*lo,* starting with you." She picked up *Marie Claire* and resumed flipping through it.

"Put that down. I'm not done with you yet." I paused. "You knew about our break-up?"

"About how you ran off with that drummer and broke his heart?" She gave me an unctuous smile. "This is Lindbrook. Everybody knew about it. He walked around the U. looking all rebellious and tortured for a year, and then he got on with his life."

"It was a bass player." I gritted my teeth. "So what happened with Sondra?"

"Well!" I watched the struggle on Sally's face as her Sigma Psi loyalty warred with her primal urge to gossip. "She kept wanting to get married, but he wouldn't."

I sat down next to her. "What? That doesn't sound like Flynn."

She sneered at me. "I guess you ruined him for everyone else. She kept hinting for a ring, and he kept saying he didn't want to talk about it—"

"Now, *that* sounds like Flynn."

"—But I told her not to feel bad because it was all your fault for scarring him for life. So she went to this psychic on Hennepin Avenue and put a hex on you."

"A hex? You're serious? But she'd never even met me."

"Yeah, but she wanted to get engaged and it was all your fault he wouldn't, so she paid the psychic to put a spell on you. To curse your love life with madmen and criminals."

I had to admit, this explained a lot about my dating history.

"Did it ever occur to you that maybe he didn't want to marry her because she was a narcissist who dabbled in the dark arts?"

She ignored this. "Anyway, Sondra finally got over it and ended up marrying Mark Churchill, but then he turned out to have major mother issues—"

"But what happened to Flynn?"

Her eyes wandered back to the magazine. "I don't know. He graduated and went off to work. I haven't seen him much since then, except when you're around."

"I thought he was at the Roof Rat every night?"

"Not until last week. He's been in Lindbrook a lot more since you showed up."

I tucked this tidbit away for later analysis. "Really."

"Yes. Look, I have to get back to the office. Daddy needs me to pour coffee and type memos." She made a face as she folded her prescription into her purse. "And I haven't decided about suing, but if you tell anybody about the antidepressants, I'll name you in the lawsuit."

"Uh-huh. So glad we had this little chat." I watched her stalk out the sliding glass doors, all flaming hair, tasteful twill, and Sigma Psi suburban rage. And then I trailed after her, even more confused about Flynn and wondering if Leah or Skye knew how to reverse hexes.

*　　*　　*

Tuesday night at the Roof Rat boiled down to me, Flynn and Ian, who had struck up something of a courtship with Skye after I talked her into rebuffing Lars. Nary a single customer. At nine o'clock, torn between abject boredom and panic over lost profits, my sister decided we needed a distraction. She ran up to the apartment to unearth, from the bottom of a closet, a 500-piece jigsaw puzzle.

Ian excused himself to go retrieve his pipe and tobacco from his car, whereupon Skye dumped all 500 pieces on the table and announced, "Flynn, I have some excellent news. I told Ian that his college department group thing could have their annual wine and cheese party here next week. Isn't that exciting?" She squared her shoulders, trying to look brisk and businesslike. "I'm doing it all myself! I am totally becoming a burned-out career woman."

"You sure are," he agreed. "But what about my big event? We're supposed to be prepping for that."

"Don't worry, we can do both," she assured him.

I jerked my head up. "What exactly is 'your big event' anyway?"

"Just a little get-together for the hockey team." He turned a puzzle piece over and over in his hand. "A little get-together with a lot of alcohol."

"Yeah, we might even hire a band," Skye said.

"With a bass player and everything." He smirked at me. "You'll love it."

My sister looked horrified. "Can't you two just be happy for once?"

"I don't know. Can we?" He turned to me, and I knew he was thinking about my abrupt departure from Main Street after he'd kissed me.

"I don't know," I muttered.

There was a moment of silence you could have cut with a knife and served in slices on little doilies.

Then Ian clattered back through the door, gazing with adoration at Skye. "Always so lovely, my lamb."

She puckered up and gave Ian a tiny, non-lipstick-smearing kiss on the cheek. "Oh, how sweet!"

As I looked around for a place to vomit, I risked a moment of eye contact with Flynn, who was laughing. But he stopped when I caught his eye and I realized that one little kiss in the rain today didn't erase the big kiss-off ten years ago.

12

On the morning of the English department cheese and wine soiree, I hauled my carcass out of bed after another night of insomnia and headed for the bathroom, but Skye cut me off to usurp the shower.

She scooched around me and turned on the hot water, shoving me back against the sink. "Ugh. Morning. By the way, your car's broken."

"My car's broken?" I rubbed the sleep out of my eyes. "What's wrong with it?"

"I was trying to get to Cannon Falls to meet Ian—"

"Yeah, and thanks for borrowing it without asking and then blowing off work, by the way."

"—and it kept making these horrible grinding noises. So I

called Lars and he said it's probably your clutch or something and you shouldn't drive it again until he takes a look at it."

"You called Lars? On the way to Ian's house?"

"Sure." She yawned and grabbed a loofah from the shelf above the sink. "He said he'll come over and fix it this week."

"I can't believe you called Lars while you were on your way to meet Ian." I shook my head. "Have you no shame?"

"None whatsoever." She tossed her towel aside and stepped into the tub. "Now get going, Faithie. You've got a million things to do today, and most of them involve cheese-slicing."

I put my hands on my hips. "*I've* got a million things to do today?"

Her voice drifted over the hiss of hot water. "Don't get snarky, I'll be working, too. While you slice all the cheese and pour all the wine and clean up for the party . . . I'll be at the laundromat."

"The laundromat? Are you sure? I wouldn't want you coming down with Chronic Fatigue Syndrome."

She laughed. "I'll even take your clothes and wash them. What do you say?"

I sighed and grabbed my toothbrush. "I say, bring on the brie."

After scouring the local grocery store and Leah and Stan's bakery, I decided that the Arts and Humanities faculty were going to have to make do with Nabisco, because English water crackers were not going to magically materialize in Lindbrook. Skye, using Lars as her chauffeur, bundled up every scrap of clothing and linen she could find and flitted off to the Lakewood Soap 'n' Suds.

"It's better than the one in Lindbrook because it has TV and they always have the Soap Opera Network on," she informed me. "I'll be back in a few hours. You better start chipping away at that cheese."

Four hours, two slabs of cheddar, one wheel of brie and countless wedges of Gouda later, my right arm was aching and my good mood was a distant memory.

Even on my best days, I was no Nigella Lawson. I unwrapped the crackers, dumped stacks of them in the center of the cheese piles, and called it an artistic choice. Then I checked the clock. Time for some tiara therapy and a little beautification before facing Flynn.

We hadn't talked much since our kiss on Main Street, and I wasn't sure how to interpret his silence. The bar had been busy, but not too busy for basic verbal communication. Was he waiting for me to make the next move? Was he pretending the whole thing had never happened? Was he conspiring with the psychic on Hennepin Avenue to curse me into oblivion?

I wandered into the bedroom to begin wardrobe selection and realized that Skye had not been kidding when she offered to take all my clothes to the laundromat. Every last one of my shirts, my pants, even my underwear had been trundled off to the Lakewood Soap 'n' Suds. My current outfit, the voluminous Cubs T-shirt I'd thrown on for cheese detail, lacked a certain come-hither allure, so I opened the top drawer of Skye's dresser in the hopes of finding at least a bra that might fit.

I reached into the deepest recesses of the drawer, hoping I might chance upon a rogue B-cup left over from her middle school days, but my hand closed around a fistful of family photos.

My throat constricted as I saw my father's face for the first time in years. I shuffled through the pictures, hypnotized by the images of my sister at seven or eight with pigtails and the same playful grin she had now. She was standing next to my father in one photo, wearing his baseball cap and mimicking his proud posture. And there was my mother, bright and blond and slightly out of focus, on her way to somewhere more exciting.

When I reached the last photo, I had to sit down on the bed. I stared at the image of myself, grinning and impossibly young in a fancy dress for my senior graduation dance. In the photos taken that night, Flynn and I looked relaxed and happy, probably because we knew that as soon as we left the house, we were heading to the creek instead of the crepe-papered high school gym. The creek bank was where we'd spent every significant high school event, camped out under the stars by ourselves and enjoying the wilderness in our formalwear. That was where, on the night of that graduation dance, we decided to shed all pretext of restraint, along with our clothes. Which had led to skinny dipping under a huge white moon, which led to sex, which led to the beginning of the end.

"I'm home!" Skye slammed the front door. I shoved the photos back into the dresser and shut the drawer.

"I'm in here," I yelled back.

She staggered through the doorway, her blue eyes peeking over a mountain of white sheets and lavender towels. "Faithie, we have to be down there in half an hour. Why are you still wearing that T-shirt?" She took another look at my face and froze in place. "What?"

I shook my head. "Nothing."

Her eyes widened with concern. "No, it's definitely something. What happened?"

"Nothing," I repeated, realizing as I said this that it was the truth. The people and places—the potential—I saw in those photographs had evaporated long ago. "Let's get dressed."

Bra-gate, as it later came to be known, began while I was still trying to pull myself together in the bathroom.

Skye rapped lightly on the door. "Um? Hi?"

I sniffed my last sniffle into a ball of Kleenex. No more obsessing on graduation dances of yore. "Yes?"

"I have some good news and some bad news. What do you want first?"

I braced myself. "The bad news. Always."

"Well . . . remember how I went to the laundromat?"

I popped my head out into the hall. "The laundromat from whence you returned not ten minutes ago?"

She shifted her weight. "Yeah. Remember how they have the Soap Opera Network there? They had this really sad episode of *All My Children* on, and Anthony was in a coma, and . . . I sort of forgot to bring your stuff back."

I narrowed my eyes. "What stuff, specifically?"

She examined her manicure. "Some of your clothes. Okay, actually, all of your clothes."

"All my clothes? Are moldering in Lakewood? Because Anthony's in a coma?"

She nodded.

"Then, Skye," I said pleasantly, "how exactly am I supposed to get dressed?"

"That's the good news." She beckoned me into the bedroom, pointing out a slim pair of black leather pants draped on the bed.

"You jest." I stared at the slinky Pamela Anderson britches.

"They're brand new. Bob bought them for me and I haven't even worn them. Aren't they the hottest ever?"

"Hot, yes. Appropriate for an Arts and Humanities faculty party, no. What are my other options?"

"Not much, because I forgot a lot of my clothes in Lakewood, too. But I did bring the sheets back. *And* the towels." She rummaged through her closet. "There's this." She held out a ruched gold lamé minidress and a red backless number.

"Dear God. Can't we send Lars back to Lakewood?"

"No. He's already setting up the bar downstairs." She gave me her patented "problems are hard" face. "You don't like the pants?"

How to put this tactfully? "I love the pants. It's just that . . ."

"Great! Put them on. I'll wear this"—she held the gold lamé up to the mirror—"and we'll be the belles of the ball."

The problem was not that the pants didn't fit; the problem was that they fit too well. The pliant leather clung to my every skin cell. After a thorough inspection in the mirror, I had to admit they didn't look half bad. For a Justin Timberlake groupie.

"Seriously, Faithie, you look so kick-ass!" Skye dug around under the bed and emerged with a pair of strappy silver sandals. "Try these on. Sensible shoes don't go with those pants."

I sighed. "In for a dime, in for a dollar. Gimme."

"Oh, and here." She handed me a tiny scrap of white cloth, which turned out to be a tube top with the word VIXEN spelled out in red rhinestones across the chest.

"I'm not wearing that!" I flung the offending hoochie rag to the floor.

"Why not?"

"Because I refuse to go down there in leather pants, stilettos, a tube top sized for an eight-year-old boy, and no bra."

"Why not?" Her blue eyes sparkled. "Flynn'll love it." She shimmied into the gold lamé.

"Skye. Focus. This isn't about Flynn. It's about my personal dignity."

"Dignity, schmignity." She affixed giant gold hoops to her ears. "What's more important, getting back together with Flynn or your foolish pride?"

"Whoa." I sat down on the bed. "Listen to me. There's no question of us getting back together. Flynn and me? Not gonna happen."

"But he kissed you—"

"A week ago, for about two nanoseconds." I flopped back against the pillows. "And he's devoted every spare minute since then to ignoring me."

"Well, maybe if you just talked to him . . ."

"He doesn't want to talk to me," I pointed out. "Which sucks right now, but is probably for the best." I rolled over to face the wall. "I'd rather he be mad at me than decide to give me a second chance and have me blow it again when I leave to go back to L.A. We've already had one apocalyptic break-up. I don't ever want to go through that again, and neither does he."

She pouted. "But if he did give you a second chance, maybe you'd decide to move back here and we could . . ."

"Minnesota and me? *Definitely* not gonna happen." The look on her face cut me to the quick, but I couldn't let her nurture the hope that I would suddenly change my mind and settle down here. "Sweetie, I love you and I came out here to help you, but I can't stay. I will suffocate here."

She seemed skeptical.

I tried to frame this in a context she'd appreciate. "Okay, imagine if you just washed a new sports bra and it shrunk in the dryer and when you put it on, it's so tight you can't even breathe."

"Ooh, I hate that."

"Well, that's what I feel like when I'm in Lindbrook."

She nodded sadly. "Except you can't take the sports bra off."

"That's right. And speaking of bras, I need to rustle up some appropriate partywear ASAP."

I ended up calling Leah. After laughing for about ten minutes, she brought over a flowing white silk blouse for me to try. "You have to remember, I've had two kids and no personal trainer. No way are my bras going to fit you. But the shirt's pretty roomy, so maybe no one will notice you're going commando."

"I hope so." I glanced at the clock and smeared on some lip gloss. "Either way, I have to get moving. Skye's already down there setting up the cheese platters and the classy plastic wine glasses."

"Good luck. Let me know how it goes." Leah tried unsuccessfully to hide her smile. "Those pants are so sassy. Flynn will definitely approve."

"That's just what Skye said." I yanked my hair back into a Health Code–friendly braid.

"It is a truth universally acknowledged that men love leather pants. Hold still." She smeared some purple shadow on my eyelids. "Are you nervous about seeing him tonight?"

My eyelid twitched. "No, I'm through with that drama. He can love me, he can hate me . . . I don't give a rat's ass."

"Whatever you say." She took a step back and gave me a critical once-over. "Stan's leaving our old pick-up truck in the parking lot. You can borrow it until your car is fixed. You know how to drive stick, right?"

"Yeah. Flynn taught me, actually." We had spent entire Sundays steering and shifting and braking, and he never lost his temper. Not when I stalled, not when I kept confusing the left and right turn signals, not when I hit pothole after pothole in my attempt to focus on second gear. He'd just stretched his arm along the back of the bench seat, craned his head around to view the cracked pavement behind us, and nodded. "Good work, Geary. You hit every single one."

"Done." Leah turned me around to face the mirror. "Tell me you don't look stunning."

With the free-flowing white silk shirt, the tight leather pants, and the high heels, I looked like a hybrid of Joan Jett and Edna St. Vincent Millay. "There are no words," I agreed.

"Now go prove me right about men and leather pants."

13

Downstairs, the wine and cheese fête had gone terribly awry.

The Roof Rat was overflowing with beer kegs and hockey banners. The cheese platters, for which I had sacrificed hours of labor and all feeling in my right arm, warred for counter space with bowls of potato chips, pretzels, and some unidentified brown crunchy substance. Flynn, decked out in his customary jeans and T-shirt, was hanging a huge Polecats banner from the ceiling. Skye, teetering in high heels on a flimsy folding chair, tacked a woven medievalesque tapestry over the bar.

I cleared my throat. "I wasn't aware the faculty members were such avid sports fans."

Skye hopped down from her chair, nearly breaking an ankle in the process. "The hockey stuff is for Flynn's event."

"Wait. I thought that was next weekend?" I turned to him for clarification, but he continued his banner-hanging without sparing me a single glance. "Right now we need to be prepping the place for professors. Think Chaucer."

"Um, actually, I kind of need to talk to you about that." Skye twisted her hands together. "See, Ian wanted to do this event today and I said okay, and then Flynn asked me about doing his event on Saturday, and I thought he meant *next* Saturday, but he meant *this* Saturday, so . . . my bad!"

"You've double-booked? Humanities professors and hockey players?"

She nodded.

"Perhaps it strikes you that we now have a crisis on our hands?"

"Nah. We'll just combine the parties." She looked staggered by her own genius. "Wine and cheese *and* beer and pretzels. Double the money, double the fun!"

I raised my eyebrows. "And how do you think Ian's colleagues will feel about this?"

"They'll love it! I mean, they're stuck in some boring office all day grading papers. I bet they're dying to meet a real live goalie."

"Right. Because there's nothing they love more in the Ivory Tower than a good, toothless brawl." I snatched up a cube of cheddar and devoured it. "You guys, we can't do this. We promised Ian that—"

"Relax, Geary." Flynn still didn't bother to turn around. "If you don't want to deal with it, you don't have to. Skye and I have it under control. Go back upstairs."

The minute things get tough, you turn tail and head for the hills.

I set my jaw and crossed my arms under my flowing white shirt. "I'll stay, thanks."

"Good." He finally glanced back over one wide, broad shoulder. And his face went from blank and blasé to hot and bothered. "What the hell are you wearing?"

I grinned. "Top half by Leah Goldberg, bottom half by Skye Geary, hair, unfortunately, a Faith Geary signature. Like it?"

"But you're not . . ." he sputtered, gesturing at the thin silk skimming my nipples. "I can see . . ."

"You can?" My hands flew to my chest, which suddenly felt completely exposed. "From *there?*"

"It's my fault," Skye said. "I just lost my head at the Soap 'n' Suds. But I think she looks fabulous. Very riot grrl."

Flynn addressed my sister without taking his eyes off me. Well, off my breasts, to be precise. "I'll tell you what she looks like. She looks like a—"

"Woman who doesn't need a scathing fashion critique right now," I finished for him, reminding myself sternly that that he could love me or hate me, I didn't give a rat's ass. "Now hand me those pretzels and let's get to work."

The Arts and Humanities faculty showed up first. They took the news quite well. The female professors in particular seemed eager to share their wine with professional athletes.

"Hockey players. Really," mused Valerie Wheeler (harpist, potter, Women's Studies). "I've been wanting to investigate the layman's view of Showalter's gynocentrism theory and this will be the perfect chance." Then she hurried off to the ladies' room to fix her hair.

Barbara, the American Literature specialist, was equally delighted. "Oh, fantastic." She rummaged through her bag and pulled out some Chinese herbs and a tube of lipstick. "A fresh new audience for my word dances. And they work out every day, you say?"

"Real men! Finally!" whooped Teresa, the studio art teacher. "Hallelujah!"

The male faculty members were less enthusiastic.

"I don't see how we're supposed to have serious conversations about curriculum development while surrounded by a herd of drunken degenerates," harrumphed Bryson (husband of Valerie Wheeler).

Frederick Gill, a reed-thin sociologist with ethereal blond hair, glanced at the kegs in dismay. "Where are we going to set up our annual chess tournament?"

Ian pulled me aside and tugged at his bow tie. "Are you certain this is a good idea? My colleagues seem most off-put."

"Are you kidding? Take a look around. You're the new hero of female scholars everywhere!" I pointed to the jukebox, where Barbara and Valerie were giggling like schoolgirls and watching the front door with the predatory intensity of wolverines.

Teresa, impatient for the pro hockey players to arrive, made a beeline for the amateur defenseman. She had Flynn backed into a corner and was fluffing her hair in his face. I hurried over to Skye.

"Go deal with Ian." I grabbed her wrist and pointed. "He's freaking out, and I have to go rescue Flynn."

"Why?" She glanced over at Teresa. "He looks fine to me."

"Shut up and get over there," I hissed. But before I could unhook Teresa's claws from my man—okay, my *ex*-man—the hockey players burst through the door, ready to get the party started.

"Flynn! Dude!" A burly thug with a shaved head and a scruffy beard clapped Flynn on the back with enough force to fell an oak. I squinted, trying to picture him in pads and a hockey jersey, and thought I recognized him as Harley McKellar, a first-string center raised in California and prone to vicious fighting on the ice.

"Sorry we're late, bud. Claude waits until we're halfway here, and then he pulls over, throws up, and goes, 'Sorry, guys, I'm too hung over to drive anymore.'"

"What could I do?" Claude, short but massive with a huge bruise over one eye, was unapologetic. He spoke with a French-Canadian accent and had an absolutely heart-melting smile. "I'll be damned if I'm throwing up in the new Benz."

The entryway was awash with testosterone, all of it flowing in the direction of my sister, who didn't seem to mind at all.

Skye pulled me into the swarm of alpha males and put an arm around me. "This is my sister Faith. Isn't she the cutest? Don't you guys love her pants?"

Ten pairs of appraising eyes immediately turned to my thighs.

"*I* love the pants," said Claude, hoisting a full stein of beer. "Here's to the pants."

Amber liquid sloshed onto the carpet, the tables, and the front of my shirt as mugs were raised in the name of black leather.

"Savages." Bryson whipped a sterling silver flask out of his breast pocket and quaffed. "Has anyone seen my wife?"

Somewhere between the second keg and the third replay of AC/DC's "You Shook Me All Night Long," the party dissolved into a free-for-all.

Harley McKellar was hunched over a tiny corner table with Frederick, immersed in a cutthroat game of chess.

"Checkmate, bud!" bellowed the six-foot-three bruiser, swigging from beer mugs in both hands.

"Rematch! I demand a rematch!" Frederick howled surprisingly loud for one so frail-looking.

Barbara was giving the Polecats center a dance lesson, Bryson was losing an arm wrestling competition to a defenseman, and Teresa was getting her freak on with Claude in the corner.

"Isn't this the most raging party ever?" Skye shrieked.

I stared. "How are we going to calm these people down before they start rioting in the street?"

She shrugged one lamé-clad shoulder. "Who cares? Valerie just told me she's having the best night of her life! She'd never even done a keg stand before, can you believe it? Stop stressing and enjoy! Flynn's got everything under control."

I climbed onto a chair and scanned the crowd. "Where is he, anyway?"

"Up on the roof. Some of the guys wanted to see if they could throw the moose head all the way to the river, but he's stopping them. They already threw the muskie. But that only made it across the street."

"Fantastic."

"Yeah! And it's all thanks to Ian! Thanks for introducing us, by the way. He's going to be my next."

I stopped gaping at Harley's bulging biceps for a second. "Your next what?"

"My next husband, of course. As soon as I track down Bob and get divorced."

A hard-bitten right-wing player sidled up to us and asked Skye to dance.

"Okay!" She clapped her hands. The neckline of the gold dress dipped dangerously low. "Conga line, people!"

She blew a kiss to Ian. He nodded back indulgently but did not, I noticed, stir from his teacup by the chessboard. She then scrambled onto the bar and everyone, athletic and academic alike, hoisted themselves up after her.

"Shake it like a Polaroid picture!" she yelled. And they did.

This was officially out of control.

"Geary."

I whirled around to find Flynn six inches behind me, staring at me with steely intensity.

Our eyes met. I was suddenly very conscious of the cool whisper of silk against my skin. I anchored the neckline of my shirt with one hand and tried to look dignified.

I straightened my shoulders, and stared right back at him. "How may I help you?"

"I need a word with you in the office."

I hadn't had enough to drink to deal with yet another kiss-and-diss fracas. "Can't we talk later?" I winced as Claude slipped on a puddle of Pig's Eye and crashed into Barbara, who fell into Bryson, who thudded to the floor and decided to curl up and take a nap right there among the bar stools. "We'll have plenty of time to talk after we take everyone to the emergency room."

"Now. Come on." He captured my wrist in his hand and tugged me toward the back room.

"Hey. Less bone-crushing pressure, please," I protested as he dragged me down the hall. "Why so grabby these days?"

No response.

I threw up my free hand in exasperation. "What now? You don't like the fact that people are having a good time and we're making money? Jollity offends you?"

He slammed the door to the back office. "Why are you still wearing that . . . *that?*"

"You dragged me all the way back here to talk wardrobe?" I planted my stiletto-heeled feet far apart and shook my fist. "You know, fashion fascism is very unbecoming in a man. Unless you're starring in a make-over series on Bravo, I don't want to hear it. I'm sorry if this outfit is a little unprofessional—"

His eyebrows arched. "A *little?*"

"But Skye left all of my clothes at the laundromat. We did the best we could. And anyway, I'm starting to like these pants." I stroked the smooth leather. "What do you want from me?"

"I want you to wear a bra, for one thing. Can't you at least put a T-shirt on under that shirt? A tank top?"

I shrugged. "I could, but I don't want to."

"Well, I want you to."

"But guess what? I didn't marry you. I don't have to wear a bra, I don't have to live in the sticks, and I don't care what you want." He looked stunned. I kept raving. "You broke up with me then, and you don't want me now, so you don't get a say. I can run around in no underwear at all if I want to."

There was a long silence.

"Are you?" He gave me a look that could only be described as smoldering.

"Well, evidently, you're the underwear expert. Why don't you tell me?" I regretted these words as soon as I said them. He took a step back, studying me, deliberating, lingering for an unnecessary length of time on my panty line.

Finally, he cleared his throat and met my eyes. "All I know is that you come downstairs wearing this white shirt that doesn't hide a goddamn thing, and the next thing you know, you've poured beer all over yourself—"

"Oh, please." I tugged the shirt around my torso, covering myself in the loose folds. "Claude *accidentally* spilled a little beer, and it *happened* to splash on my shirt, but . . ."

"You thought that was an accident?" he scoffed. "It's bad

enough that you march around flaunting your chest—"

"Hello? I'm flatter than Lara Flynn Boyle?"

"—but when I have to hear about it in locker room gutter talk . . ." He clenched his fists. "I can't even repeat what Claude said about your . . . your . . ."

My temper swept in and vanquished the last traces of my common sense.

"I don't care what Claude said about me. Okay? I'm sure it's no worse than what I hear every time I walk down Hollywood Boulevard." This did not seem to placate him. "I'm a single girl at large in the big, bad world, and if you don't like hockey players looking at me, you shouldn't have invited the whole team down here." I smacked my palm down on the desk in frustration. "Flynn. I cannot keep doing this. I hate this."

He glowered. "Which part?"

"All of it!" I started pacing the floor. "This is bullshit. I'm so sick of arguing. I know you don't trust me anymore, but you could at least pretend to like me."

He tipped his head back and inhaled deeply. "I do like you."

"No, you don't."

"Sure I do."

"You don't act like you do. You can't even look me in the face when you say that."

He looked me in the face. "Come here."

"Why? So you can put a petticoat on me?"

But when he opened his arms to me, I let him pull me against his chest. I breathed in, trying to store up the scent of laundry detergent, summer springs, fresh-mown grass—*eau de* off-season hockey player.

His breath stirred the curls near my ear. "Hey, Geary?"

"Yes?"

"Maybe I do like this shirt after all."

He kissed me.

I wrapped my arms around his neck and kissed him back. Because, as it turned out, I *did* give a rat's ass.

Everybody remain calm. This is a kiss, this is only a kiss. Nothing more, nothing less. You are just having a nice little reconciliation smooch. With a lot of tongue.

While my mind raced, my senses thrilled. Endless chaos in endless cities, and I still craved him. His scent, his taste, his warmth. But his body wasn't familiar to mine anymore. He'd grown up and filled out. We shifted and curved together, getting reacquainted.

He broke off the kiss and sighed onto the top of my head. "What are we doing?"

I let my cheek rest against his soft cotton T-shirt. "Nothing that will come to any good."

"Does this change anything?" He traced patterns on my back through the thin white shirt.

I kept my eyes closed. "I don't know," I admitted, so softly I could barely hear myself over the music drifting in from the barroom. "But I missed you."

"I missed you, too." He caught my chin and tilted my face up.

We were both breathing hard in a sort of post-work-out pant.

"God, ten years." I leaned in closer, ready for another kiss.

He pulled back an inch or two. "There's something I have to ask you . . ."

Oh no. Birth control, STDs, who knew what mood-ruining horrors were lurking at the end of his sentence.

"If you had to run away, why didn't you run away with me?"

The answer to this question, if I'd ever really had one, had long ago gotten lost in the shuffle of fear and anger. So I just smiled and said, "It's not too late."

"What do you mean?"

I took a deep breath. "Want to run away with me?"

He thought this over for about half a second. "Okay. Let's get the car."

"Right now?"

He shrugged, tossing me a rakish James Bond grin. "Yeah. Why not? Don't tell me that Faith Geary, single girl at large, is all talk and no action?"

While I tried to process this astonishing turn of events he started kissing my neck. "Let's go," he urged.

"Where are we going?"

"My apartment." His words said Minneapolis, but his tone said unbridled lust and passion.

My body was primed to go forward, but my mind was reeling back in the equivalent of emotional whiplash. How had we gone from weeks of razor-edged civility to unbridled carnality in the space of ten minutes?

More importantly, how could I know when we'd suddenly

do another one-eighty? I stepped back, letting the cool air rush in between us. Decade-old grudges don't vanish just because you get some.

But, damn, he looked good. And old habits die really, really hard.

"Let's go." He pressed his lips against my temple and eased his hand into the waistband of my pants.

My eyes snapped open. "What do you think you're doing?"

"I'm just checking out the underwear situation."

I risked a glance at his eyes, and then I laughed. "Take me away from all this."

And he did. His hand was instantly out of my pants, grabbing my fingers, and leading me toward the back door. Because, really, who needs a solvent small business when you've got physical chemistry raging out of control?

"We're leaving," he announced to Skye. "Together. Right now. See you Monday."

Her only comment was: "Oh my God, go for it."

He led me out into the cool night air. "You're going to go upstairs and pack whatever you need. Then we're getting in the car and going straight to my place." This was his Last Word tone—there would be no deviations from this plan.

I nodded. "Okay."

He looked surprised at my easy compliance. "Okay. Well, then, get over here for a second."

I scooted closer into his heat and stared up at the huge white summer moon. Why couldn't life come equipped with a "freeze frame" function? I'd just stop things right here and walk away with a happily ever after. Before I sabotaged myself or our pasts screwed up our future.

"Are we sure this isn't going to end in scandal, bitter reproach, and smashed crockery?" I asked lightly.

He stopped laughing. His eyes were sharp and bright in the moonlight. "That's up to you."

I tossed makeup, a few random articles of Skye's clothing, and the sultriest of her lingerie into a brown paper bag.

Flynn raised his eyebrows as I clattered down the steps. "Nice luggage." He opened the passenger side door. "You ready to go?"

I decided not to consider this question on too many levels. I was packed, right? "Yes."

"Good. I checked on the bar and everything's fine. One of Skye's many admirers is helping out. The quiet guy? Looks like a bouncer with a migraine?"

I winced. "Lars?"

"Yeah. So let's go."

He kissed me, one of his hands stroking my cheek in a gesture that I'd never witnessed anywhere but onscreen in insipid romantic melodramas and in real life with Flynn.

And then he suddenly pulled away, leaving me with a damp breeze on my lips and a taste for more.

"All right. Enough of that. Let's go," he said. That little muscle in his jaw was twitching again.

"What?" I stared at him. "I thought you were a *guy.*"

"I am. So what?" He ushered me into the truck's cab.

"So get your priorities straight." I watched him walk around to the driver's side.

He climbed in and slammed the door. "I do have my priorities straight. First I get you out of Lindbrook, then you can have your wicked way with me."

Something was definitely wrong. The Patrick Flynn I knew did not break off in the middle of heated kisses come hell, high water, or the Cubs winning the World Series. Rather, our usual routine had been that I would toss out a few token protests, and then we would make out like our ship was sinking.

A slick tendril of panic and doubt unfurled in the pit of my stomach.

"Did I do something wrong?" I asked.

"Of course not. Don't worry. We're fine." But his voice sounded flat as he started the truck. He reached over and pulled me across the seat so my shoulder leaned into his. I managed to keep my mouth shut and let him re-establish physical contact at his own rate.

"So," he said, "tell me more about this juice bar of yours."

Okay. Not sixty seconds ago, he had practically been ready to take me up against the side of the pickup truck and now he wanted to chitchat about juice?

No doubt about it. Sondra Cutler was getting her money's worth on that voodoo curse.

"Well . . ." I sketched him a very appealing—and very selective—description of what I'd been doing since high school. I left in the juice bar, the "Street Food" column, and Europe. I left out the isolation, the moody liquor-soaked boyfriends, and the insomnia. "What about you?"

"You heard. Went to college, played some hockey, started working." He shrugged.

I was starving for the rest of this story. "That's it?"

"What do you mean, 'that's it'? That's ten years' worth of activity."

I jabbed him with my elbow. "What about all the details?"

He stared at me. "I just gave them to you. What else do you want to know?"

"Oh, you know . . ." *Just for example, out of idle curiosity . . .* "Like dating for example. Did you have lots of girlfriends?"

"Did you have lots of boyfriends at the juice bar?" he countered.

I exhaled, a weary sigh originating at the soles of my feet. "Flynn, let me explain something to you. Some men are like Fords or Hondas. Chevy. Like a rock. You get the idea."

"Not really." But I could see a smile tugging at the corners of his mouth.

"This truck, for example. Ford. It's not exactly a status car. But it always gets you where you need to go. It starts in sub-zero temperatures. You can fit all your baggage in the back without a problem. Now, some men—the kind of guys one wants, ideally—are the Fords of the male world."

"I see."

"And then there are the sports cars. They have leather interiors. They look cool. They go fast. But they aren't always reliable. It's like that old joke: if you get a Jaguar, you have to buy two. One for you, and one for your mechanic to follow you around in."

He raised an eyebrow. "That's an old joke?"

"It is in L.A. Anyway, the problem with sports cars is that they look good, but their performance is sketchy. They'll leave you stranded at four A.M. in the middle of an icestorm. You can't take them anywhere because if they don't throw a rod, they'll get themselves stolen."

"What about Mercedes?" he countered. "They're dependable."

"It's an *analogy*. Work with me." I gave him a look. "What I'm trying to say is that I spent too much time with Fiats when I should have been looking for Fords."

"Fiats," he repeated.

"It's a teeny Italian sports car."

"I know what a Fiat is," he said dryly.

"Well, I've had enough of them," I said. "I am at the point in my life where I'm starting to appreciate Fords."

He seemed nonplussed.

"*You* are a Ford," I supplied helpfully.

"I am a Ford?" I couldn't read his expression in the shifting shadows. "I see. May I propose a theory of my own?"

"Please do."

"You are a loon." He waggled his eyebrows at me. "Instead of thinking of car analogies, you should be thinking about how you're going to win me over after all these years."

The man had a point.

14

We crossed the county line at 12:08 A.M.

"It's like something out of *The Blair Witch Project* out here." I stared at the inky silhouettes of pine trees against the sky.

"That's what I remember about you," Flynn said. "Always the soul of romance." Ten minutes later, white city lights glinted among the sprinkling of summer stars, and soon we were weaving our way through Saturday night uptown traffic.

Flynn turned the truck down a quiet street and pulled over in front of a long, low brick house. The sidewalk was lined with family homes, small apartment buildings, and tall shade trees rustling in the breeze. The very heart of white picket fence territory. He cut the engine and turned to me.

There was no doubt about it: falling into bed with this man was just insane. We had been apart so long, we had no idea what was going on, we had no idea what was *going* to go on—

"Follow me." He opened the driver's side door. Bathed in the moonlight, his face, his eyes, and his body were an intriguing blend of the familiar and the unfamiliar. He didn't only look like the guy I'd left—he looked like the one I wanted to find.

So I followed him. I made a conscious decision to put the white picket panic attack on hold, open the car door, and get my ass in gear. Surely all this apprehension would serve a purpose. It would help us to slow down, set a pace. We could have a nice rational discussion over dinner and a few glasses of wine, and then we'd just see where the night might take us.

As if.

He strode purposefully up the steps to the brick building, then ushered me through the massive front door (solid oak complete with ye olde brass letter slot) and down a dark hallway. He didn't turn on the lights. When we arrived at the foot of a wide, shadowed staircase, he placed my hand on the massive carved banister and led me up to apartment 2B.

He unlocked the door and I brushed past him into the pitch-black, groping blindly on the wall for the light switch.

The door slammed behind me and he wrapped his arms around my waist, pulling me back against him. My body woke up in the dark, replacing hesitation with heat. I kissed the side of his face and felt his smile against mine.

"Hi," I whispered.

"Hi," he whispered back, nibbling my ear.

This felt good to the point of paralysis. I wanted to turn around and wage a full frontal assault, but I also wanted to stay anchored against him while his hands roamed all over the front of me.

In the space of a heartbeat, he had me facing him and backed up against the wall. We were tangled up, completely cornered. An abrupt rush of chilled air swept in between us as we yanked at each other's shirts.

In the distant recesses of my brain, my rational mind was tapping its foot and warning that this was probably not so smart. Like *it* had such a spotless track record. So I ignored it and concentrated on some of my other body parts.

We stumbled through the blackness together, finally collapsing on a soft down comforter. I felt crushed by the weight of his body but somehow this was not as claustrophobic as I'd thought it might be.

His technique had improved considerably over the past ten years. And my senses were heightened by the heady mix of discovery and déjà vu. Turns out, the body has its own memory.

"God," was his only comment in the first few moments of afterglow.

"I know." I gave him a kiss and smiled against his lips. "I thought the male sex drive decreased after eighteen?"

He yawned. "Yeah, but the difference is about as noticeable as an ice cube melting in hell."

*   *   *

Later that night, I tripped through the semi-darkness to Flynn's bathroom, which was exactly what I expected. Clean and empty, with threadbare gray towels and no frills. The shelf above the gleaming white sink held a razor, a toothbrush, and a roll of athletic tape. A single bottle of shampoo stood next to a bar of soap on the edge of the bathtub. At least he was *using* shampoo these days. As a teenager, he used to claim that a bar of Irish Spring was all a real man needed for daily ablutions. "It's shampoo and conditioner in one. Just add water. What could be easier?"

Before I flipped the bathroom light off, I peered down the hall and saw the telltale glint of a wide-screen TV. Over which, if I wasn't very much mistaken, hung a poster featuring a hockey player. Just imagine the treasure-trove I could unearth while he slumbered away in the next room. The possibilities were staggering. What did he read now? What did he eat?

No need to get carried away and ransack his home immediately. There'd be plenty of time for that kind of psychosis later. Like tomorrow.

Back in the air-conditioned bedroom, I curled my toes against the varnished hardwood floor and groped around for something to wear. My hands closed on his T-shirt and I pulled it over my head.

He had lapsed into one of his deep, comalike sleeps, and I knew from experience that he was down for the count. This was the time of night when my insomnia usually kicked up, but tonight I felt utterly exhausted. I edged onto the mattress, shivering at the friction of the crisp, chilled sheets against my bare legs. His body heat kept the air conditioning at bay as I reached out and touched his wrist so I could feel his pulse in the dark—a strong, steady Morse code assuring me that everything would work out between us.

He was such a peaceful sleeper. I had forgotten that about him. The ebb and flow of his inhalation pulled mine into the same rhythm, and I snuggled against the contours of his body, falling into a sleep so deep that I would not have thought it possible without a prescription.

Everything was perfect. For about eight hours.

15

I woke up disoriented, blinking into consciousness after the first night of real sleep I'd had in months. Sunlight streamed in through the tree branches crisscrossing the window. My limbs were tangled up with Flynn's and I turned my head to look at him. He was still sleeping, his breathing deep and even, and I noticed that the tips of his ears were sunburned. I lay still, trying not to wake him while I drank in his calm, unguarded features.

It occurred to me that, unless one is in love with a man, one does not generally rhapsodize over his sunburned ears. Do the math, and you arrive at the same conclusion I did.

But I did not panic. I did not flee the premises. And that, along with my sudden affinity for sunburned ears, was highly unusual.

I waxed poetic about ears for another three minutes. Then I just wanted him to get up and ravish me. So I draped myself over him like a chinchilla coat and began stroking his cheek.

"Mmm?" he said, part sleepy question, part growl.

"Good morning, good morning to you," I sang into his sunburned ear.

He threaded his fingers through my hair and tugged lightly. "What are you so happy about?"

I stroked my way down his chest and stomach. "You."

He opened his eyes and gave me a disheveled grin. "Since when are you a morning person?"

I leaned over to kiss him.

"Wait," he said, stopping me with a frown.

I slid my bare legs against his and mirrored his frown. "What?"

"Nothing. I just don't think we should . . . do this yet."

I rolled away from him with the sheet clutched around my chest. A cold front was creeping into my core. "Do *what* yet? Cast your mind back—we already did this last night."

I felt him turn toward me. "I know," he said.

"So?" I knotted the sheet in my hand.

He sighed. The mattress shifted as he lay back, moving away from me. "Last night was probably a mistake."

All molecular motion ceased.

"Wait, Faith. Before you freak out, and I know you're about to, let me explain." He rested a hand on the nape of my neck, but I shrugged him off.

I was trying to rally the troops. Inhale. Exhale.

"Last night was incredible, obviously," he said slowly. "Incredible. But I don't want to just jump in and have everybody take for granted that this is now a really serious relationship."

"Everybody?" I repeated. "Define 'everybody'."

"Look. I don't want a replay of last time. I mean, I'm really relieved that you're even here this morning."

"Well, isn't that good?"

"No. I shouldn't be *relieved* that you stuck around for the second act. That should be a given, not a cliffhanger. I can't pretend that the past never happened. We shouldn't do this"—he gestured to the tangled bedclothes—"until we work out what we need to work out."

"Well, you're a day late and a dollar fucking short on that one." My voice was high and clipped. "Were you not *here* last night? You initiated it, you never said anything about nonescalation or whatever, and you seemed to have a fine time."

"True." He sounded utterly calm and controlled. "However—"

"*However* what? *However*, you decided you're not attracted to me anymore?"

"Faith—"

"*However*, I was just a one-night stand?"

"You know—"

"Or how about this one? *However*, you're still trying to punish me for what I did when I was eighteen and even stupider than I am now?" I choked on the end of this sentence.

His hand was back on my neck, smoothing my hair. "I'm

not trying to punish you. Would you stop being so irrational and listen for a minute?"

I shut up, but only because his unmitigated gall left me speechless. So this was how crimes of passion started. A woman who has been grievously wronged points out the obvious, and then the guy busts out the I-word.

"It's not that I don't want to sleep with you. I obviously do. To the point of losing my good judgment." He paused for a moment, I assumed to savor his conquest of the dizzy broad who should have known better. "I'm not trying to punish you. I'm not saying last night shouldn't have happened at all, or that we shouldn't get involved. We already are."

"*However?*" I asked, icicles dripping from every syllable.

He sighed again. "However, we need to slow down."

I thrashed around in the sheets like a trout on the bottom of a rowboat. "Oh my God! Are you actually going to lie there, in bed, with *no pants on,* and tell me that you think we need to slow down?"

He set his jaw. The stubble, which had looked so masculine and sexy fifteen minutes ago, now seemed sloppy and Neanderthal. "We do need to slow down. There's a lot of stuff we still haven't dealt with."

Just my luck to find the one man in the Western World who *wanted* to deal with relationship issues.

"What ever happened to not wanting to talk about it?"

His stubborn look was intensifying. "I would rather slow down and give this a chance to work out than crash and burn again."

How subtle. The crash-and-burn finger pointing right at me. My blood began to boil.

He remained impassive. "If we're going to do this, we're going to do it my way this time. I admit that I got a little, uh, carried away last night. That was my fault. But things are going to be different from here on out."

"I didn't realize you were such a control freak," I bit out.

"I told you, I'm not trying to punish you or control you or confuse you. All I want is to establish a solid foundation before we start throwing up walls and support beams and roofs."

"When did we start with the construction analogies? And what the hell does that even mean? You're saying my foundation is faulty?"

He rubbed his forehead. "I can't tell yet. I hope not. I hope to hell it's not, Faith, because the last time we collapsed, I spent years recovering. I do not ever want to do that again."

"Oh." This took the wind out of my sails.

Now he was scrutinizing the ceiling. "I didn't know what happened to you. I had to ask your mom where you'd gone. I had to get Skye to tell me about California and Hank." I winced at the sound of that name coming out of that mouth.

"I know," I said softly. I wanted to touch him, but I couldn't bear the possibility that he'd shrug me off like I'd shrugged him off.

"All I knew was that I'd had sex with you and I wanted to marry you and you disappeared. You just took off. I didn't know if you were ever coming back. I didn't know a damn thing." His expression was completely neutral, his words even and measured.

"But *you* broke up with *me*," I reminded him. "When you

knew what I was going through at home, when you knew I needed you so badly. And afterward, well . . . I wanted to call you. I wanted to explain so many times, but . . ."

We lay there in silence, wary and raw under the harsh morning sun. I could hear the faint sounds of traffic outside, everyone on their way to somewhere else.

"But you didn't call. For a while there, I was worried you had gotten pregnant."

I had never even considered this. The idea of him thinking that, staring up at the Minnesota sky while I streaked off towards the Pacific, made me ache.

"Flynn." My voice was steady. At this point, words were all I had to prop myself up with. "I'm sorry. I am sorry a million times over. But I cannot change the past."

He looked at me. "I'm not asking you to change the past. I'm asking you to figure out the present. Do you even know if you're staying in Lindbrook? Or for how long?"

"Uh . . ."

"I just want to be a little more confident about the future before we build on the foundation."

I glowered at him. "Will you please stop comparing me to a construction site? It's really very insulting."

"Fine," he agreed. "We'll use your car analogy. I don't want to be a Ford."

"But Fords are good!"

"Sure, good for *you*. I'm glad you think I'm dependable and tough and roomy enough for all your so-called baggage. But what do I get out of it?"

I sensed a trick question. "What do you *want* to get out of it?"

"I am more than your trusty backup. I am more than the guy you call when your 'Fiat' breaks down and leaves you stranded at four A.M."

"Of course you are." I clasped my fingers together.

His expression was dubious. "We'll see."

"We'll see what?"

"We'll see what happens." He resettled his body under the few scraps of covers I'd left him. "Let's table this for now. Do you want to use the shower first?"

I gathered the sheet around me and stalked off to the bathroom.

While the steaming water coursed over my skin and the industrial-grade shampoo sudsed in my hair, I tried to hold on to my anger and ignore the searing pangs of guilt.

He had hurt me this morning, but I knew he had a point. I couldn't be trusted with other people's hearts. I couldn't even be trusted with my own.

Flynn and I spent our post-sex, post-argument Saturday afternoon watching the Cubs game on TV. We were not really speaking to each other, although occasionally we would speak *at* each other. It was like we had never left middle school.

"Please pass the popcorn," I said. "If that's not moving the relationship too fast for you."

"Here you go. But could you do me a favor and stop drooling over Kerry Wood? You're going to flood the living room."

"I'm not drooling over him," I lied. "You seem to have mistaken me for someone who has any use whatsoever for men."

"I seem to remember you having plenty of uses for me." He said this matter-of-factly, without a trace of a taunt, then returned his attention to the TV screen. "Why the hell is Sosa all the way back in the outfield?"

I counted to ten, then did my best Grace Kelly impression. "Won't you please excuse me?"

He stood to let me by. "Sure. Where are you going?"

"I have to make a call." I closed the bedroom door behind me, snatched up the cordless phone and dialed.

It rang. And rang.

And then my last resort, my only port in the storm, came through.

"Hello?" Skye's voice was thick and heavy with sleep.

I frowned. "Dude. Aren't you up yet?"

"Faithie!" She yawned. I could picture her back in Lindbrook, all flopsy and frail in her pj's. "I'm exhausted. I was out so late last night. Those hockey players were really fun. And then I was talking to Lars for a while. He cleaned up the whole bar after the party."

"Why would he do that? Doesn't he know you're with Ian now?"

"Yeah, but, you know. He's one of those 'nice guys' you read about. But who cares about me—how was *your* night? Did you get any?"

I rolled my eyes. "Nicely put."

"Did you?"

Fifty miles away, I blushed. "You are so vulgar."

"You did! I knew it! Are you in looove now?"

"Not so fast."

"Why?" she demanded. "What happened?"

"Well." I sat down heavily on the mattress. "That's what I'm calling about. I know business and you know men, remember? So, I need help. A lot of help."

"Uh-oh. What'd you do to him this time?"

"Nothing! Why would you assume that *I* did something?" I waited for the beat of two breaths. "Never mind, don't answer that. Look. I thought everything was fine, and then this morning it disintegrated into a total shambles."

"Why? What's the problem?"

"All right. Last night we drove up to his place, and then we did things that I *never* thought I'd do in Lutheran Land—"

"No details!" she yelled. "You're my sister and he's like my brother, and I don't need the visual!"

"Fine. And then we went to sleep, and I woke up all blissed out this morning, and I did not bolt—"

"You didn't what?"

"Bolt. Run away. You know." I crossed my arms and gave the bedroom wall a look of defiance.

She paused. "Do you usually? Bolt? The morning after?"

"Well . . ." Sometimes I forgot how much I'd sugar-coated my reports of California to my family. "Yeah. Occasionally."

"God, you're weird." Her mouth was full now, probably with untoasted Pop Tart. "But okay, you didn't run away. Good girl. You want a cookie for that?"

When did she get so uppity? "Listen, missy—"

"Right, okay, that's not the point. I get it," she conceded. "What's the problem? This time?"

I sighed. "After all that, he just spurns me this morning! He rebuffed my advances and said we had to 'slow down,' whatever that means."

"Huh."

"I know! I finally smoked him out of the grass, and he ran into the underbrush! He was supposed to come to *me!*"

Another pause. "Huh."

"And then he went off on this irrelevant tangent about building a house and dealing with our old issues and not rushing into things."

"Wow." She sounded impressed. "That's very mature of him. That actually makes pretty good sense."

I held the receiver away from my ear, stared at it for a long moment, then pressed it back up to my ear. "No, it doesn't! It makes sense to do that *before* you sleep with someone, not *after*. Now it's just a slap in the face, because obviously he sampled the merchandise and he didn't like it. He's got sexual buyer's remorse."

She ignored this. "Where are you now?"

"We're both watching the Cubs game in his living room and pretending to be functional adults."

"Who's pitching?"

I sighed. "Kerry Wood."

"He's such a hottie."

I checked my watch. "But what should I do?"

"About Flynn?"

"*Yes,* about Flynn. I'm so humiliated. He thinks I'm an architecturally deficient chippy."

My sister cleared her throat and took charge. "Two things. First of all, you have to stop dealing with man problems over the phone. Get off the line and suck it up, Faithie. Be a marine and fight the good fight."

Wait a second. Hadn't we had this same conversation when I was in Florence, telling *her* what to do?

But she wasn't finished. "Second of all, he does not think you're a chippy. He's probably just scared that you'll take off for California again."

I groaned. "Why must everyone keep bringing that up? That was a really long time ago."

"Yeah, but have you guys talked about your plans for after the summer?" she asked.

I did not have an answer for this.

"See?" She was triumphant. "He probably doesn't want to deal with all that again. But you can change his mind. It's easy. Just seduce him."

"That's your answer to everything? Weren't you listening? He doesn't want to be seduced."

"Of course he does. All men want to be seduced. Just calm him down and get him to stop thinking so much."

"And how exactly do I do that?"

"Well, to calm him down, just be nice." Her tone suggested it was time to increase my medication dosage. "Pretend you're wearing the homecoming crown. Be sweet and reassuring. Don't be snarky."

"And as for getting him to stop thinking?"

"Duh. Alcohol." She giggled. "This whole 'slowing down' thing is hogwash. Take him out for a pitcher of beer after the game and you're good to go. End of story."

I tapped my foot. "If only it were that simple."

"It is that simple. I'm telling you! Homecoming queen plus alcohol equals helpless man-slave!"

I did not ask her how she could be so sure of this equation.

"Look, I'm hungry and I have to go. Do what you want. I'm just afraid that if you two don't get it together, once and for all, like normal people, you're going to freak out again and head for the hills. And then both of you are going to be really sad."

I sighed. "Maybe I *should* just head for the hills. Save us both a lot of hassle."

There was a long pause.

"Don't say that. You can handle this. Don't run away again, okay? Flynn loves you. I love you."

"Love" was not a casual word in the Geary family. Even Skye, who got assigned the bubbly, peaches and cream role, hardly ever said "love." I cradled the phone against my ear, but there was dead silence on her end. "Okay. I won't run away."

"Okay!" A smile bounced back into her voice. "Now go drench that man in liquor, have fun, and be safe!"

16

Skye's romantic advice, while time-tested and all but guaranteed to succeed, lacked one tiny but crucial ingredient: a scrap of human dignity. I had to face facts. Despite what the beer commercials aired during the Super Bowl would have one believe, getting a man trashed and then leaping on him like a panther from the trees is not going to enhance one's long-term sexual magnetism. If Flynn didn't want to be with me, I certainly wasn't going to beg and/or slip him a roofie.

I decided to stick to my original plan: play by his rules, new and unfathomable though they were, and beat him at his own game with my frosty poise. If he wasn't attracted to me, I'd still get out of this with the tattered remains of my self-esteem, then leave the state. And if he *was* attracted to me . . .

well, he'd have to do some serious groveling to prove it. I was thinking along the lines of roses, rare gems and many lavish apologies.

Either way, I had the upper hand. My plan was diabolical in its simplicity. Foolproof. Right?

"What time is it now?" I leaned into the cool breeze blowing off Lake Weyburn as we strolled along the shore.

Flynn checked his watch. "We're five minutes closer to death than the last time you asked that. What's going on with you?"

I took off the baseball cap he'd insisted I wear (along with half a bottle of sunscreen) and let my hair whip around in the wind. "Nothing. I just want to make sure we have time to change before dinner."

"We do." He stopped his progress through the sand and plunked down on the dunes, tugging me down next to him. Sunset at the lakeshore. Very romantic. Now if only we could drum up some sweeping background music and two adults who could discuss a relationship without making reference to cars, home repair, or other Time-Life book topics.

We sat in silence and watched the waves.

He would always be my first love, but the problem with that title was that it was a one-shot deal. We could never go back to the way things were when we were younger. He'd changed and I'd changed . . . but had we changed enough to overcome the flaws that wrenched us apart in the first place?

He cleared his throat. "Okay. If the reservations are at eight, we should get going."

"Yeah." The flaming summer sun reflected in his eyes, but I saw twin autumn pools underneath, deep and still and cool.

"I'm starving," he warned. "Is this place going to be some post-modern dive where you can only get wheatless pasta and vegetarian sushi?"

I struggled to my feet, ignoring the outstretched hand he offered to help me up. "It should be great. Leah recommended it. She said it reminded her of some organic fusion bistro in San Francisco."

He shook his head and tossed me his sweatshirt. "Well, that answers that question. Any chance we can pick up a pizza on the way?"

Normally, I would have gotten swanked out in some fail-safe, black-on-black outfit, but upon returning to Flynn's place, I discovered that my Saturday night packing job had been as disorganized as my thought process. My options were limited to what I'd "borrowed" from Skye's bureau: sweatpants, T-shirts and lingerie. Oops. Should have skipped the Cubs game today and hit the mall. Ever resourceful, I threw on a simple gray silk chemise. Technically underwear, but who really allows themselves to be hemmed in by such arbitrary categorizations?

Doing the best I could with my overachieving hair, strappy silver sandals, the could-pass-as-a-dress chemise, and a lot of false confidence, I tried to transform myself into a sultry siren à la Catherine Zeta-Jones.

When I emerged from the bathroom, Flynn, who had completed his wardrobe and grooming routine in four minutes flat, was kicked back watching ESPN. He turned his head and took his time looking me up and down. This is what he said:

"Aren't you ready yet?"

Then he turned back to the game.

I would bet the Roof Rat that Catherine Zeta-Jones has never heard "Aren't you ready yet?" in her life.

I retreated to the bathroom, stared at myself in the mirror, and wondered what was going on with him *now*. The chemise, though bearing a Victoria's Secret label, was a perfectly respectable slip that fell to just above the knee. And okay, my skin was alternately sunburned and chalky white, my hair was in a state of anarchy, and I was still flatter than Lara Flynn Boyle. But I looked the same as I had last night and he'd wanted me then.

Screw it. I was done letting him jerk me around. Hell would freeze over before I'd humiliate myself in front of him again.

"Let's get a bottle of red wine," I suggested the minute we sat down at Café Guaio.

The low ceilings, dim lights, and dusty brick walls lent the place an intimate, speakeasy atmosphere. Black and white photos of the Rat Pack adorned the entryway and little green tendrils of ivy twisted to the ceiling.

Flynn had donned one of his newer gray T-shirts for the evening, and as a couple, we looked very grim and very goal-oriented. We were really applying ourselves to the task of having a pleasant evening.

"You want red wine?" he asked. "I thought you didn't like red wine."

"I didn't like red wine in *high school* because I always drank too much of it and threw up. But I like to think I've gotten a little more sophisticated since then."

While he flagged down the waiter and ordered a Shiraz, I glanced around at our fellow diners. They all appeared to be in full Catherine Zeta-Jones mode. Our table remained the lone desert island of tension in a sea of celebration and general joie de vivre. This whole "slowing down" thing didn't seem to be working out so well.

The wine arrived just as I was about to head to the ladies' room to escape the awkward silence between us.

Flynn filled both our glasses halfway and we clinked them together, meeting each other's gazes with equal parts speculation and suspicion. "Here's to building a solid foundation."

Gag.

I took a small swallow of wine and tried to dredge up something to talk about. Something other than: sex, betrayal, cars, houses, bass players, and small business failure rates.

"Hey! Would you like to hear the story of how I got lost in the catacombs in Rome?"

By the time a server finally deigned to take our dinner order, I was somehow, inexplicably, on my third glass of Shiraz. I wasn't really hungry anymore, but I was feeling much more sociable.

"You know what?" I asked the server, who politely waited with pen in hand. "I'm just going to have a peach martini."

Flynn raised an eyebrow. "You sure that's a good idea?"

"I have more good ideas before nine A.M. than most people have all day." I took a delicate, ladylike sip of the wine and tossed a saucy grin his way.

"Fine. It's your funeral."

A warm rosy flush spread through my body, smoothing down the sharp ridges of tension. I poured myself another glass, dribbling a spotty pink trail on the tablebloth. "Oops."

Flynn refrained from comment, but gave me a very pointed look.

"What?" I demanded. "Do you have something you'd like to say?"

He half-smiled and toasted me with his water glass. "I know better than that. There's no point in telling you to do anything right now, because you'll either ignore me or do the opposite. You're contrary enough when you're sober, but now? Forget it."

I gasped in outraged modesty. "That's not very chivalrous."

He pushed my hair away from the open flame of the candle. "But it *is* true."

The waiter reappeared with my martini and Flynn's steak. I rocked back into my chair, swamped for a moment by the swirls of smoke and music and light. The conversations going on around us blended into one thick hum.

By the time he finished his meal, I was practically Dorothy Parker: wry, chatty, with bon mots galore. Perhaps wine was the *true* secret to social success.

"Wow," I said out loud, "Dale Carnegie must have been a raging alcoholic."

He stared at me. "What?"

"Oh . . ." He couldn't hear my inner monologue. Right. "Yeah, see, I was just thinking about how to win friends and influence people, and . . ."

"You and the red wine. Some things never change." He shook his head. "I think you've had enough, tiger."

I rolled my eyes. The world went spinning off its axis. "To pura—to *para*phrase William Blake: 'You never know what is enough until you know what is too much.'"

I had had way too much. I kept my eyes closed during the ride back to Flynn's apartment, trying to ignore the cloying sweetness of the fruity martinis rising in the back of my throat.

He frog-marched me into his bedroom like Fred Astaire slogging a doped-up Ginger Rogers. I winced and rubbed my eyes as he snapped on the glaring overhead light.

"Ugh. Mayday. Turn it off." I gave up trying to balance on my sandals and leaned back against the closet door.

"Hang on one second." He crossed the room to the lamp on the bedside table. The room went soft and muted as he turned off the overhead light.

I threw myself down on the bed. "I can't walk another step in these heels."

He sighed and crouched down next to me. "You're impossible."

"It's part of my charm."

He tried to figure out the complicated criss-cross straps of my sandals. "Do me a favor, Geary. Next time you decide to go swimming in wine, wear more practical shoes."

"Sorry." But I couldn't even get it together enough to lift up my head, let alone slip my toes out of the designer stilettos. "That Stuart Weitzman is a crafty one."

"Okay." The nerves in my feet tingled back to life as he tossed the sandals to the floor. "I'll be back in thirty seconds. Try to not to fall asleep or do any permanent tissue damage while I'm gone."

Half a minute later, he was shaking me awake. "Hang on a second. Drink this before you pass out." He shoved a glass of water in my face.

I scowled up at him. "Huh-uh. I'm tired."

"I know you are, sweetheart, but if you don't hydrate, you're going to be even more miserable in the morning." He stroked the hair back from my temples.

I knew he was going to keep hounding me until I complied, so I sat up and drank. Then I rolled over onto my stomach, tugged the hemline of my silk chemise down, and propped my face up on my hands. "Hey. You want to know a secret?"

He looked guarded, a man with one hand on the fire extinguisher and one hand on the emergency brake. "Probably not."

"Remember those tattoos we got in high school? I still have mine." I yanked down the low-cut back of my dress to expose the masterpiece in question, a little red heart overlaid with a black capital *F.*

He glanced at it, then studied the wall behind my head as if committing the wallpaper print to memory. "Of course you still have it. Where did you expect it to go?"

"I could have had it removed," I pointed out. "Body mutilation is *so* last millennium. Lots of people had their tattoos lasered off. But I didn't."

He nodded. "Good to know."

I pressed my cheek against the comforter. I could smell the alcohol on my own breath. "Do you still have yours?"

He seemed to be counting the floorboards. "Yeah."

I bounced into a sitting position. "Let's see."

"You want to see it?" He looked skeptical, but began untucking the gray T-shirt from his khakis. "Why do you want to see it?"

"Because every time I wear a midriff-baring top or try on clothes in a communal dressing room, someone asks what the *F* is for in the heart, and I have to go through this long explanation. I just want to make sure the other half is still around." I folded my legs, dropped my hands on my knees, and waited.

But he had gotten derailed earlier in my story. "How often do you wear midriff-baring tops?"

I shook my head and braced myself against the ensuing dizziness. "That's not the point of the story."

"They have communal changing rooms for women?" He seemed fascinated by this prospect.

My patience ran out. "Shut up and take it off, baby." I tugged at the hem of his shirt and he acquiesced, slowly pulling the shirt over his head.

I tried not to stare. Our encounter last night had been a breathless, blazing dance in the dark, but now I had an opportunity to really ogle him. And the view from here was pretty damn good.

There it was, bold and clear against his back. The thin black circle with a lowercase *f* inside. The trademark *f*, we'd called it. The anarchy *f*.

"That still looks fabulous." I leaned over and bestowed a loud, wet kiss on our trademark.

He froze for a moment, then pulled away and stood up. "Okay, that's enough of that."

Foiled again. He was backing toward the bathroom, and I sat back and sighed. Didn't even make a token effort not to stare. "Why?"

He held out yet another glass of cold tap water, then leaned against the wall and folded his arms over his bare chest. "Because you're in no condition for any of this. I thought you were passing out?"

"No. That was a vicious rumor." I drank the water and tucked my bare feet under the pillows. "I'm so glad you still have the tattoo."

Now he was smiling back at me. "Why?"

"Because of Brunelleschi," I said earnestly.

He sat down next to me and wrested the empty glass out of my hand. "God, I can't wait till you sober up. What the hell are you talking about?"

"Well, you see . . ." I said. And that was when I threw up.

17

The damp washcloth felt cool and comforting against my forehead. Sadly, I had no such panacea for my ego.

My stomach had settled down and my head no longer felt like it was in danger of floating away in a sea of red wine. But my body was sweaty and shaky under the steady hand Flynn had placed on my back. I tipped my head forward, hiding my face with my hair.

He rubbed my back. "Feeling better?"

I nodded and swallowed, grimacing against the sharp, acidic aftertaste in my throat. *"Never* let me order red wine again."

"Here, drink this."

I sipped the water he offered and waited. Sipped again. He was still rubbing my back, not trying to get me to look at him.

Which was good, because I didn't want to see the disgust in his face before I hurled myself out the nearest window.

"Faith?" He waited. "How you doing?"

I coughed feebly. "Sorry about this. They didn't do such a good job with me at finishing school."

"No need to apologize. We will never speak about this night again. Now. You were saying?"

I groped for a tissue and blew my nose. "About what?"

"About some Italian guy?"

I started to laugh. "Patrick Flynn, you are so honest-to-God *nice*. It's unnatural. Why? Why do you have to be nice to me?"

He arched an eyebrow. "You want me to be mean to you?"

I chewed my lip, thinking this over. And then, obviously still *T*-rashed, I gestured expansively at the mess we'd made of the bedroom. "If you just gave up on me, at least I wouldn't like you so much. I realize it's very high-maintenance of me to ask, but it's the least you can do, really."

He caught one of my hands between both of his. "You are, no question, the most impossible woman I have ever known." He pulled me back against him, and we reclined in a jumble of pillows and quilts and low lamplight.

"You were saying," he prompted. "About the Italian guy."

I relaxed into him, my head on his chest. *I was saying, I was saying . . .*

"Oh, yeah. I was going to tell you this thing about when I was in Florence. But it might be irrelevant."

"Why start worrying about that now?"

"Why, indeed? Well, while I was working in Florence, I

heard this story about the city cathedral." I closed my eyes and tried to marshal a linear thought process. "Actually, this story is right up your alley. It involves architecture and building foundations."

"Do not start with me," he warned.

"Seriously. Back in the day, early fifteenth century or so, they decided to build this huge cathedral in Florence." I paused to see if I still had an audience. "I promise this has a point. They wanted their new cathedral to be better than Siena's, because the two cities were having this big rivalry. Cats and dogs. USC and UCLA."

"Got it."

"So they drew up the plans for this elaborate church that made Siena's cathedral look like a Popsicle-stick birdhouse, and they decided to build this huge dome over the main altar."

"Mm-hmm." He was absently stroking the side of my neck.

"Which was all fine and dandy, except that the base for the dome was a big octagon, and the diameter was something like a hundred and fifty feet," I explained, pausing to hiccup. "And no one had ever built a dome that big before. No one even had any idea how they *might* build one. But they just went ahead and started construction anyway."

"Just like that."

"Just like that." I hiccuped again. "They went ahead and started building the rest of the church and figured that, sooner or later, they'd find a solution to the dome problem. But then they finished the base, and they were up a creek without a paddle." I lapsed into sleepy silence.

"Because . . ." he prompted.

"Oh." I blinked. "Because they still had no clue what to do about the dome. A dome made of stone would crush the base, and anyway, they couldn't figure out how they'd support it during the construction process. And of course, by this time, they were the the punchline of every joke in Siena."

"Of course."

I yawned and stretched against him. "And then Filippo Brunelleschi waltzed in and saved everyone's ass. He'd been studying old-school architecture with Donatello down in Rome. And he realized right away that the typical dome wouldn't work on this church. So he designed this system of arched ribs to support the stone they were building with. And then, toward the top of the dome, when stone got too heavy, he started putting bricks in this herringbone pattern. So the dome was supporting itself, instead of just crushing the base."

"Genius," Flynn said. "And the point you promised earlier in this gripping tale . . . ?"

I yawned again. "Well, now the cathedral is the most famous building in Florence. And it's only there because those city planners had the moxie to go ahead and start without knowing how to finish. They figured that, this being a church and all, God would provide when the time was right. And He did—in the form of Brunelleschi, who, by all accounts, was kind of a diva."

"High maintenance, you'd say?"

"Very." I could feel the first faint stirrings of tomorrow's hangover pounding at the base of my skull. "And after you called me in Florence, every time I walked by that cathedral, I thought of you."

"I see," he said, not sounding like he saw at all.

"You are my arched, brick herringbone dome," I declared dramatically. "I don't really have a plan, I don't know how to build a good foundation or whatever it is you think we need, but we can figure something out. So that's my story. And it even involves architecture and good foundations. You happy?"

"I'm *interested.*"

This was not the show of unbridled enthusiasm I'd been hoping for. "But . . . ?"

"But my opinion of this morning remains the same."

A door slammed shut inside me. While I tried to pull away from him, he held me, gently but firmly, where I was.

"I know your opinion of this morning remains the same," I fumed. "It's not enough if I apologize, or if I try to clean up my act, or turn one-handed cartwheels down the hall. You are determined to stick to your plan. I would expect nothing less. I am *not trying* to change your opinion of this morning."

"Yeah, you are," he said in that mild Midwestern tone.

"And how dare you assume that I would *want* to change your mind, anyway? You kicked me to the curb, and now you're like, circling the block to make sure I'm still out there, all sad and lonely like a lost little kitten."

"You paint quite a picture." I could hear the smile in his voice.

"Let me assure you, I am not going to just sit out on the curb, trying to grab onto the tailpipe for another ride. How dare you?"

"I don't," he said. "Let's get some sleep."

"Fine." I resumed my struggles, and this time he let me go. I rolled over to the edge of the bed, keeping my back to him.

He turned off the lamp, plunging us into darkness. My eyes were wide open.

"Good night, Geary." His voice reached out like a caress through the night.

"Didn't we *just* talk about this? Quit being so damn nice to me."

"I'm trying."

"Try harder." I writhed around, attempting to get comfortable on the small strip of bedsheet I'd allotted myself. Unfortunately, my calves and feet were mired in the blankets directly over the patch of mattress left damp from cleaning up after the Brunelleschi Incident.

"Hey!" I whispered, still buzzed, half hoping that Flynn was already asleep. "My side of the mattress is wet."

"Uh-huh."

"It's really cold. And gross."

A long pause. And then, thick and hushed through the dark: "There's room on my side. You can scoot over if you want to."

I scooted. But I did not fling myself into his arms, preferring to pretend that I still had a modicum of pride left. We lay there, side by side, separated by approximately two molecules of space and a widening gulf of wills.

I wondered how long it would take him to drop off to sleep so I could get up, throw up again, and start battling with my usual insomnia.

"What?" he whispered through the dark.

"*What* what?" I whispered back.

"I can *hear* you thinking," he said. "It's distracting. Knock it off."

"I'm not thinking," I lied.

"Yeah, you are. You're going existential over there. Don't deny it. It's like trying to fall asleep with Friedrich Nietzsche having a breakdown three inches away." He paused. "What's on your mind?"

I sighed. "You really want to know?"

"Yeah."

"Okay. What would you say is your worst flaw?" I asked.

He started to laugh. "Is this a job interview?"

"You asked what's on my mind, I'm telling you. What's your worst flaw?"

"What's *your* worst flaw?"

"I asked you first."

"Okay." He paused for a minute. "Stubbornness, I guess."

"Stubbornness. That's a good one." I nodded.

"Okay. Now yours."

"Well . . ." God, I was tired. All that alcohol, on top of the nausea-induced electrolyte imbalance, suddenly hit me like a ton of bricks. Worst flaw. Pick a card, any card. I decided to start small. "Other than my weakness for wine and the inability to be quiet when other people want to sleep, I'd have to say . . ." I trailed off into the first wispy fogs of sleep.

"You'd have to say?" prompted a voice in the distance.

"I'd have to say commitment problems."

*   *   *

I woke up at 4:45 A.M. on the dot. The glowing green digits on the alarm clock were the only things visible through the darkness. I'd slept for roughly ninety minutes. Felt like fifteen. I flipped over and curled into the sheet, which is when my bare foot brushed against Flynn's leg.

I froze, and my rational mind reached for the sky. Last night's events came back in bits and pieces.

Commitment problems?

Oh. My. God.

I had sucker-punched myself once again.

There was no way around it. I had squandered the last vestige of my reputation as the smart, responsible member of the Geary family. Compared to me, Skye was ready for a Supreme Court nomination.

But the bigger issue here was the one sleeping next to me. If memory served, and I was horribly certain that it did, this man had wrung me out, cleaned me up, tucked me in, and listened to all my disjointed gibberish. For the past few weeks, I'd tried so hard to convince him that I'd blossomed in California, that I'd figured life out, that I'd improved with age.

But now he knew the awful truth: I was just the same as I'd been at eighteen—needy, erratic, and unable to accept defeat graciously.

The chances that he would wake up this morning and decide that I was the perfect woman and his only chance for happiness seemed exceedingly slim. He admitted it himself: he was stubborn and unforgiving. He was never going to trust me again.

Like it's *so* difficult to fall in love with someone who has sex with you, refuses to marry you, leaves you, comes back ten years later and then pukes on you, yells at you, and sends you off to the land of nod with tales of commitment problems. Whatever.

It was just like I'd told Skye: the Faith and Flynn Reunion Tour was not gonna happen. And there was only one way to avoid further humiliation.

I bolted.

It took me five minutes to get a taxi and another twenty to get to the airport. Looking like Little Orphan Annie with a ferocious hangover, I approached the woman at the Northwest ticket counter.

"I need a ticket for the first flight to LAX, please." I dug through my purse and unearthed my wallet. "I will give you money. Credit cards. Unprecedented quantities of frequent flier miles."

Just as I was about to offer up my firstborn child, I realized two things. One, all my stuff was still at Skye's apartment and the Soap 'n' Suds Laundromat. Two, my car was still parked in front of the Roof Rat. And three, I couldn't do this. I simply could not hop a jet plane and spend the four-hour flight back to Los Angeles imagining Flynn waking up without me.

This wasn't a matter of free will. I simply could not spend another day feeling like I'd felt when I left him the first time. I wasn't the woman he wanted me to be—hell, I wasn't the woman *I* wanted me to be—but I couldn't keep running away.

Fuck a duck.

"Never mind. There's been a slight change of plans," I told the ticket agent. "Where can I get a cab?"

The sunny morning was already starting to steam into stifling humidity. I checked my watch: 6:08 A.M. With any luck, he was still asleep.

But if I had learned anything from my recent adventures in Lindbrook, it was that luck was not on my side these days. I had to be my own backup. I needed an alibi. So. What possible reason might one have for traipsing out into the wild blue yonder at the crack of dawn?

"I'm back, and I brought breakfast," I announced, flinging a brown paper bag on the bedside table and setting down two Styrofoam coffee cups.

"You what?" Flynn asked. He stretched under the white sheets, looking tired and disoriented. Excellent.

I opened the blinds halfway, flooding the room with light. The varnished hardwood floor looked like a war-torn Bloomingdale's, with lingerie, mismatched shoes and rumpled T-shirts everywhere.

When we got disheveled, we *got disheveled.*

I handed him a bagel and one of the coffee cups, trying desperately to avoid eye contact.

"Here. Coffee. You still take it black?"

"Yeah. Thanks." He sat up and took the cup from me. "Where'd you go this morning?"

I smiled as glibly as possible. "I told you. I'm your personal ambassador to Starbucks. Mmmm, bagels!"

He gave me a long, piercing look. "Well, if you want to discuss it, let me know."

"Discuss what?" I fled into the bathroom to collect my toiletries and my composure.

He didn't answer.

I was dreading the ride back to Lindbrook, envisioning a nightmarish, hour-long dissection of my infamous commitment problems, interspersed with interrogations about my early-morning whereabouts.

But these fears proved unfounded. While driving to Lindbrook, he refused to even look at me, preferring to stare stonily at the road, bitter and seething through the morning after.

Well, at least this time I was dealing with *him* instead of a toked-out bass player.

A dubious victory.

18

"It was a total fiasco. We should both be awarded purple hearts for making it through the weekend." I scowled up at the overhead lights in the Cannon Falls Stop & Shop.

"Don't you think you're being a little melodramatic?" Leah asked, unloading her grocery cart onto the conveyor belt.

"No. If anything, I'm understating. He was all over me on Saturday night, he was standoffish on Sunday, and by this morning he was repulsed. We're right back where we were ten years ago."

"Oh, come on." She wedged a jug of milk in between a box of cereal and a jar of applesauce. "You were nervous, you had a little too much to drink, you got sick, and you brought him coffee this morning. So what?"

My cheeks burned with shame. "He barely said a word to me this morning, just stared at me like I was his shiv-packing cellmate. He's definitely pissed."

"Let me get this straight. You guys are now sleeping together without having sex."

I nodded. "Yes. And apparently, we're not speaking, either."

"It's like you skipped the courtship and went straight to marriage." She grinned. "Don't worry, this will all blow over. Just give it a few days."

"Maybe, maybe not." I cleared my throat. "I may have left out a few minor details."

"Like what?"

I considered telling her about the frantic five A.M. airport run, then decided that the rest of this story made me look bad enough. So I just stuck to the part about my drunken treatise on Italian architecture and my prima donna mattress complaints.

" . . . And then, after I started in with the mattress, he said, all sultry, 'Well, my side is dry, why don't you come over here?'"

"Ooh." She leaned over the handle of her shopping cart. "This is getting good. Why didn't you tell me this before?"

"Because nothing happened! I wasn't sure if that was supposed to be some kind of sexual overture or what, so I rolled over and we just lay there, an inch apart, all night."

"You *weren't sure* if that was supposed to be an opening? What were you waiting for? A burning bush in the desert?"

"I swear to God, at the time it felt ambiguous."

"You are beyond help." She tilted her head. "But if he was

offering to share his side of the mattress last night, why is he mad at you this morning?"

"Well . . . because of all the things I just told you."

"But that doesn't make any sense. None of that was really that bad. Are you sure you haven't left anything out?"

Like trumpeting my commitment problems from the rooftops?

Like fleeing to the airport at the crack of dawn and then lying about it?

Like behaving like a bipolar eighteen-year-old instead of a well-rounded woman who's changed her ways?

"Nope, that's it."

"Uh-huh," Leah said. And then she gave me the same suspicious look I'd gotten from Flynn five hours ago.

"All right! All right! I confess! I left a few things out." As we wheeled the cart out to the parking lot, I recounted the whole sordid tale of my aborted attempt to escape via Northwest Airlines. "He doesn't know where I went, but he knows I left this morning. So now he thinks I haven't matured at all since the first time things got rough and I fled the scene."

"Why on earth did you go to the airport?" Leah asked.

"I was ashamed of myself and scared to face him this morning. So I freaked out and made everything worse." I rummaged through a brown paper grocery bag until I happened upon a bag of M&M's. "He's obviously disgusted with me, and I don't blame him. I'm horrible at being close to people. Just ask the ticket agents at Northwest." I ripped open the candy wrapper and crammed a handful into my mouth.

"At least you returned to the scene of the crime," she ventured. "The last time you ran off, you just kept on running."

"I don't think he's putting that positive spin on it." I helped her load groceries into the trunk of the Camry. "But you know, I'm not the only one bringing something to the table of dysfunction. That man has some major trust issues."

"Well. You did break his heart."

"When we were teenagers! And he broke mine! After a fascist marriage proposal!" I flung an M&M across the parking lot in exasperation. "Why doesn't anyone focus on *that* part of the story?" I threw up my hands and turned to Rachel, who was trying to tug her white sunbonnet off. "It's all over. We had our chance, we screwed it up six ways from Sunday, and that's just the way it goes. One less thing to worry about when I get back to L.A."

"That's the spirit," Leah said dryly. "You know, your worst flaw is not commitment problems. Your problem is that you sabotage yourself."

My jaw dropped. "I . . . you . . . that's . . . I do not!"

"You do." She nodded sagely. "Speaking of which, what *are* your plans, Faith? How much longer will you be out here?"

"I'll be here until we get the bar sorted out," I hedged. "Maybe two more weeks. I think the Roof Rat is going to be okay, actually. Profits are up, we refinanced the mortgage to free up cash flow, and I worked out a new payment plan with our vendors. Now I just need to hire a new manager who won't rob Skye blind."

I closed the trunk while she strapped Rachel into her car seat. Leah looked at me. I looked back at her.

"Well," she said, starting the car and heading for Lindbrook. "At least you learned a valuable lesson from all this."

"And that would be . . . ?"

"Don't ever let Skye do your laundry again."

We arrived at the Roof Rat and I was hauling my grocery bag out of the trunk when I heard Skye's voice from across the street.

"Faithie! You're back!" She waved, all breezy and blond in a gauzy pink minidress, then paused at the curb, craning her neck to study my state of hung-over exhaustion. "So? What happened? How did the rest of the weekend go?"

"Think hell. Then double it."

"Oh, no! Tell me everything." She darted out between two parked cars and made a beeline for Leah's Camry.

I heard, rather than saw, the collision. One second I was watching the flutter of her pink skirt as she raced into the street, and the next second I caught a flash of blue motion out of the corner of my eye and started screaming at her to stop.

Which she did, smack-dab in the middle of Main Street.

And Sally Hutchins's bright blue Mazda Miata plowed right into her.

Skye lay there for a moment, a still life in pastels on the cracked gray asphalt. I stared at her, frozen, praying for her to start breathing.

And then she started screaming like a banshee. My circulatory system resumed operations.

She rocked into a sitting position, cradling her right shoul-

215

der and hand with her left arm, looking for all the world like a toddler who'd been shoved down on the playground.

Sally wormed away from the Miata's airbag, stumbled out into the middle of the street, and joined Skye in the upper-octave caterwauling. Her expression was equal parts mortified and murderous.

Doors popped open up and down Main Street.

Skye stopped her ear-splitting aria long enough to holler "You reckless bitch!" at Sally. Then she burst into tears.

"Stop being such a drama queen!" Sally hollered back. "It was an accident! It's not like anybody's dead!"

I threw down my grocery bags and started toward Sally, balling up my fists.

Leah materialized at my side, clamping a restraining hand on my shoulder. "Faith, honey, calm down. It was an accident."

Sally managed to look snotty and supercilious despite her pained expression. "Ow. I think the airbag broke my wrist."

"Quit your whining!" Skye yelled. "You broke my whole body!"

"Well, you're the one who came busting out into the middle of the road."

"Well, *you're* the one who can't drive for shit!"

We were attracting an audience. The lunch crowd at Cherry's Café spilled out onto the sidewalk to witness the bloodbath.

Still shaking, I walked out and knelt down next to my sister, blocking her from the stares.

"Okay. You're okay," I said to myself as much as to her.

"How do you feel? Does your head hurt? Does your back?"

Sally interrupted us. "I'm sorry, all right?" She *did* look as contrite as a hinterland debutante could possibly condescend to look. "It was an accident. But I was trying to find you anyway, Skye. I have to tell you something."

Skye tossed her curls and winced, clutching her shoulder. "Well, you found me. What?"

Sally lowered her voice, perhaps in deference to the fact that half the population of Lindbrook was either trying to listen in or already on the phone with the town sheriff to report the accident. She crouched down, still cradling her wrist in her left hand. "You know Ian Hammond?"

My sister tossed her hair, quite self-assured for someone recently laid low by a Miata. "Yes, I do, as a matter of fact. I'm his girlfriend."

"Well, so am I," said Sally.

There was a thirty-second break in the conversation while we took turns staring at each other. The hot asphalt was digging into my knees, but I put my arm around Skye and waited.

Finally, she smoothed her skirt and straightened her one good shoulder. "What?"

Sally gave a quick, irritated sigh. "Open your ears. I said I'm his girlfriend, too."

"I heard you," Skye snapped. "But that's impossible."

"Excuse me, I think I know who I'm sleeping with," Sally hissed, glancing around to make sure no one overheard. "Ian and I have been seeing each other for two months."

Which would trump Skye's two weeks. She glared at Sally. "But I just spent all yesterday with him at Flatbush Lake."

"This makes no sense," I pointed out.

Sally winced and cradled her wrist. "Of course it makes sense. The man's a pathological liar."

"You're nuts," my sister declared. "If you were his girlfriend or whatever, why is he dating me?"

"Are you sure he's really dating you?" Sally sniped.

"I think *I* know who *I'm* sleeping with," Skye shot back.

I put my hands over my ears. "Please. No more. Ladies, can we continue this in a more appropriate place, like a doctor's office? Leah, can you drive us to the hospital?"

"Sure. But I think we have to call the police and report this first." She dialed her cell phone.

"Well, I just do not get this," Skye fumed. "There must be some mistake. How would I not know if you and Ian were dating?"

Sally rolled her eyes. "Because he wanted to keep it secret. And so did I. My mother would go nuclear if she knew I was dating someone older than my dad. And it's not like we were exclusive." She narrowed her eyes. "Especially once *you* came along. I can't believe you didn't figure it out. Honestly, how stupid are you?"

"Hey! Don't call her stupid!" I warned.

"That's why you ran me down like a dog in the street?" Skye asked. "You were coming to tell me about you and Ian?"

"No. I was coming to tell you that his *wife* just showed up. He's married! Can you believe it?"

Skye blanched. "Married?"

"His wife just showed up from London. She's this old British hag named Portia. I met her downtown this morning."

I sat down hard next to Skye.

This was my doing. I had practically forced my only sibling to take up with an unprincipled, over-read chamomile junkie.

"No way!" Skye raged. "He's *married?*"

"For twenty-five years!" Sally said.

"Are you sure she's not, like, his *ex*-wife?"

"Do ex-wives wear big diamond rings on their left hands?"

I tried to round up the wounded. "That's enough. We're going to the emergency room at the clinic. Leah's driving. Get in the car, pronto."

Sally curled her lip at me, but she started toward the Camry.

I put my arm around Skye's waist and tried to haul her up into a standing position. "Okay, let's move it. We've got to get that shoulder checked out." But she was segueing into hysterics. It was long overdue at this point.

"Wait! We can't go yet!"

"Sweetie, you can't just sit here in the middle of the street all day."

Big round tears were forming in the corners of her eyes. There was no way to head this hissy-fit off at the pass.

"I can't go to the hospital like this! I have to talk to Ian first. Why would he do this to me, Faithie? Why? This has to be a mistake."

I leaned my forehead against hers, trying to take on some of her anguish via osmosis. "We'll get it all sorted out. After you go see a doctor."

"No! I want to talk to him now." She felt so thin and breakable in my hands. There was so little padding protecting her fragile spots. "Sally's lying," she insisted. "I need to talk to Ian."

"You are going to the hospital. Right now. I will drag you there myself if I have to." And it looked as if it might come to that.

But she *was* going. She was all I had. She was the only person I had ever been able to take care of, the only person who counted on me. And I had thrown her to a Beowulf in sheep's clothing.

"Don't make me beg," I begged. Due to the uncertain nature of her injuries, I could not simply sling her over my shoulder like a sack of potatoes and throw her into the car. I grabbed her hand. "Come on."

She shook her head again and started to cry in earnest.

I could see Sally pouting through the windshield of the Camry. Leah was stationed in the driver's seat, keys in hand. Rachel was gurgling in the backseat. And the Geary sisters were causing a scene at high noon in the middle of Main Street. How could I possibly take action without making matters worse?

Skye was squirming around like a garter snake on amphetamines when a shadow fell over us. A tall shadow with broad shoulders.

"I'll take it from here," said a deep male voice. I turned around and smiled, ready to welcome Flynn into the melee.

But it wasn't Flynn. It was Lars. Immense and impassive, he scooped my sister up without jarring her shoulder or heeding her vehement protests.

He nodded at Leah. "I'll meet you at the clinic."

Skye took a deep breath and batted spiky wet eyelashes at him. "Hi. Listen, I really appreciate this and all, but I really can't leave yet. I have to go find—"

"Faith will go. Then she'll meet us at the clinic." He turned his gaze from her to me.

"Forget it. I'll stay put until the cops get here, but then I'm going straight to the clinic," I said. "Who cares about Ian when you could be—"

"Come on, Faithie!" my sister pleaded. "Go talk to him. *Please!* Go talk to him and then come tell me what he says. Bring him with, if you can."

And since she was so agitated, I found myself agreeing. This calmed her down sufficiently to allow Lars to bundle her into his truck. I waved to my sister and smiled grimly.

Go get him. Finally, an idea with merit.

19

Finding Ian's house was almost too easy. All I had to do was dash up to Skye's apartment, call our old next-door neighbor and ask for directions.

"That old English guy?" Mrs. Dupree, my mother's close friend and the one-woman Page Six of Lindbrook Minnesota, paused to take a drag on her cigarette. "He lives over on Hilgard Avenue, right next to Maggie Polk. Big white house with green trim."

"Great," I said. "Thanks a lot, Mrs. Dupree."

"Now what's this I hear about you and your sister starting a brawl in the middle of Main Street?"

"No time to talk. Thanks! Bye!"

As I headed out the front door, I noticed the answering machine. I'd had to buy a new one after Skye's unfortunate trial-by-toilet debacle. The little red light was winking away, and the digital display announced three new messages.

Flynn.

Except wait. What if it wasn't Flynn? Odds were good that he was never going to call me again.

This was no time to get sucked into the will-he-or-won't-he-call-me quagmire. How selfish could I get? The smart move here would be to revert to my original position, i.e., *I don't give a rat's ass,* and take care of business.

So I left the machine light blinking and ran out the door. Right now I had to focus all my energy on my sister.

And, of course, on the double-crossing professor.

The house was just as Mrs. Dupree described it—big, white and boxy, with green trim. There was a huge porch with spindly railings and lots of sun-dappled shade from the tree branches arching over the roof. I half expected Ward and June Cleaver to come traipsing out the front door.

I rang the bell.

A hulking, honey-colored retriever lumbered down the hall, barking all the way. He planted himself on the other side of the screen door and bared his teeth.

"Roland, no. Quiet." A tall, maternal-looking woman appeared behind the growling guardian of the threshold and repeated "quiet" in a clipped, British accent. She had a wedding band on the appropriate finger.

Portia, no doubt.

This woman bore very little resemblance to the "old hag" of

Sally's description. Though perhaps guilty of having achieved middle age, she was by no means old. Rosy and round, with thick dark hair pulled back into a French twist, she wore a crisp yellow sundress and a knotted silk scarf that I knew she hadn't bought in Lindbrook.

She nodded at me through the screen but didn't smile.

All my plans for self-righteous ranting and merciless revenge went right out the window. "Uh, hi. Are you Portia Hammond?"

"I'm *Mrs.* Hammond, yes." She maintained eye contact through the screen but did not open the door.

"I'm Faith Geary . . ." I trailed off.

She looked unimpressed. "How do you do, Faith."

"Not so well, actually. I need to . . . is your husband at home?"

"He's at a teaching conference in the city at the moment." She laid the gold-ringed hand on Roland's head and tilted her face at me. There was a definite smirk in those brown eyes. "Are you the latest?"

"Excuse me?"

"Well, I assume you've come either to carry on with or about my husband. In either case, he's not at home. You're welcome to leave a message." She cracked the door open and clutched Roland's collar.

The foyer was full of dark wood and muted blue accents. I stepped in, trying to reassess the situation. "Mrs. Hammond, I am definitely not Ian's latest. But do you know what he's done to my sister?"

Her smile was icy. "I might be able to guess, yes."

I stared at her. "Well . . . doesn't it bother you?"

"May I offer you a cup of tea?" She gestured back toward the kitchen.

"No, thank you. Listen. I know I just met you, and I don't want to interfere with your personal life, but this concerns you, too." I took a deep breath. "Ian has really misrepresented himself to my sister. And one of her good friends." All right, the 'friend' bit was a shameless lie, but it added dramatic effect.

She nodded. "A muffin, perhaps?"

"No, thank you." I pressed on. "Aren't you outraged?"

She smiled again and pretended to try to hide it. "Should I be?"

"Yes! Really, how *dare* he?"

She scratched Roland behind the ears. "Your sister is one in a long line. Dr. Hammond has been diverting himself with his students since his first faculty appointment in London. Really, ducks, why do you think he finally had to come to the States to teach?"

This *would* explain why he was teaching in the boonies. And the hasty departure from the University of Chicago.

"Well, why didn't you leave him?" This sounded cheesy and canned, even to my own ears. I was so confused and taken aback, I'd resorted to lines memorized from bad TV.

"Ian and I reached an understanding many years ago. I've become accustomed to a certain lifestyle, you might say. We have children."

The second jaw-dropper of the day. "You have children?"

"Three sons. The youngest just left for university. So I thought I'd pop over to see Minnesota. Lovely scenery, isn't it? Quite unspoiled."

"Stop changing the subject!" I sputtered. "How can you be okay with all this?"

She gave me a pointed look. "He is my husband. My loyalties naturally lie with him, and your sister should not date married men."

"But she didn't know he was married!"

She shrugged. "Then she must be quite thick. Any one of his friends or colleagues could have told her." She paused and gazed past me out the front door. "Very warm today."

"I want—I *demand* to talk to Ian. I'm waiting here until he gets back!"

"Young lady. This is not a film clip from *Showdown at Shadow Gulch.*" She pushed the screen door open with a squeak. Roland pricked up his ears and growled low in his throat. "Good day."

So much for subtlety. I had no idea when I had lost the upper hand, but I knew I was getting the boot. I backed out the door and made a face at the dog. "Fine. But I'll be back tomorrow. And I'll sit on your front porch until I've talked to Ian."

That was when Roland bit me.

It wasn't like that scene from *Cujo,* full of frothy fangs and split-second lunging for the jugular. The dog was almost casual about it. He just stuck his neck out and chomped before I could jerk away.

One second I was raving at Portia, and the next, I was looking in open-mouthed horror from my left arm to Roland, who had resumed a sitting position, licking his chops in the canine version of a sneer.

Small red tidepools were welling up on my forearm. I had no idea about first-aid procedures for dog bites. I gaped at Portia, who raised her eyebrows in theatrical bewilderment.

"I can't imagine what's gotten into him," she said. "He's never done anything like this before."

"Your dog just devoured half my arm, and that's all you have to say?"

"Let me get you a towel." She shooed Roland down the hall and returned with a thick blue dishcloth from the kitchen.

I snatched it from her and wrapped it around my arm as tightly as I could. I didn't know whether pressure was good for the wound, but I didn't want to look at it anymore.

"I'm sure you'll be fine. He hasn't got rabies. Ian keeps all the veterinary shots up to date." She stood on the other side of the door and folded her arms.

And that was the end of that. I realized I was not going to get any apologies or explanations, and I didn't want them from her, anyway, so I tied the ends of the towel around my arm and returned to my car.

En route to the clinic, my mind kept fixating on the answering machine light blinking away in Skye's kitchen.

Sick and obsessive? Perhaps. But better to speculate for twenty minutes about phone messages than about what kinds of nasty little microbes might be lurking under that dishtowel.

*   *   *

When I arrived at the Raylor Memorial Clinic, I found Skye and Sally waging a full-fledged catfight through the thin yellow curtain separating their treatment areas. Before I even got past the frazzled nurse in the waiting room I could hear the accusations and counter-accusations flying.

"Well, at least I didn't *knowingly* two-time somebody and then try to kill them with my car."

"Give me a break. I was only going like ten miles an hour. If I had wanted to kill you, trust me, I would've."

A fed-up-looking doctor in a floral print dress and a white coat bustled out of the room.

I peeked through the yellow curtain to find Skye, sulky and supine on a metal exam table with her shoulder exposed and alarmingly swollen.

"Are you okay?" I rushed to her side. "What did the doctor say?"

She stopped pouting at the ceiling and looked at me like I was about to part the Red Sea. "You're back! Did you see him? What'd he say?"

I glanced around the sterile white room and fixated on a jar of cotton balls resting on the shelf above her head. "Well. I didn't get to talk to him directly. Listen, what did the doctor say about your shoulder? Do you want me to call Mom?"

"Don't change the subject." Her eyes were huge. "What's going on? Are you hiding something from me?"

"I went to his house," I admitted. "He wasn't there. But his wife was."

"So he does have a wife?" She sighed, then tried to make

the best of this. "Did she say he'd left her for a beautiful blonde?"

"Or a stunning young redhead?" Sally piped up from the other side of the curtain.

"Not exactly. We'll talk about it later, okay? It's kind of a long story. Now, seriously, how's your shoulder?"

"They think my collarbone's broken, and two of my fingers." She held up her right hand. The fingers she kept so carefully moisturized and manicured were twisted and livid.

"That looks awful. Are you in horrendous pain?"

She grimaced and nodded slowly.

"Well, so am I," Sally proclaimed. "The airbag broke my wrist."

Skye went from kitten to cougar in two seconds flat. "I'm *so* sorry you hurt yourself running me over with your car."

I could see why the physician had looked so harassed.

"What happened to Leah and Lars?" I asked.

"Leah had to go pick up Rex. She said you should call her tonight. And I told Lars to stay in the waiting room. He was making this big deal about doing something useful." She raised her voice. "So I asked him to go call Sally's insurance company and see if we can throw her in jail." My sister stopped threatening litigation long enough to gawk at me. "Faithie. What happened?"

Startled, I followed her stare to the blue dishtowel tied to my forearm, which I'd momentarily forgotten about in all the excitement. There were dark wet splotches seeping through the fabric. I tucked my arm behind my back and squeezed her hand. "Oh.

Nothing much. I sort of had an accident. Don't worry about it."

"What happened?" she pressed. I could tell she was dying for more details about what had transpired at the Hammonds'.

"Nothing," I said firmly. "Let's move on."

And we did. "How cute was Lars when he dragged me off to the hospital? Let me tell you something about that boy—you could break bricks on his pecs."

"Hold it right there." I clapped a hand to my forehead. "Are you or are you not currently in the E.R. because of a love triangle worthy of Aaron Spelling? Don't you think it's a little early to be discussing *Lars'* pecs?"

"It's called a transitional man," she said loftily. "He's going to help me at the bar from now on. Plus, he can shut up for three minutes at a time, which is more than I can say for Ian."

"Somebody say 'amen'," intoned the disembodied voice of Sally Hutchins.

The physician returned, X rays in hand. She pinned these up to a lighted box mounted on the wall and pointed at the abstract jumble of black and white lines.

"Your right clavicle is broken," she told Skye. "We're going to line it up and set it now. You'll need to keep your arm in a sling for three or four weeks."

"How's my wrist?" Sally yelled through the curtain.

"Still broken. We'll discuss it in a minute," the doctor yelled back. She turned to me, raising her eyebrows at my tea towel tourniquet. "If you'll excuse us."

"Of course. Skye, I'll be right outside if you need me." I headed for the waiting room pay phones.

*　　*　　*

There was no message from Flynn. Of course.

I wasn't surprised; I knew I wouldn't get off that easy. I had made this mess, and I needed to clean it up myself. No *deus ex machina* miracle was going to magically reconcile an inveterate grudge-holder and a commitment-phobe. Unfortunately.

The first message was from Ian, telling Skye he'd have to cancel a date tomorrow because "something's come up." The second was Sally, sounding like a cross between Joan Crawford and Donald Duck, commanding Skye to call her back immediately. The time stamp placed this call at a scant thirty minutes before the Main Street Massacre.

The third message was from my editor, who, I was relieved to hear, was not demanding to see a final draft of the Tuscany piece. In fact, he didn't mention Italy at all.

"Faith! We just finished some meetings, and we've decided to go ahead with a whole special issue on the Southern California cuisine scene." I pressed the receiver against my ear. "Mostly Los Angeles. Maybe a little bit of Santa Barbara and Orange County. Your scene. So you can stop complaining about how much you hate it out there in the wilderness because we need you back in civilization. Give me a call as soon as you can."

I kept listening to the soft whirr of recorded silence after he stopped talking.

Lars would be only too happy to pick up where I'd left off with the Roof Rat. He'd do anything for Skye. And no matter how socially inept he was with the customers, he couldn't be any worse than I was.

I could say my good-byes, hop in the car, and in a few days I'd be back in California. In a desert full of flowers where it was too dry for mosquitoes and the smog only enhanced the vibrant colors of the sun setting over the ocean. I could trade Lindbrook's volatile weather and small-town scrutiny for the balmy warmth and anonymity of Los Angeles. I could swap Thompson's Dry Goods for the Beverly Center. I could be free. And no one could claim I was running away. My glamorous career beckoned, and I had to follow.

But for some reason, I did not respond to this news in what I knew to be the appropriate fashion (i.e., doing backflips down the hall while singing "Going Back to Cali" at the top of my lungs). Flynn was still M.I.A. and I missed him. And I'd miss him more if I went back west, more than I did the first time because now I'd fully appreciate what I had lost. Every time I listened to some jackanape at Koi go on about how his Milan photo shoot just hadn't panned out yet, I'd think about what I'd left behind.

And Flynn would never go with me. Even if, through some odds-defying feat of diplomacy, I managed to win him back, he was one of those stalwart Minnesota natives who harbors a love of their arctic motherland that borders on the fanatic. I thought back to the conversations we'd had about hockey and fishing and family values, how intense he'd looked when he talked about his job. He belonged here.

But it was more than that. I'd miss Leah and Stan and Rachel and Rex. I'd miss the wide-open silence of country evenings, the joys of dressing down and driving a really crappy car with pride. And I'd miss Skye. We were just getting to know each other as adult friends instead of siblings allied against adversity. She was the best part of my fractured family, the weakness that forced me to be strong.

I had a history with Flynn and Skye. They knew all the twists and turns I'd taken early in my journey, and why. No matter how close I might get to someone else, I would never find that same shorthand understanding that comes from sharing a past.

Something inside me had shifted during the past few weeks. I didn't know if the change was good or bad, but it was permanent.

"Dammit, dammit, son of a bitch." I rested my head against the rough beige wallpaper that smelled of antiseptic and stared through the glass doors at the end of the hall. Beyond the asphalt parking lot was a vast expanse of cobalt sky streaked with clouds. The horizon under which I'd grown up now seemed almost as wide and fresh as the Pacific or the Mediterranean.

And then a shaded silhouette appeared, as they say, out of the blue. I knew it was Flynn before I could discern his face—his stride and his posture were like kinetic fingerprints.

Pieces of me that I'd kept separated since I first left Lindbrook started to collide. Whatever had happened in his apartment, whatever he must think of me right now, he had come. Probably more for Skye's sake than mine, but he had come when I needed him. That was enough for the moment.

So I did what I always did under duress. I ran.

I ran down the hallway and into his arms with no regard for

personal space or good manners. I was trusting him to accept—
for the moment—all my contradictions, to ignore his better
judgment, and to catch me when I threw myself at him.

And he did.

He paused for a second, his body absorbing the impact of
mine, and then he wrapped his arms around me while I buried
my face in his soft gray T-shirt. He smelled like the promised
land mingled with traces of laundry soap. And in that moment,
I fell right back in love with him. So simple, yet so complicated.

He stood there for a second, just letting me hold onto him
in the hushed taupe waiting room. And then he stepped back
and picked up my left wrist.

"What the hell happened to your arm?"

20

W here to begin? Just imagine a movie called *My Sister, Her Lover, His Wife, and Their Dog, Roland*. Imagine the movie gets an 'R' rating for explicit language and vicious animal attacks."

His eyebrows shot up and his grip on my forearm tightened. "That's a dog bite? When exactly did this happen?"

I blinked at the blue dishrag, sort of surprised to realize that it still hurt. "About an hour ago. I guess."

He slid his hand under my right elbow and steered me back to the urgent care clinic. "Let's get this checked out before you go Old Yeller on me."

"I did nothing to provoke this," I said, anxious to clear my name as an animal lover.

"No one's saying you did." He nodded at the waiting room receptionist, who rolled her eyes, turned up the soft-rock radio station, and handed him a clipboard to fill out. "I just don't want to have to drag you out to the backyard and shoot you."

"I was taking care of Skye," I explained.

"Yes, and I'm taking care of you." He filled out my name and local address on the clipboard, then handed it off to me.

The form asked for my permanent address. That was a head-scratcher. "How did you know we were here?" I asked.

"Are you kidding? A Sally Hutchins, Skye Geary, and Ian Hammond love triangle? With car crashes and hysterics? It was all over town in ten seconds flat. My voicemail's overflowing with messages from 'concerned citizens' who 'just thought I'd want to know' what my business partners are up to."

I slumped into the Naugahyde chair. "So everyone knows about the Ian thing?"

"If you guys wanted to keep it a secret, you shouldn't have been screaming about it in front of Cherry's Café at lunch hour."

The phrase "lunch hour" reminded me. "Hey, shouldn't you be at work? It's Monday."

He squeezed my shoulder. "I'd say this qualifies as a personal day."

The next hour was a blur of detailed questions and unappetizing medical procedures. The same physician who had just sentenced Skye and Sally to overnight observation in the upstairs clinic (in a shared room, God help us all), attended to me. She introduced herself as Dr. Shelbourne and got right down to brass tacks.

"Have you had a tetanus shot in the last five years?" she demanded, flushing out my gaping lacerations with water and yellow fluid from an unlabeled plastic bottle.

"I'm not sure," I said, wincing anew at the sight of my mangled flesh. Roland had been quick but thorough.

"Try to remember." Dr. Shelbourne was clearly at the end of her tether with the Roof Rat Delegation.

I racked my brains, then said, "I don't think so." Flynn gave me the same look that his grandmother used to give us when we forgot to wear our mittens in January.

"Well then, after I wash this out, you're going to need a few stitches, and we'll give you a tetanus booster. I'm also going to prescribe a cycle of antibiotics to prevent skin flora. Are you absolutely, positively, one-hundred-percent certain the dog is current on his rabies vaccinations?"

"That's what the owner said." I swallowed hard as the doctor broke out a silver tray full of scary-looking sharp steel instruments.

"So you know for sure it was Ian's dog?" Flynn wanted to know.

Dr. Shelbourne threw up her latex-gloved hands. "This is more of the famous Ian's work? He must be quite a guy. Tell him he's responsible for eighty percent of my paycheck today."

Flynn commenced pacing. "What did he say when the dog bit you?"

"Well, nothing, because he wasn't there. Only his wife."

He stopped pacing and resumed staring. "His *wife?*"

"Yeah, it turns out he's married. Come on, you need to keep

up with the gossip mill," I chided. "Skye begged me to go over to his house and find out what the hell's going on, but his wife answered the door and she was really not very sensitive about the whole situation. So then the dog bit me, and she threw me out so I wouldn't bleed on the carpet. Ian never showed up."

"That's it," he decided. "I'm killing him."

"No," I corrected, *"I'm* killing him. You have to wait your turn."

But no one got around to killing Ian that afternoon. By the time Dr. Shelbourne finished with me, it was nearly five o'clock, so Flynn and I made a quick trip to Cannon Falls to pick up my antibiotics and dinner for the invalids.

"Listen." I cleared my throat as we returned to the clinic's parking lot. "About this morning . . ."

"Later." He cut the engine and shoved one hand into the drugstore bag. "One thing at a time. Start the antibiotics." He refused to meet my eyes while I fumbled with the child-proof cap.

Changing the subject and ignoring me. How novel.

We figured that Sally and Skye would need either heavy tranquilizers or nonstop refereeing to survive a night together in the same room. Flynn agreed to wait out in the hall while I poked my head in the door, armed only with contraband cheeseburgers and chocolate milkshakes.

The overhead light was off, but I could see that the room was decorated in tones of unrelenting gray. A tall metal tray with a vase of daisies and a plastic water pitcher separated twin beds. The whole place reeked of industrial-strength cleansing fluid.

I could make out Skye's yellow curls and Sally's very red hair gleaming through the dusk. The only sound was the drone of the TV on the far wall. Two pairs of eyes blinked owlishly at me in the fading light.

Either they had already beaten themselves senseless and were resting up for round two, or I was missing something here.

"Dinner? Anyone?"

No response. I perched on the edge of Skye's bed and tried again. "Nice flowers."

"Lars. He brought them by and now he's opening up the Roof Rat for the night. Isn't that sweet?"

"Ssshhh!" hissed Sally from her bed by the window.

"We're trying to concentrate," explained Skye, battered and bruised but looking quite alert amid a pile of white linen.

I followed their rapt gazes to the TV, which was tuned to the Home Shopping Network. A hypnotic female voice was extolling the virtues of what was, bar none, the ugliest piece of jewelry I'd ever seen in my life. Four enormous hunks of pink stone were set into a garish explosion of gold curlicues and diamond chips in what was presumably intended to be the shape of a butterfly. The gemstone equivalent of a black velvet Elvis portrait.

"We're going to buy it," my sister whispered.

I smiled and waited. But she was not kidding.

"Neither of us can afford it on our own, so we're going to split the cost and share it," added Sally, regarding the butterfly with the same awed, solemn reverence as she would the lost Romanoff treasures.

I looked from Skye to Sally to the TV. "Oh my ears and whiskers."

"I know! Isn't it fabulous? Now, sshhh! Sshhh! I have to hurry up and call because we only have two minutes left!" Skye turned on me with her lost kitten eyes. "Thank God you're here. Can I borrow your credit card?"

"Skye . . ."

She clutched at her arm sling. "Please! My Visa's maxed out—I need yours. Please! We'll pay you back! I promise."

"We *will* pay you back." Sally chimed in with all of Skye's conviction and a lot more authority. "In three easy installment plans, just like the screen says. But we have to buy it today. They're almost sold out, and it is a very valuable piece."

"Pink tourmaline," chirped my sister.

I dropped the brown-bag dinner on the nightstand near Skye. She dug out a milkshake and sucked on the straw until her cheeks hollowed out like a Dickensian orphan. "We're down to forty-five seconds and there's only a few left! Please!"

"How much is it?" I peered back at the TV. *"Oh my God."*

Sally put a calming hand on my arm. "I know that $569.99 sounds like a lot, but it isn't, really. Not when you figure we're splitting it two ways and paying you back in three installments."

So Sally Hutchins and my sister, dueling divas since the 1994 homecoming court, had been united by their newfound loathing of unctuous English professors and their love of tacky jewelry. I thought I could detect the hand of divine intervention modeling the merchandise on QVC.

I handed over my wallet.

"Oh, I love you, Faithie!" Skye blew me a kiss and lunged for the phone. "This is gonna be so cool. We'll even let you borrow it sometimes! Wait. I can't dial with one hand."

"Give it to me. I'll do it." Sally snatched the receiver away.

She ordered the hideous bauble in my name and thoughtfully added on a 14-karat gold chain. I left when they started an argument over who would get to wear the butterfly first and headed back to the hallway, where the real battle with Flynn was still to come.

"You're still alive. That's a good sign." Flynn looked up from the newspaper and a cup of coffee.

He always seemed so strong and comfortable in his own skin—he made even this sterile, blank hospital hall feel safe and familiar. I wanted to throw myself into his arms again, but that moment had passed.

We were back to wary looks and long, uncomfortable silences.

"Here. I got you a cup of coffee. Two sugars, no cream." He handed it over.

I took a seat on the hard plastic chair next to him. "Not only are those two not scratching each other's eyes out, they're making joint jewelry purchases. On my credit card. I guess five-hundred and seventy bucks is a small price to pay for world peace."

He leaned back in his chair and grinned. "Skye always knows just how to handle you."

I watched the steam from my coffee unfurl into the atmosphere. "It makes me so angry, what Bob and Ian did. How can they not love that girl? How can they do that, just drop her and leave?"

I nearly bit my tongue off as that sentence left my mouth, but he didn't make any comment about my desperate bid for freedom this morning. Or ten years ago.

"Has she heard from Bob yet?"

"No. She's barely mentioned him since I got here. It's hard for us to talk about. Maybe even harder for her than for me. Everyone expects her to be the smiley, breezy one who doesn't take anything seriously."

"Because that's your department?"

"So I'm told." I took a sip of coffee. "I just worry that she's gotten trapped underneath all that blond. People see her running around giggling and they don't think she'll be hurt after stuff like this. But you should have seen her eyes today when Sally told her about Ian. It broke my heart."

He reached over to grab my hand, but changed his mind at the last second and ended up giving me an awkward and somewhat stinging pat on the knee. "She's stronger than you think. And she's smart enough to know what she needs. Right after Bob left, she called me and asked for help."

"Which you, of course, provided."

"I could pitch in with the financial aspect, but she really needed more help on the emotional front. So I convinced her to call you."

I smiled. "You realize, of course, that her phone call—her *collect* phone call—cost me more than dinner at L'Orangerie."

"Where?"

"L'Orangerie." I shook my head. "Los Angeles. Never mind."

"Well, I bet that the phone call and L'Orangerie put together are still cheaper than that necklace in there."

"You think it's funny now, but wait until you see this thing. It's like something Cher would wear to the Oscars."

I studied his face and realized I was still missing huge pieces of this puzzle. The fireworks between us had died down this morning, but now that the volatile explosions were gone, so was the spark. He was closed and unreadable, and I seemed to have misplaced my Psychic Male Decoder Ring.

I gulped my coffee and tried to replace the sinking sensation in my stomach with reheated Folgers. "You were so great to help us out. To help *me* out this afternoon. I really appreciate that. But, and forgive me for pointing this out, you seem to be a bit standoffish now."

"I'm not a glutton for punishment." He devoted all his concentration to refolding the newspaper.

I turned both palms out. "I can see the anger and disappointment in your face every time you look at me."

"I'm not disappointed in you," he said. "You are who you are."

"Oh, *that's* nice. Listen, I don't know what to say to you. "When I first got here, I was scared I was still in love with you, and I was scared I wasn't. And I was so ashamed of myself. It was like a really bad country western song. I pretty much just wanted to throw up every time I saw you that first week."

"Good to know," he said. I couldn't bring myself to look up at his face, but his voice sounded like he was smiling.

"And speaking of throwing up . . ."

"Yes?"

"About last night." My entire face was probably Ferrari red. I should have let Ian's dog finish me off when I had the chance.

"Yes?" Of course he couldn't make this easy for me.

I swilled the final cold sips of my coffee. "I am really, really sorry."

He laughed out loud.

I glared at him. "Knock it off, I'm being serious. That was so irresponsible and immature and just very unrefined. I suppose I've lost some of my charm for you, but I promise you it will never happen again."

He was still laughing. I think I preferred the grim stoicism.

"May I ask what the hell is so amusing?" I demanded.

"The look on your face when you were making the transition from Brunelleschi to, quote, 'losing your charm'."

"I'm *trying* to apologize. Why must you torture me?"

"I'm not torturing you." He paused. "Right now. I had a great time last night. Between the tattoos and the architecture lecture, you were very entertaining." He gave me a look which, under better circumstances, I would have classified as a once-over. "And you really should consider wearing that little gray dress more often."

"Oh, really?"

"Definitely. It makes up for a lot of character flaws." He cleared his throat and went on. "And just so you know, I've seen you be a hundred times less charming than you were Saturday. Like the first night you were back in town, when you took one look at me and took off running."

I resumed communing with my Styrofoam cup. "That was different. There were many extenuating circumstances. Like the fact that you told me to quote, *get out,* unquote."

"Okay, then, what about when we were five and you threw a bowl at me and cut my chin open?" He pointed to a tiny white scar on his jawline.

"You had that coming," I objected. "How quickly we forget. You held me down and colored all over my face with a brown marker."

"And I did a fine job," he retorted. "You looked like a very small, very cute lumberjack. Talk about charming."

"Yeah, well, your grandmother didn't seem to agree."

"True." He nodded. "You're incredibly charming when you're not leaving me in the dust."

The sugared coffee aftertaste turned bitter in my mouth.

He slid a hand under my chin and nudged my face up to look at him. "I don't know where you went this morning and I don't know why you went, but I'm not angry."

I went very still. "Why not?"

"Because I know how you work."

"No, you don't."

"Yeah, I do. You either have no reason for something, or you have a *huge* reason. When you leave me, it's because you need to. It's part of who you are. I accept that."

"Why do I suddenly feel hugely insulted?"

"You shouldn't. It takes two to tango. I've made plenty of mistakes in this whole thing."

I licked my bottom lip. "So what do you think now?"

"I don't know." But he looked grim.

I held my breath as I waited for the inevitable, for what I should have expected since our hit-and-run reunion in the back room of the bar.

But then he pulled me closer, mindful of the freshly-bandaged dog bite between us, and kissed me.

All my anxiety about the look in his eyes, and Skye and Ian, and my editor's new assignment dissolved for a moment. I wrapped my nonmangled arm around his neck and kissed him back.

I loved him. Without shame, without boundaries, without any clear idea of where this was all going. Not wisely but too well, and all that. I had no defenses left and I didn't care.

And by the time we came up for air, I realized that I should probably keep this little epiphany to myself. At least until I could take a stand on the nebulous matter of my future and the burning question of *location, location, location.*

But all that could wait a few hours. I sighed and relaxed against him.

He cleared his throat. "Someone needs to be at the bar tonight. I better—"

"Shut up out there, you guys. We're trying to watch this!"

Skye hollered. I heard Sally murmuring, then Skye yelled, "Oh yeah, Faithie, come in here for a second. I need you to run an errand, like right now. Flynn, you stay out there."

"Oh, no." I handed my wallet to him and stood up. "Do not, under any circumstances, let her at my MasterCard."

"Good luck." He gave me a snappy salute. We'd figure out our new relationship soon enough. But first, back into the QVC abyss.

21

Fifteen minutes later, as per Skye's request, I pushed open the front door of the Roof Rat and braved the gauntlet of raised eyebrows and stalled conversations. But I didn't have time to deal with all the inquiring minds. Flynn had walked me to the car and sent me off with a promise that we would discuss That Which Needed Discussing tonight. We were going to ditch the inpatients as soon as I got back.

The bar had a big crowd for a Monday night; apparently half the town had shown up in the hopes that Skye or I would be staging a scandalous sequel to our Main Street matinee.

Someone even turned off the jukebox when I made my entrance. Very Old West.

The men put down their glasses of Pig's Eye and pushed

back their John Deere caps. The women started fiddling with their jewelry and pretended to be looking at each other while they eyeballed at me.

At first, I couldn't account for the gawking. It wasn't like *I* was a key player in this little drama. I was merely sister to the star. But just as I was about to chalk it up to desperate small-town gossip-mongering and proceed with Skye's errand, I felt a puff of warm air on my back as the front door closed again.

And the evening wind brought with it a whiff of Earl Grey.

He wouldn't. Ian would not have the gall to show up at my sister's bar while she was in the hospital, sharing a room with his other girlfriend. I mean, the man had a Ph.D., right? He was indiscreet, not idiotic.

But then I remembered Portia saying he'd been at a conference in Minneapolis all day. If he hadn't gone home to his wife before coming here, maybe he hadn't heard about Skye and Sally.

The crowd had settled into a hungry silence. The Roof Rat had become Lindbrook's Coliseum, and I was the gladiator du jour.

"I'd recognize that hair anywhere. Fair Faith, are you all alone tonight?" I'd only heard him use that tone of voice with Skye.

I whirled around, one hand on my hip. "What?"

"Well, I don't see Skye or Flynn about. We'll have to entertain ourselves somehow." He chuckled and clamped a dark wood pipe between his lips. Alistair Cooke on the prowl.

Was he . . . was he *flirting* with me?

I gaped at him. "Are you kidding me?"

"Join me for a cup of tea." He patted the seat beside him and wrapped a hand around my wrist. His skin felt dry and soft, like wax paper.

I jerked away. "Listen, you . . . you *Twins fan,* you. Would you like to know why Skye and Flynn aren't here? They aren't here because they're holed up with Sally Hutchins. At the Raylor Memorial Clinic. And would you like to know what they're discussing?"

His eyebrows skyrocketed and he pushed his chair back. "I can't imagine—"

"You are such a slut!" I said. A collective gasp from the crowd.

He recaptured my wrist and forced a laugh. "My dear—"

"How dare you treat my sister that way?"

His gaze bounced around the bar as he realized we were currently center ring at the circus.

"Back off, Faith." Lars, who was stationed behind the bar, had finally registered an identifiable facial expression. He looked furious.

"I will not back off! My baby sister is all mangled in the hospital, and I'm taking it out of his hide!"

"I mean, back off so *I* can get at him." Lars started out from behind the bar, rolling up the sleeves of his denim shirt.

Ian fled into the night. He left his pipe, still smoldering, on the tabletop.

In a blur of blond, Lars reached the door before it closed behind Ian. He moved with a shocking amount of speed for one so monolithic.

I hesitated by the cash register, unsure if I should complete my assigned errand and rush back to Skye, or stay put and try to maintain order in the bar, or hurry out to see the beating to end all beatings.

Some decisions get made for you.

"Get him!" shrieked a tiny brunette, toppling her barstool as she raced out the front door.

"Yeah! Fight!" Her date waved his fist in the air like a communist peasant with a mullet and a farmer's tan.

"Fight! Fight! Fight!" The bloodthirsty mob stampeded toward the parking lot, delighted with the latest turn of events. It might be too early for hunting or ice-fishing, but it was always fist-fighting season in Lindbrook.

Ever committed to customer satisfaction, I followed the crowd into the swampy night, where Lars was gaining on Ian in the parking lot.

As the bar patrons and a fresh swarm of mosquitoes gathered under the streetlights, Lars reached out and caught the back hem of Ian's tweedy gray blazer.

"Oooh," said the crowd.

Ian whipped around, his arms pinwheeling.

We all leaned forward into the rank smell of gasoline and garbage, waiting for the fists to start flying.

Ian tried to struggle out of the jacket, but Lars reeled him in by his tailcoats.

"Aaah," said the crowd.

Lars's mouth formed a perfect O as Ian sank his teeth into Lars's hand.

"Cheater!" The petite brunette put both hands on her hips. "Biting's no fair!"

The mob grumbled threateningly as it closed in on Ian. Since the path back to the bar was clogged with a sea of onlookers, he high-tailed it toward the back alley, his Brooks Brothers loafers clicking on the asphalt.

A yellow Volvo screeched into the alley, cutting off his last route of escape. He froze in the glare of headlights as Portia Hammond slammed out of the car.

I rubbed my eyes against the blinding headlights and by the time my vision adjusted, Portia was chasing her husband back toward the bar, pelting him with hardcover books. Even in high heels and a dainty silk scarf, she had quite the pitching arm.

"Aha!" She unleashed a torrent of *Orlando, Mansfield Park,* and *Great Expectations.* "I thought I'd find you here! Slouching around the pub with a two-bit floozy!"

We all froze except Ian, who dropped to his knees and curled into a ball under the onslaught of literature. "I can explain!"

She snatched a fresh supply of missiles from the car. We all flinched as she let loose with a massive copy of *War and Peace,* which narrowly missed his head.

For a woman who had assured me that her husband's infidelity was no big deal, she certainly seemed to be riled up.

"How dare you humiliate me like this? It's one thing to lie, but to flaunt it so publicly . . ." She wiped a strand of brown hair back from her forehead, dived back into the Volvo, and emerged with a book the size of Albania.

"What is that?" asked the brunette in a hushed tone of awe.

I squinted at the boxy tome as Portia advanced on her husband. "Dear God. I think it's the Riverside Shakespeare."

"The what?"

"The Riverside edition of the complete works of Shakespeare," I repeated.

The crowd erupted into horrified whispers:

"That thing must be a million pages!"

"And it's hardcover! Look at the corners!"

"I'm too young to see a cold-blooded murder."

But it was too late to miss the massacre. Portia grabbed Ian by the ear and yanked him into a standing position.

"Please," he quailed. "Not the Riverside! Anything but that!"

She stepped back, got a running start and whomped him right in the stomach.

"Woah." Even Lars winced as Ian doubled over.

The rubberneckers had been reduced to a collection of blinking eyes and hands clapped over mouths.

"And there's more where that came from." Portia seemed pleased with her handiwork. "Now get in the car, and be quick about it, you mangy cur. We'll finish this when we get home."

Ian staggered toward the Volvo, threw himself inside, and doubled over in his seat as his wife slammed the driver's door and peeled away.

"Show's over." I tried to herd everyone back into the bar. "Nothing left to see here."

"Want me to go after them?" Lars offered. He picked up Ian's pipe in a huge callused fist. "If you watch the bar, I can meet him back at his house and return this *properly.*"

I shook my head reluctantly. "I can't. I'm here on a mission from Skye, and she wants me back at the clinic ASAP."

At the mention of Skye, his expression melted into the Viking version of dewy eyes. "How's she doing?"

"She's feeling a lot better, and I think she and Sally are actually bonding. She says thanks for the daisies." While she hadn't actually uttered those words, I felt sure she had *meant* to thank him.

"Does she need anything?"

"That's why I'm here. She and Sally have evidently decided to throw themselves into the business, and she wants to go over last week's receipts." I grinned at his look of bewilderment. "I, too, was stunned. But you never know with Skye."

"Yeah." He smiled, totally besotted.

"It doesn't pay to ask too many questions. And she's all worked up as usual, so I'm just going to grab them and get back to her."

He shoved his hands in his pockets. "She'll be back home tomorrow, right? Does she need anything else?"

Maybe my sister wasn't so bad at choosing suitors, after all.

"Honestly, your working here tonight is by far the best thing anyone could do for her," I said. "You're saving our collective asses. Thank you so much."

He shrugged. "It's nothing."

"No, really. Thank you." I wanted to apologize for judging him, for taking away what he loved and giving it to a social disease with an advanced degree, but he didn't know I'd told Skye to dump him and now didn't seem like the best time to bring it up.

So I just grabbed the receipts from the back room, hopped in the car, and headed back to Flynn.

The Home Shopping Network had moved on to iolite and tanzanite rings by the time I returned to the clinic. Submerged in darkness, Sally and Skye slouched into their pillows, glued to the screen with the glazed expressions of recent cult converts. Moonlight filtered through the curtains and mingled with the bluish glow from the television.

"Here you go. A little something for the walking wounded." I tossed the rubber-banded pack of receipts on Skye's bed and looked around for Flynn.

She sprang into action. "Great! Now we have his credit card number!"

Sally started to cackle like she was brewing up some eye of newt. "Ian just became a huge fan of tanzanite jewelry."

I had unwittingly become an accomplice to a felony.

"Well . . . Godspeed, girls. Give me a call from jail." I turned to my sister, who had assumed secretarial duties for the looting and plundering of Ian's credit line. "Where's Flynn?"

"I dunno. He left."

I blinked. "He left? When?"

"Like twenty minutes ago." She salivated over the incredibly low price of $499.99. "He seemed kind of mad, actually, and he left. I think you're in trouble."

"Why would he be mad?"

"I dunno."

I sat down. "Okay. Skye. I need you to stop and talk to me

for a minute. What exactly happened? Did you two have a fight?"

"Of course not." She finally tore herself away from the TV. One look at my face, and she started to apply herself to answering the questions at hand. "I thought *you* two had a fight, because . . . Let's see. He went to get us some Skittles from the machine, and then he called the Roof Rat to make sure you and Lars didn't need any help, but no one answered, and then I asked him to check my messages to see if Ian had called. Which he had, with some lame story about a conference in Minneapolis. He's probably reading a sonnet to some skank right now. I mean, how dumb does he think—"

I cut her off. "Hold on. Back to Flynn for a second. What happened then?"

"Then nothing. That's all I know." Her forehead wrinkled up. "Are you okay?"

I tried to find a loophole before succumbing to despair. "Did he say when he'd be back?"

"No. Oh, but he did say to tell you that he couldn't meet up with you tonight."

"Does he want me to call him?" Grasping at straws never hurt anybody.

She shook her head. "I don't think so. He seemed really mad."

"About *what?*" I exploded, pounding the mattress.

"I don't know! He just started muttering about how he's an idiot and how he'd had it with you." She regarded me with a blend of concern and reproach. "What'd you do?"

"Nothing!" I racked my brains.

"Well." She picked up her pen and gave me a disapproving look. "I've hardly ever seen Flynn get mad, and he certainly doesn't just storm out over nothing. So you'd better fix whatever you did."

What could be worse than throwing up all over him and then stealing away to the airport in the dead of night? I went over our last conversation with a fine-tooth comb, but I couldn't figure out what I'd done wrong. We made an agreement! We were going to fish or cut bait! Good lovin', we hardly knew ye!

I had to call him right now and get to the bottom of this.

But before I made it to the door, a tall, willowy woman stalked into the room. She wore a crisp linen pantsuit and a facial expression that suggested she had just gotten a whiff of the stables behind the polo field.

This looked like the kind of woman who would dial up the I.N.S. the moment her newly immigrated housemaid spilled a drop of '97 Cabernet Sauvignon Reserve on the white carpet in her den. The kind of woman who might have more than a passing acquaintance with vicious sorority hazing and *The Rules*.

"Well, Celeste, I hope you're proud of yourself." She dug a pack of Virginia Slims out of her handbag, glanced at the NO SMOKING signs, and threw it back in. "The news is all over town, your father is spitting nails, and I have to face everyone at the country club supper on Friday." She drummed her fingers over her pants pocket and waited. Skye and I cowered on the bed.

Sally didn't look away from the TV. "Hello, Mother."

"Don't you 'hello, Mother' me. Do you know what people are saying about you and Ian Hammond? Your father is the mayor of this town. How could you do this to us?"

"This is my roommate, Skye, and her sister Faith," Sally said before she turned the TV volume up. "My wrist is broken, thanks for asking."

Mrs. Hutchins stopped fuming long enough to grace us with a brittle smile. Her face looked strained, but it was hard to tell if this was due to stress or the tightness with which she'd yanked her white-blond hair back into a chignon. "Please forgive me. I'm Julia Hutchins. My daughter has ruined the family name in less than a day, so I'm a bit upset. You two look familiar . . . were you some of Celeste's little friends in high school?"

"Your name is Celeste?" Skye asked Sally, deftly changing the subject.

Sally opened her mouth, but Julia cut her off. "Yes. I named her Celeste because it's a beautiful name and it has lots of nice, straight lines. It would look fabulous in print, under a TV anchorwoman, for instance. But her father insists on that trailer-trash nickname, and she goes along with it just to annoy me."

Sally rolled her eyes. "Mother, who ever heard of an anchorwoman named Celeste Hutchins?"

"Well, your name wouldn't *be* Hutchins if you had married that nice Ben Coleridge, now would it? Celeste Coleridge is a perfect name for an anchorwoman." Julia turned to us. "I told her over and over to marry that nice boy from that nice family, but no. She insists on tramping around with ancient married men and disgracing me in front of all my friends. You see what I have to live with?"

One could see why Sally might develop a bit of a chip on her shoulder, living with this woman.

"I spoke with your doctor on the phone, and she said you're going to be fine, but your father insisted I skip bridge night and come see you, so here I am. I brought you something to read." Julia produced a pile of magazines from her voluminous leather tote. She pointed to a blurb on the cover of *Glamour.* "There's an article in here on how to attract worthwhile men."

Then she narrowed her eyes at my sister, who looked even more sweet and vulnerable than usual with her golden curls and blue arm sling.

"Here, Celeste. I brought your makeup bag, too. You never know when you might meet an eligible doctor. Not that you'd want him, unless he had a wife and a rap sheet as long as my arm. And turn the light on when you're reading. Don't you know how terrible that is for your eyes?"

I escaped out the door while Skye stared in abject horror at the dark side of the Avon Lady.

I communed with the dial tone for a minute, listening to the thin gray hum. Then I got down to business.

The phone rang and rang. Four times. Five. He didn't have an answering machine at home. Vintage Flynn.

Six times.

"Hello?"

His voice surprised me. I startled under the glaring fluorescent lights in the hallway, then leaned against the wall. "Flynn. Oh, thank God."

"Didn't Skye tell you not to call me?" His tone was flat and final.

"No. But she said you stormed out and said that I shouldn't go over there, which—"

"She's right."

This bounced around in my head for a moment.

"But, um, why—"

"Look." There ensued a long pause on his end. "I don't want to make this into a huge deal."

"Too late." I twisted the phone cord around my index finger until the tip went purple and numb. "I have no clue what's going on here. I thought we'd agreed to talk about things. Didn't we?"

"We did."

"And you kissed me. Not two hours ago."

"I did." He ended this statement on a rising inflection, clearly censoring the rest of what he had to say.

"Then what is going on?" I waited for an answer I wasn't sure I wanted to hear.

"I just can't do this anymore. The whole thing is a game to you. The hot and cold, cat and mouse, advance and retreat thing. You don't take it seriously, and I do."

I practically hyperventilated at this. "How can you say that? I do take it seriously."

"Come on, Faith." This was clearly a dismissal, his final word on the matter, but his tone was still a caress. "You don't need me. You never will. I know you want to go back to California."

I watched the seconds tick by on the black clock on the white wall.

"See? You can't even deny it," he said.

"You're right—I can't deny it. And why shouldn't I leave when you won't give me a single reason to stay?" I struggled to keep the frustration out of my voice. "This is insane. You won't forgive or forget. Nothing I do is ever enough. But you expect me to give up my whole life for the remote possibility that this relationship will ever happen. And how can *you* accuse *me* of being unreliable? You were fine two hours ago and now—"

"I heard the message from your editor when I checked Skye's phone messages for her," he said. "I know you're going back to L.A."

"Oh." Where to begin with this? "Well, that doesn't mean—"

"Were you even going to tell me before you left?"

"*Yes,*" I said, stung. "I mean, no. I mean, I don't even know what I'm going to do about that . . ."

"I have to go."

There it was again: his Last Word tone. I lost my head and played my trump card in a desperate bid to keep him on the line.

"Wait. Flynn, please. I love you. I—Let's get married." It was out before I could stop it.

For a long minute, I didn't hear anything except our breathing overlapping through a sea of wires and metal.

"*What?*"

Swallowing back rising waves of panic and dread, I sagged against the wall. But I was willing to do whatever I had to in order to keep him on the line. Even something that felt utterly wrong, that jarred the deepest parts of my soul.

Now I knew exactly how he had felt ten years ago.

"I want to get married." I forced this out in hot puffs of air.

"No, you don't." He laughed dryly. "You just want to eat your cake and have it too."

"I do. I do want to . . . to get married." I tried desperately to convince myself that this was the truth, but my body betrayed me. My palms were soaking wet, my hands were shaking, and my head felt light and woozy.

"Don't do this," he said. "Don't lie to me. Don't lie to yourself. You need things that you can't find here." There was a long, agonizing pause. "Please don't call me again." He put the receiver down gently. I was left with the snick of disconnection, a brief silence, and the dial tone.

I didn't know where to go or what to do.

In the name of self-preservation, I drained the cold, charged fear inside me until things were officially under control. Then I redialed his number. (Being "officially under control" seemed to involve having no pride whatsoever.)

This time he didn't pick up.

22

I returned to Skye's room to find that Julia Hutchins had given up tormenting her daughter in favor of sawing away at her own manicure with a nail file and muttering about thankless children. Sally had apparently been forced to submit to an extensive makeover and now peered out from beneath slabs of mossy green eyeshadow. She handed Skye a copy of *Modern Bride*.

"Here, you want this?" she offered, scowling at her mother. "Someone who actually has a boyfriend should read it."

"I can always dream, can't I?" Julia smiled grimly.

"No thanks." My sister waved the magazine away. "I'm through with the whole marriage thing for a while."

"You are?" I asked, stunned into speech. Sometimes when God closes a door, He lobs a FedEx package with a big red bow through the window.

"You're back!" She scrambled off the bed to meet me in the doorway. "Hey, let's go hang out in the lounge down the hall. I'm sure these two want to be alone."

She hustled me out the door.

"Thank God we're out of there," she gasped, still within earshot. "Is that woman a bee-otch or what?"

"Skye, shhh." This was more of a reflex than an outraged appeal to etiquette.

"No wonder Sally's in such a bad mood all the time." She slipped her good arm through my good arm and tugged me toward the patient's lounge. More variations on the theme of windowless white. "But I'm going to fix all that. I asked her to come bartend at the Roof Rat."

"Can we afford that?" I asked automatically.

"Oh, sure." She beamed. "Lars is going to work for practically nothing. He's such a hunky, upstanding hunk."

"And yet you're not up for *Modern Bride?*"

"Don't be ridiculous. I'm *so* not ready to get married again," said the woman who, not five days ago, had declared that Ian Hammond was 'her next.' "At least, not to a good guy. And since I'm sick of bad boys, I guess I'm sick of marriage. But it'll be interesting to date someone with morals for a change. Do you think I'll have to start going to church?"

I sat down at the metal card table in the lounge and tried to look enthusiatic.

"Hey? Are you okay?" She frowned at me. "Are you even here? It's like the light is on at the Motel Six, but the guest has checked out."

"I'm fine, sweetie. What do you feel like doing? It's up to you." I gestured to the game boxes strewn about on shelves and counters.

"What do *you* want to do? Uno? No, boring. Monopoly? No, you always kick my ass. I know!" She pulled a red-sided jigsaw puzzle box from the middle of a stack of board games and tossed it on the table.

The top of the box boasted a picture of Florence's Piazza del Duomo, with the cathedral right in the center, arching up toward the sun with that big, brick, herringbone-patterned dome.

She pried the lid off and dumped all five hundred pieces in the middle of the table. A jumbled heap of white, orange, blue, and gray.

I started to cry.

I didn't *burst* into tears; it was really more like a traitorous leak that got out of hand.

"Oh no!" She stared at me, hand clapped to her mouth. "What's wrong? What did I say?"

I put my head down in my arms.

The folding chair scraped against the floor as my sister sat down next to me. She threaded her hand through my hair. "It's okay, Faithie. Tell me what's the matter. I can take care of you."

I pulled away from the hand stroking my head. I couldn't stand to be touched right now. "Skye. You are such a sweetie."

She brushed this aside. "I know. But what's the matter?"

"Flynn and I . . ." I swallowed. "Flynn doesn't want to see me any more."

"Ever?" The girl had quite a way with words.

I nodded. "Ever. He called everything off tonight." I picked up a piece of blue horizon and pinched it between my fingers.

My sister looked horrified. "Why? I thought you two had finally worked it out."

I sat up straight. "It's complicated. Basically, he doesn't trust me."

"Trust you to what?"

I shrugged. "To stick around. To be the kind of person he thinks I should be. He doesn't want to risk anything. He thinks I'm the same person I was when I was eighteen."

"Well, that's just nuts," she said authoritatively. "Look how far you've come. All the way back to Minnesota."

"Against my will," I reminded her.

"Yeah, but you're here, aren't you? Taking care of everything. You seem pretty reliable to me."

I thought of his flat monotone on the phone. "He doesn't see it that way."

"That is so weak sauce."

We fiddled with the puzzle pieces for a minute, constructing asymmetrical mosaics. She didn't look up when she said, "Well, what are you going to do now?"

I knew what she was really asking. "I don't know. I honestly don't. But I'm thinking about going back to L.A. And I want you to come with me." I saw the expression on her face and rushed ahead. "I mean it, I want you to come. You'd love it there. We could wait a few months until the Roof Rat's back in the black, then sell and reinvest out there."

She pursed her lips, considering this. "But I have everything I want right here."

I went back to our little mosaic. "Just think about it."

"I will." She nodded. "Because you know what? *I* trust you. I know that doesn't mean much, coming from someone who trusted Bob, but . . . I'll make you a deal. I'll think about moving to California if you think about staying here. I know you secretly like it here, even though you won't admit it. Don't feel like you have to leave just because of Flynn. That's what you did last time, and look what happened."

We gazed at each other for a moment, smiling. She was right. I didn't have to live my life as a reaction to the mistakes my father or my boyfriend made. I was older and wiser and this time, it was up to me.

"Men." She shook her head. "Put a tent over that circus."

Skye and Sally fell asleep around ten o'clock, their faces still bathed in the glow of the Home Shopping Network. I sat next to my sister until I could tell from her breathing that she was down for the count.

I groped for the remote control and turned the TV off. Now I could see the night through the window, but it seemed foreign and distant. Sitting there in the dark, staring at the crack of light under the door, I tried to figure out where to go. I couldn't stay here—I was already in flagrant violation of all visiting hour regulations. And I couldn't go back to the apartment. Even if I hurried up the back steps without peeking into the bar, I'd hear the jukebox and the chatter in the parking lot all night. With every muffled glass clink and waft of cigarette smoke, I'd think about the night Flynn found me hiding under the desk and all the things that had gone wrong since then.

So I got in the car and headed for the Goldbergs'. Because nothing in this life was certain except death, taxes, and domestic tranquility at Leah's house.

Leah threw the door open. "Faith! Thank goodness you're here! Everything's gone cattywampus." Her face was bright pink with exertion and her jeans were streaked with mud.

A pungent odor drifted down the hall. I crinkled my nose. "What is that smell?"

"Hans Gruber got sprayed by a skunk!" howled Rex, sprinting up behind his mother in Winnie the Pooh pajamas and stocking feet.

"Rex, honey, I told you not to leave him alone in the bathtub." She looked like she'd spent her day on the front lines of a swamp war. "That stupid mutt somehow got out of the yard and ran into a skunk, and I had to chase him all over the neighborhood through the woods and the creek, and I don't know how I'm ever going to air the house out."

"Hans is skunky! Hans is skunky! Pee-eww!" Rex hopped around his mother's legs with his black hair flopping all over his face. The child was clearly wired. He looked ready to throw his hands up in the air and jitterbug.

"Rex, get back in that bathroom, *now,*" Leah ordered as she ushered me inside. "Anyway, you couldn't have picked a better time to come over. I'm in desperate need of an extra pair of hands. Stan had to run out and get more dog shampoo and supplies. Do you have any idea how much tomato juice and vinegar it takes to wash a shepherd mix?"

"No," I said truthfully.

"A lot. And it's way past Rex's bedtime, but I needed someone to help me with the darn dog." She wiped her hands on her jeans, grimacing at the state of her outfit.

It was nice to know people with normal, real-world problems. Man pitted against nature, dog against skunk. Bedtime truants and tomato juice droughts. I shifted gears from intense self-pity and frustration to a dog-grooming frame of mind.

"Okay." I started pulling my hair back into a bun. "Show me to the victim."

"He's in the bathtub!" shrieked Rex, a veritable human superball.

"Eli! Bathroom! Now!" He scampered down the hall, and she turned back to me. "Faith, what's the matter? Is Skye okay?"

"Her collarbone's broken, but she's doing fine. I think she and Sally may actually become friends."

"Then why do you look like death warmed over? Is this about Flynn?"

"I guess." I squared my shoulders and summarized the evening's phone conversation.

" . . . And he told me not to call him again." I twisted my watch around and around my wrist. "Ever."

She exploded into a mother-bear rant. "That's the most passive-aggressive thing ever! To lead you down the primrose path and then dump you like that? That's the most vicious, angry, hostile . . ."

My watch band tore, leaving me with two ragged straps of black leather. "Don't say that about him. He wouldn't do that. He would never string me along like that. He had a good reason for what he did."

"Oh really? And what might that reason be?" She put her hands on her hips, indignant as only a mom caked in mud and eau de skunk can be.

"I think he finally gave up on me. I pushed him away too many times. I'm paranoid and emotionally stunted." I dug my sandal toe into the carpet. "But the problem is that, somewhere along the way, I fell back in love with him and now I'm really up a creek without a paddle. Because I think it's really over this time. You should have heard his voice."

She reached out to hug me, but I shied away.

"Sorry about the smell," she said. "Rex and I are probably as bad as Hans by now." She turned toward the bathroom. "Prepare to get wet."

At that moment, Hans Gruber raced out of the bathroom, a furry streak of brown and red headed for the living room. Rex was in hot pursuit. "Mama! Mama!"

"*Nooo!*" screamed Leah. "Not the living room! I just had the carpet cleaned!"

All three of us dashed after the dog, but we were too late. We froze in the doorway and looked on in horror as Hans, leaving a damp red trail in his wake, leapt atop Leah's one "good" cream-colored sofa and shook himself dry. Droplets of skunk-scented tomato juice spattered the walls, the ceiling, the furniture, and the curtains.

And Rachel started wailing upstairs.

Leah covered her eyes and groped for an appropriate, family-friendly expletive. "Oh . . . *no.*"

"Hans Gruber, how could you?" yelled Rex, arms akimbo. "Who's gonna pay for all this?"

Leah and I looked at each other and started to laugh, the kind of degenerate cackle heard in mental institutions.

"Don't worry, Mama. I'll get him." Rex tugged at the dog's collar, which only prompted Hans to collapse and roll on the embroidered sofa cushions.

Leah dabbed at her eyes with the hem of her T-shirt. "I'll get Hans, honey. Go grab some paper towels, okay?" She turned to me. "Faith, could you go up and get Rachel back to sleep? She's teething these days—she probably just needs to be rocked back to sleep. There's a teething ring in the freezer."

I had never in my life put a baby to bed, but this hardly seemed like the time for such petty objections.

Holding Leah's daughter brought me back to myself. She smiled when she saw me, even though her eyes were still glistening with tears.

"Hi," I whispered, waving the teething ring.

The light from the hallway caught her silky brown curls and huge brown eyes, and she reached for me, so I picked her up. I sat down in the old-fashioned rocking chair, cradling her warm little body against me. We settled into the shadows, rocking and humming to each other while she gummed the cold plastic ring.

I closed my eyes and leaned my head back against the chair. Rachel smelled like baby powder, applesauce and sleep all rolled into one. Downstairs, there was barking and splashing and yelling, but up here there was only the whisper of the summer breeze through the tree branches by the window.

She curled up sleepy and heavy against my chest. This, then, was why people liked babies—the symbiosis of souls, the bridging of gaps too big to fill with words.

I felt both completely trusted and completely trustworthy for the first time in recent memory. The simple truth of this surprised me. I was not someone who deserved to be given up on.

The baby stirred against me and looked up. Our eyes met in the dark, and she replaced the ring in her mouth with her thumb, waiting, I supposed, for me to sing her a lullaby. Sadly, my lullaby repertoire was quite limited, so I settled for singing "Copacabana" and "My Cherie Amour" in the most soothing way possible. She seemed satisfied and surprisingly uncritical of my choice of material. Score another point for the infants of the world.

The plan was to sleep over in Leah's guest room and regroup tomorrow. The guest room part went off without a hitch, but sleep presented more of a challenge. We got Hans Gruber cleaned up and banished to the basement by midnight. The Goldbergs were all asleep by twelve-thirty. I lay in bed and watched the digital clock next to my bed tick off the minutes for the next two and a half hours.

By three A.M., I was thrashing around with pernicious insomnia. Despite my best efforts to distract myself by rattling off state capitals and decorating my fantasy beach bungalow in Malibu, my mind kept wandering back to Flynn. He kept popping up, unbidden, in Sacramento, Honolulu, Boise, and in the sunny yellow bedroom of my beach house.

I threw in the towel at three-fifteen. Careful not to wake the family, I slipped out the front door and into the night. The minute I opened the door to my car, I knew where I wanted to go. I wanted to go back to the beginning, back to where I had taken that first, fatal wrong turn that had redirected the entire course of my life.

23

I saw him silhouetted in the headlights before I even cut the
VW's engine. He was sitting in the wet grass under the huge
white summer moon, watching the river rush past and tossing a
baseball up in the air. Just tossing it and catching it, tossing it
and catching it.

Apparently, I wasn't the only one with insomnia tonight.

He didn't turn around or interrupt his solitary game of
catch, but he knew it was me. Who else could it have been at
this hour of the night, at this particular latitude and longi-
tude?

I turned off the headlights and got out of the car. The summer night was hushed but alive with crickets and mosquitoes
and the cool breeze rising off the river. Blades of grass tickled

my toes through my sandals as I stood on the overgrown dirt road I'd taken to get here. Our old stomping ground.

I took two steps toward Flynn and waited.

I could see the tension straining the shoulders of his T-shirt, which was bleached even paler than usual by the moonlight.

Given the fact that it was the middle of the night and I hadn't expected company, I was decked out in a pair of Leah's old white seersucker pajamas and a terminal case of bedhead. I smelled vaguely of shampoo and wet dog, and my left arm was wrapped in a fresh bandage.

It was just me, shipwrecked but salvageable.

I walked up behind him and plucked the baseball out of the air, mid-toss. "You remember when we tried to learn how to play out here?"

He didn't look up. "I remember you hitting the ball into the river every single time you made contact with the bat. I had to wade in with you to get it because you were scared of leeches."

My smile surprised me. "That fear was not unfounded. Remember the first time we went skinny-dipping in here? When you . . ." The sentence died in my throat, because it brought to the surface the things that had gotten us here in the first place. The sex on this sand and the quicksilver panic of the morning after and the rest of our lives without each other.

"I remember a lot of things we did out here," he said.

I looked at him. He looked at the water.

I sighed and sat down next to him in the rich, damp dirt. I rolled the baseball between my palms. "Well. What now?"

He still refused to turn away from the river. "I specifically asked you not to contact me."

"It's not like I stalked you down," I countered. "This river was my idea, not yours."

"Right. That explains why I got here first." We listened to the water lapping at the sand by our toes. "Let me ask you this, Geary. Were you even planning to say good-bye?"

I stopped fidgeting with the baseball and looked him right in the eye. "Knock it off."

"I guess that answers that question." He nodded and got to his feet. I couldn't see his eyes, but his posture was casual. He seemed to consider breaking my heart a jeans-and-T-shirt kind of event.

I stood up too, wiping my palms on my dirt-streaked pajama bottoms. "Don't just dismiss me like that. I think I deserve a little better from you after everything we've been through."

The moon reflected in those deep autumn eyes. "You know, I used to be able to read you like a book," he said. "You couldn't hide anything. The worst poker face in the world. I really liked that about you. But I guess you got better at hiding or I got a lot worse at finding, because I really misjudged you this time. I really thought you had changed."

"I have. And if you can't see that . . ."

But he was shaking his head, his expression one I hadn't seen for a very long time. He looked stark and stripped down to the essence of himself. "I just can't keep breaking up with you."

"Then why the hell *do* you keep breaking up with me?" My voice broke on the first word, so I let my temper take over.

"I don't. But it's kind of a moot point—you leaving me, me leaving you. It still leaves us both in pretty much the same place, doesn't it?" He gestured to the vast expanse of dark wilderness. "Right here, having this same old conversation. Tell you what. I've been sitting here all night, collecting mosquito bites and trying to figure this whole thing out. Why don't you try it for awhile?" He turned and started to walk away.

"That's it? 'Tag, you're it' and you cut and run?"

"Smarts, doesn't it?"

"Flynn, just give me—"

"More time to decide what you want?" He stopped and turned back to face me. "I gave you ten years. And we're right back where we started. Except now I feel like twice the jackass, because I'm older and wiser and you got me again."

"I did?" Did he mean what I thought he meant? Or was I just being delusional in my attempt to get something—anything—positive out of this conversation? "What do you mean, I 'got you'?"

"But that's my own fault," he continued, as if I hadn't interrupted. "I believed what I wanted to believe, instead of what was right in front of me."

"And what was right in front of you?" I demanded.

"I'm never going to be able to give you what you want. Just go back to L.A. We don't need a big, drawn-out scene."

"Why do you keep insisting that I'm going back to California?" I demanded. "Why do you insist in making up my mind for me?"

He narrowed his eyes. "So you're not going back to L.A.?"

I heaved the baseball out at the river with all my might. "This isn't about L.A. This is about you refusing to trust me. Ever. It's all or nothing with you. It always has been. So that's what we both have now. Nothing."

Through my shame and my sorrow, I thought I could detect a glimmer of hope in his eyes. "You're not going to L.A.?"

I threw my hands up and surrendered the last of my pride. "Of course not, you dumbass! Don't you think I've learned one single, solitary, goddamn thing in the last decade?"

He threw me a small, grudging smile. "I do wonder about that sometimes."

"Well, for your information, I've learned a lot." I straightened my muddy pajama shirt cuffs. "But it doesn't matter unless you see it, too. If you can't trust me for who I am now, then please go right ahead and walk away because you never *will* be able to give me what I want." I closed my eyes, but I could still see the glow of the moon through my eyelids.

He watched the waves ripple out from the baseball's watery grave. "I want to trust you. But I can't be your Ford or whatever it is you feel like reducing me to. I'm not just the backup plan. I'm not perfect. And you've decided not to need anyone. You've built this little fortress for one. What do you need me for?"

I crossed my arms and peered down at my innumerable shortcomings. The ill-fitting pajamas flapped in the wind, alternating patches of grime and wet with the occasional stray leaf clinging to the seams. "Flynn, of course I need you. And it scares the hell out of me. You were closer to me than my family. Everywhere I went, I carried pieces of you with me. You're like my own personal Brunelleschi project, which I think I explained to you right before I lost it in Minneapolis, when I also needed you."

I went for broke under the huge white moon, praying that he would want to step off this precipice with me.

"Don't say these things if you don't mean them." His voice matched his face, a sharp contrast of light and dark.

"How could I not mean them? I'm lost without you. I mean, honestly, look at me. Really look at me." I leveled my gaze and tied the errant tails on my pajama top around my midriff.

And then I finally admitted it to myself and to him. "I'm afraid to love you, okay? I admit it. But I'm not a lost cause."

He took a few steps closer to me. "I know you're not a lost cause."

"Then don't give up on us." My voice was almost as soft as the leaves rustling above us.

Our bodies were half a foot apart. I took a deep breath and reached out to close the distance. My fingers grazed his cheek, trying to memorize the feel of that face in the damp breeze. My heart beat through my entire body, pulsing out to the ground and the sky.

We drank each other in under the stars. I was barely touching him, but I felt emphatically, electrically alive.

"I want to stay here with you," I said. "And I can say it all day and night, but words don't mean anything. You'll have to let me show you."

And there it was. The sum total of all I had to offer: a promise I couldn't back up with anything more substantial than the moonlight.

"How can I say no to that?" He stroked my cheek. "Especially when you look so good in those pajamas and I can see right through them."

You just can't argue with that kind of logic.

He brushed his lips across mine. I could feel every inch of him through my seersucker ensemble.

Then he pointed to the creek and grinned. "Now would you please go get my baseball?"

This time, I recognized my opening. "Not me. There's leeches in there." I batted my eyelashes, the picture of squeamish femininity.

"But do you know who signed that baseball you so carelessly tossed in? Ryne Sandberg."

"Well, I guess poor Ryne'll have to stay in the briny deep, because no way am I wading into leech territory," I said. "Old phobias die hard, you know."

"I'll go in with you." He whispered this offer into the hollow between my ear and my jaw. "And you know what? I don't think leeches even like Californians. Too smoggy."

"You go first, then." I nudged him toward the riverbank.

His eyebrows shot up. "Oh, ladies first. I insist." He caught me by the waist and started purposefully toward the river.

"Hey! You said you'd come with me," I protested, digging

my heels in, with the result that my sandals lodged in the dark, loamy earth while my feet tripped off toward the river.

He scooped me up into his arms and strode ankle-deep into the water, unmindful of his scuffed brown Timberlands.

"Flynn, seriously." I wriggled around like a worm on a hook, and he wasn't even out of breath. "Listen to me. If you drop me in there, I will beat you like a rented mule. Do you know how cold it is in there?"

My bids for freedom resulted in an accidental knee to his ribcage, and we went down, tumbling into the river together. The water was warmer than I'd expected, tepid but fresh like a summer bath. Which was fortunate because we were both drenched, our hair plastered against our necks, our clothes plastered against our skin.

"Nice work, tiger." He had cushioned my fall with his body, and I could feel his thighs under mine.

"Thank you, darling."

We kissed and kissed. Things were getting out of hand very quickly. Realizing that we were in danger of drowning at the rate we were going, he pulled me back to the riverbank, where we tossed our wet clothes on the grass and followed them down. This may not sound very romantic, but trust me, what it lacked in hearts and flowers, it made up for in raw, shameless passion.

Our eyes met in the dark, gleaming and feverish while we moved against each other. My heart raced and I could feel things shattering inside me. It was a regular bull in a china shop in there.

"We can't do this unless we're sure," I said.

And then we did, and it was like coming into myself, coming back to myself. Somehow that night, drenched in moonlight and river water, I found a new way home.

Afterward, we lay tangled up in each other, sprawled out on the hood of my car as we watched the stars shift on the horizon.

"So you really want to stay here?" He cradled my head against his bare shoulder.

"I really want to stay here." I pressed my lips against his chest.

"Well, it's about damn time." He paused. "But don't stay here just because of me. I refuse to argue for twenty years about how I didn't value your work and killed your career."

"You think we'll still be together in twenty years?"

He kissed the top of my head. "Won't we?"

I could picture it. Closets stocked with high heels and white T-shirts, the Oxford English Dictionary, and ice-fishing gear. A chi-chi, purebred dog named Wayne Gretzky or Gordie Howe. "I've been giving it a lot of thought. I can still write in Minnesota. And I'm thinking about trying to take some more classes. At the U, whatever. Accounting and management stuff. I seem to have small business in my blood." I waited for him to mock me.

He squeezed me tighter. "But won't your editor be disappointed about the California assignment?"

"Oh, I'll do a few snappy pieces on hearty Midwestern fare and he'll get over it. Besides. I have a little secret for you: I jet lag practically unto death." I curled up into his warmth. "I want to stay in one place for a while. With you. Even though you're so stubborn and bossy."

"Aw." He laughed. "I have to wipe away a tear."

"The real question is: Are you willing to bear with me?"

He smiled up at the stars. "Geary, I am a lifelong Cubs fan. What do you think?"

"I think you're in for a lot of trouble," I said.

"Hey, they finally made the playoffs last year, right? Hope springs eternal."

24

The crisp September breeze aired out the apartment, wafting away the dust and fresh paint fumes.

"Hey, Geary."

I surveyed the bowls, glasses and wadded-up balls of newspaper strewn all over the kitchen floor, then gave up unpacking in favor of following his voice.

"Yeah?" I wandered down the hall in bare feet, boxer shorts, and one of his gray T-shirts.

He was sitting on the floor of the screened-in porch, reading the morning paper amid stacks of unopened brown boxes. "You know what would go great out here? A hammock."

I leaned against the doorway and looked out at the lush

green lawns and pastel chalk scribblings on the neighbors' sidewalk. "Shouldn't you be unpacking?"

He nodded and filled in a crossword puzzle answer.

I sat down next to him, stretching out in the early autumn heat. He pulled me into his lap and I relaxed into him. "This place is really great. Unbelievable. How did you find it?"

"I have many hidden talents."

"I'm serious. This is about eighteen times bigger than my studio in Santa Monica and it's like, pennies a day."

"Welcome back to the Midwest."

He truly had demonstrated considerable prowess as an apartment-hunter, securing us the upper story of a duplex in Minneapolis' uptown district, close to the university and within walking distance of Lake Calhoun. The empty white rooms and sealed cardboard cartons held endless promise and possibility.

Currently, our furnishings consisted of what Flynn had brought from his old apartment: a bed, a big-screen TV, a ratty brown armchair, and a coffee table he described as "the Platonic ideal of flat," which he had made himself with a log, a wood plane and infinite patience.

"Aren't you excited to start redecorating?" I asked hopefully.

He shook his head. "Don't even talk to me about decorating. I'm still recovering from your outrageous wardrobe demands. All those boxes marked 'Clothes, misc.' What the hell is the 'misc.'? Bricks? Lead?"

I considered this. "There might have been a few shoes and books in there."

"Steel-toed boots? Hardcover encyclopedias? It's lucky for you I'm so manly and muscle-bound."

"I'm high-maintenance, but I'm worth it," I assured him, rubbing the base of his neck.

By the time the doorbell rang, we'd gotten ourselves into something of a compromising position. I groaned and started to extricate myself from his arms.

He tightened his hold on me and murmured into my mouth, "Ignore the barbarians at the gate."

I laughed and deepened the kiss before pulling away. "We can't. They're very persistent barbarians."

Sure enough, we could hear Skye at the other end of the apartment, knocking and yelling, "Hey! Are you home or what?"

Flynn got to his feet and pulled me up after him. I straightened my shirt, brushed off my shorts, and headed for the front door.

Life and noise flooded in.

"I love this place," Leah said, handing me a tower of bakery boxes and kissing my cheek. "Great neighborhood. And did you see the shoe store down the street?"

"Hey, guys. Rex spent all morning making you something, so he's a little excited." Stan trooped in with the kids, and true to form, Rex was cranked up to eleven.

"Faith! Flynn! Faith! Flynn! Is this your new house? Do you guys have a bathtub? Does it have claw feet?" Rex tugged on Stan's hand. "I drew you something for the wall." He handed me a fingerpainting emblazoned with bold streaks of primary colors and gold glitter.

Skye breezed in with Lars on one arm and Sally on the other. " . . . So the whole thing really made me think about life and death and what it all means, you know?"

"Oh me, too," Sally agreed. Both of them spared me a glance and a "hi," then went back to their discussion.

"I mean, when you hit me with your car, I just started to have some second thoughts about stuff." My sister lifted one hand to heaven and the other to her heart.

"Absolutely." Sally bobbed her head up and down.

"And I think, when I die, I want my tombstone to say 'Skye Geary: Often imitated, never duplicated'." Lars and I locked gazes and nodded a stoic greeting.

Bringing up the rear was Hans Gruber, with tail wagging and paws clicking on the stairs.

"We brought the family mascot," Leah explained. "I hope that's okay. If you want, we can leave him in the car."

"No, he's fine," Flynn said. "Maybe he can sniff out the box with all the cooking gear in it."

"Yeah, I'm sorry this place is such a wreck," I said, nodding at the chaos on all sides.

Everyone streamed into the dining room, leaving Flynn and me holding the door and Rex's painting. He squeezed my hand and grinned at me. "Aren't you glad we have all this extra room?"

"Yeah. God, this place is going to be Grand Central Station." I kissed him again, curling my toes against the smooth cool floor tiles.

He slung an arm around my shoulder and together we

joined the horde gathering in the dining room. Leah handed Rachel to Sally, then sliced the coffee cake and doled out cookies while Hans Gruber sniffed joyfully at all the boxes and crumpled newspaper. Skye, hanging off a blissed-out Lars, debated the merits of pink versus peach blusher with Sally, who was gingerly trying to maintain her grip on Rachel without breaking a nail. Rex spun around in staggering circles while Stan explained how gravity worked.

"Do you like my picture?" Rex asked me as he tumbled to the ground in a giggling heap.

"I do. In fact, I'm going to put it up right now." I headed to the kitchen and hunted around until I found the tape. The walls in the hallway were empty and white, except for a single framed print we had hung up last night upon arrival. An old sepia photograph of the Piazza del Duomo in Florence, with the belltower and the arched dome patterned with light against the morning sky. Our little joke.

I taped Rex's modernist, mixed media piece up next to it. Although perhaps less subtle and classic, the fingerpainting balanced the photograph nicely. The red and blue streaks and the sprinkled glitter offset the muted gray and the careful straight lines. I took a step back and looked at the newest addition to our home.

And then I went back to my family.

UP CLOSE & PERSONAL WITH THE AUTHOR

WHY DID YOU SET THIS BOOK IN RURAL MINNESOTA?

A few reasons, I guess. One, I wanted to write a book for all the women out there who love characters like Carrie Bradshaw and Bridget Jones but don't live in a big city and wear Manolo Blahniks. You can live in Wisconsin and drink Pig's Ear beer and still be fun and fabulous. It's all in the attitude! Also, I'm lazy. I went to college in a small town in Minnesota, loved it, and used that town as the inspiration for the fictional setting of Lindbrook. Finally, I needed it for the plot. How else was I going to work in scenes like "Free Beer 'Til Somebody Pees"?

TEENAGERS IN LOVE: CAN IT REALLY LAST?

There's something special about first loves—something pure and intense and kind of obsessive—and maybe that's why they don't usually endure into adulthood. First loves embody a kind of innocence that we can't take into adulthood . . . and most of us wouldn't want to! When you're seventeen, you're not thinking about whether the hot guy who asked for your phone number has commitment problems, mother issues, or a good credit rating. You're just starry-eyed and awash in endorphins. And afterward you grow up, smarten up, and get all world-weary and suspicious about dating.

Though I don't personally know anyone who married her high school sweetheart, I do know a few couples who broke up, went their separate ways, and then reunited as adults. Isn't that part of the reason why we attend high school and college reunions? We *have* to find out what happened to our old flames. Did your evil ex-boyfriend get his just desserts (i.e., a raging case of herpes and a yearly IRS audit)? Is that guy you admired from afar in biology lab still cute? And if he is, is he single?

BUT, AS YOU SAY, MOST PEOPLE *DO* EVENTUALLY GET OVER THEIR FIRST LOVES. WHY DIDN'T FAITH AND FLYNN?

I would agree that most people eventually *move on* after their first serious relationship. But the idea of reuniting with our first love is a pretty widespread fantasy. Books and movies like *The Great Gatsby, Romy and Michele's High School Reunion, Persuasion,* and *The Big Chill* all focus on the desire to track down old loves and resolve emotional issues from the past.

As to why Faith and Flynn had so much trouble letting go of their relationship and moving on to other partners, the tattoos pretty much sum it up. Those monogrammed hearts are the physical manifestation of the marks they left on each other. Neither had the heart removed—though it's possible with laser technology—but both of them hid it from view. Sometimes our romantic mistakes push us forward to the next stage in our lives, but sometimes they hold us back. By keeping those tattoos, Faith and Flynn were signaling that they weren't ready to let go of the past, even though they were angry and hurt. Nothing like a good dose of emotional ambivalence!

FLYNN AND LARS BOTH QUALIFY AS THE STRONG, SILENT TYPE, WHILE IAN, THE ARTICULATE MAN OF LETTERS, IS A TOTAL JACKASS. CARE TO COMMENT?

As someone who's dated her fair share of jackasses, I learned the hard way that actions speak louder than words. It has been my experience that men who are prone to making flowery speeches about how your eyes remind him of the sun rising over the Seine are trouble. Ditto for men who need half an hour every morning to put exactly the right amount of gel in their bangs. I like 'em stoic and sincere. No primping or posturing. As my brother put it, "A good guy only needs seven minutes to buy a pair of pants: one minute to locate them in the store, two minutes to try them on, and four minutes to leave."

WHY DIDN'T FAITH AND FLYNN GET MARRIED AT THE END OF THE BOOK? DO YOU THINK THEY EVER WILL?

They didn't get married because, quite frankly, they weren't ready. Faith, who started the story in complete isolation—almost self-imposed exile—managed to surround herself with a close-knit community of friends and family by the end. I think that's a pretty drastic change in and of itself! The story focuses on their romantic reconciliation, but before Flynn gets up the nerve to propose again, they've got a lot more rebuilding to do. You know, boring stuff like doing the laundry together and having stupid little arguments over who used the last coffee filter and forgot to buy more. Ah, true love . . .

Will they ever tie the knot? Probably. I can see it all now: a small outdoor wedding, maybe by the river, Faith in a simple white sheath dress, Skye in the frilly pink bridesmaid dress she'd insist on wearing, Leah and Stan providing a wedding cake complete with a little Cubs cake topper. (Flynn, of course, will be wearing a white T-shirt with his tux.)

Then don't miss these other great books from Downtown Press!